# Coffee Shop Girl

### KATIE CROSS

KCW

# Contents

# Chapter One

BETHANY

"This place needs to burn to the ground."

My barista, Anthony, shoved a coffee mug into the sink as he stomped away. Milk splattered the floor at his feet as he tore around the cabinet, heading for the door. The bitter scent of burnt coffee lingered in the air.

Halfway into the Frolicking Moose Coffee Shop, I stopped. "What happened?"

A car pulled up at the drive-through window, the driver peering into the mayhem I'd just walked into myself. I set aside my purse, taking in spilled chai powder, a broken mug on the floor, cream on the counter, and a few hastily tossed dollar bills next to the register, which lay open—bills spewing from the wrong slots.

Anthony held up his hands. "I'm done. This place is a freaking disaster. Not even an MIT genius could work here." He started to back away. "The espresso machine stopped working, and the register won't shut. Again. I burned a batch of coffee while following the ridiculous directions you gave me, and three people have been waiting for ten minutes out there. Five have already driven off. Oh, and the steamer probe is busted."

I used my hip to push the cash drawer closed, but it kicked back out. The lights weren't registering. The words *espresso machine* sent a prickling sensation down my back. "Did you grind the beans?" I asked.

"What?"

"Did you put ground espresso beans in the machine, Anthony?" I whispered.

"Yes!"

Half-hysterical, I hurtled to the machine. "We covered that yesterday! There's already a grinder. Now all the espresso drinks will have grinds in them. We'll have to rinse the whole thing out."

"Whatever. I'm done. You don't even have to pay me, Bethany." He walked backward now, steps away from disappearing forever. "I'm out."

"Wait!" I called. "Please, not today. Give me just one hou—"

The front door slammed shut.

Panic pulsed through me. Why did he have to do this *today*? Today, when I had the biggest meeting of my life!

I quelled the fluttery sensation in my stomach, squared my shoulders, and let out a breath. I'd get through this and still attend my meeting with Dad's old chum. My absolutely life-altering appointment.

Good thing I'd worn my favorite lipstick today. There's no power like a woman with the right shade, even at eight o'clock in the morning.

"All right," I said, keeping my voice modulated. "It's okay. I can still meet with Dave and get the funding I need to start the—"

A *bang* on the window brought me out of my spiraling anxiety.

"What's going on in there!" A scowling, white-haired man shielded his eyes from the sun. He squinted from beneath bushy eyebrows. "Where's my coffee?"

Customers.

Right.

I could do this. Moderating disasters was my jam. Thanks to Mama, I'd been doing it my whole life. Tearing an apron off a hook, I slipped it over my pantsuit and bustled over to the window in knock-off Louboutin high heels. The bells on the door jangled, admitting someone I barely saw out of the corner of my eye. I called out, "Just a minute!" over my shoulder.

"Hi there." I turned back to the drive-through and pasted on a bright smile. "Just a quick shift change. Sorry about that. What did you order?"

"A cappuccino."

My gaze returned to the inert machine. I paused, then held up a finger. "Ah . . . those aren't available right now. The machine is . . . prepped for the cleaners."

He scowled. "Fine. Black coffee."

"I can do that! The last batch of coffee burned, but I'm putting a new pot on. Would you mind waiting?"

The old man flipped me the bird and punched the gas. His tires squealed away. Stunned, I blinked, then let out a long breath. One down. Three cars waited behind him.

The first driver pulled up with an angry glare, and I clenched my teeth. Fantastic. Mrs. Jones, the wrathful old lady that the whole mountain town of Pineville feared.

"Good morning, Mrs. Jones," I said with a forced smile.

"My coffee ready yet?"

"Brewing now!"

Her nostrils flared. "I've been in line for fifteen minutes."

"I understand, and I apologize. I—"

"I didn't give my order to you."

"No, Anthony—"

"Did he quit? Is your business falling apart? You'll never be your father, you know. You're doomed to fail."

My jaw tightened until I thought my teeth might break.

Heart pounding, I let out a long breath. "The coffee will be another eight minutes."

Ten, actually, but let her wait.

She rolled her eyes. "I'll make it myself. It would probably be faster to harvest my own beans."

With that, her ancient Cadillac window eased upward, then her car inched forward. I threw myself back into the shop, dumped the coffee out, and frantically poured water for a new pot. A movement out of the corner of my eye caught my attention as I reached for the last of the ground coffee beans.

A tall, broad-shouldered man stood at the counter. Sooty hair, caramel eyes, a dark shadow of stubble on his face. He wore a white T-shirt and a pair of jeans. Underneath the thin white material, I could just make out a hint of tattoos on his left shoulder. The ink trailed to his elbow.

I swallowed hard, taken aback, and forced myself to look back at the coffee maker. The last thing I needed was a large, Viking distraction.

"Just a second," I croaked.

He kept his eyes on the chalkboard overhead, which I doubted Anthony had updated with the flavor of the day.

*Please don't ask for amaretto,* I thought. *Please don't ask for—*

"Do you have amaretto?" he asked.

With a grimace, I said, "No, that was from yesterday, and we ran out. I believe today is . . . peppermint?"

"Is that a question?"

"Everything is a question today," I said with a sigh, then headed back to the window, my heels clicking against the floor. "Hold that thought, please."

I arrived at the window just as another car drove through without stopping, the driver's lips pressed into a thin line. Relief slid over me like cool water when a familiar SUV pulled up. Jada, a middle-aged woman I thought of more like a mother than a friend, peered out at me.

"Rough day?" she asked, lips parted in a dazzling smile. The woman always had perfect teeth set in her dark brown complexion. She'd lived in Thailand for six months doing humanitarian work as a doctor, and she'd still came back with her grin sparkling. She toyed with the end of a long, thick braid that rested on her shoulder.

I slumped against the window. "Anthony just quit, and everything is broken, including myself. In good news, I dreamed about Jason Momoa last night."

She grinned. "That'll offset any bad day. I'll take my usual scone, then. Who needs coffee?"

My nose wrinkled. "No one. Gross. I can't believe my dad made a living selling it. Scone is free of charge." I grabbed one from a nearby shelf and shoved it at her without a bag. Then I flipped a light switch on the wall that turned off the OPEN sign out front.

"I'm late to see my patients," she said with a wink as she threw a twenty into the shop. "Talk to you later."

No other car came up behind her, so I spun around with a deep, bolstering breath. Time to tackle Mr. Viking, get him *something*, and send him on his way so I could officially close and take stock of this madness. This utter, chaotic disaster was drowning me in stress and debt, preventing all my professional advancement into the beautiful world of real estate.

*Thanks, Dad.*

Setting aside that unfortunate thought, I stepped up behind the open register. "What can I get you?"

His gaze dropped from the board, meeting mine. My breath caught, but I fought through it, forcing myself to maintain eye contact. His eyes were liquid gold. I'd never seen such a color before.

"Macchiato."

"We are fresh out of that."

"Caffe latte?"

My voice quieted to a squeak. "That too."

A flicker of amusement passed over his face as he reached into a back pocket. "How about you tell me what you do have?"

"Scones," I said, "and bottled water. Until I can figure out the mess that my now-former employee left behind, that's about as much as you'll get. Eventually, I'll have coffee again for you, but it may take . . . fifteen minutes at this rate."

"Breakfast of champions." He tossed some cash onto the counter. "Scones and water sound great."

I slid it back. He had to be kidding. The scones could double as hockey pucks, but I'd take whatever mercy he offered.

"On the house."

He left the money on the counter as he turned to sit down. My fingers itched to take it, but pride forced me to leave it there. The last thing I needed to be doing was turning away money.

But still . . .

My eyes darted to a clock that featured a prominent salmon Dad had bought while fishing in Alaska. Then I sighed. Nope. Already missed the scholarship meeting with Dave.

Slumping, I leaned against the counter.

Dang.

"Do you have internet?" the Viking asked. His voice rumbled low and deep, like a roll of thunder sliding across a mountain meadow. Despite my desire to get rid of him, I wanted to wrap myself in it.

"Yes. The password is on the board. Do you want the scone warmed?"

"Sure. Thanks."

He settled onto a table with his back to the door, leaving his chiseled face in full view. I fought off a swear word and left the cash sitting there. I *really* didn't want him to stay. Could I force a customer out?

No.

Dad would turn over in his grave, then reach out and slap me.

With a sigh, I grabbed a new water bottle from the mini fridge beneath the counter, warmed a chocolate chip scone on a plate, set the cash next to it, and delivered them to him without looking at his golden eyes.

He was already tapping away at his computer when he said, "Thanks."

When I turned to go, my eyes snagged a flash of something near the floor. Loose pants. Thin, specialty shoe. Odd kink in the material. I knew those signs very well.

Prosthetic leg.

Interesting.

Grateful to return behind the counter, I made sure the OPEN sign was still off, braced myself for whatever I would find, and set to work. At least Anthony walking out meant I wouldn't have to pay wages, though shutting down in the middle of rush hour meant I'd lose half of my usual sales for the day. Maybe they'd balance out.

Trying not to total up the lost money of all those cars sailing by, I started mopping up spilled milk on the floor so I could clean up glass shards from the broken cup. I lost myself in the task.

*I will not cry.*

Not again. There had been enough crying in the last eight months to satisfy a lifetime. Still, my mind wandered back to Dave. To the pitch I had planned for the last two months.

A deep throat clearing caught my attention. I gazed up to see the Viking at the counter again. His broad shoulders blocked out the rising sun behind him, casting him in silhouette.

"The internet is turned off."

"What?"

His lips tightened, but I couldn't tell if it was amusement or annoyance now.

"Sorry." I straightened. "Sorry. That wasn't about you or . . . I mean . . . give me a second."

Muttering under my breath again, I stood up, hands milky, and slipped into my closet of an office just down a short hall. Sure enough, the blinking lights were dead.

Wait.

Register wouldn't shut.

Wi-Fi off.

"Ha!" I called. "Got you now, sucker."

"Excuse me?"

"Sorry! Not you. Not . . . that was . . . excuse me just a moment. Need to flip a breaker."

Properly horrified now, I slipped out of my office and down the hall, toward a set of spiral stairs that led to the attic where I lived. My feet were already starting to ache in these shoes. I kicked them off into my attic bedroom and started back up the steps to the very top.

Five minutes later, I crawled out from an access to the electrical panel, dust clinging to my recently dry-cleaned outfit, and returned to the annoying *beep* of the register.

"Should be up in a moment," I called and ducked back into my office. With my forehead pressed to the wall, I let out a deep breath, and muttered, "One problem down, 4,153 to go."

I reached for my lipstick.

Just another day in the life of the owner of an almost-decrepit coffee shop in the middle of the mountains.

One that had just missed her golden opportunity to pursue her ideal life.

# Chapter Two

MAVERICK

This girl had no idea.

First, those pants—whatever they were— fit her a little too well.

Second, this place needed a reboot. Or death by accidental fire.

Third, no coffee in a coffee shop? She had to be kidding.

The place smelled like thirty pots of the darkest brew had been burned. That only made everything worse, including the musty smell of old guy. So many fish knickknacks littered this place that I expected her to offer me halibut as an option.

In fact, the majority of the decor here seemed to be dusty fish memorabilia and curling pictures of locals holding dead animals. What appeared to be an original hardwood floor hid beneath a layer of age, and it seemed as if every table needed a book to stabilize it.

This place couldn't be more perfect.

Despite the situation and a grumpy lady at the drive-through, the barista held herself together pretty well. I pegged her for the owner, though I couldn't imagine why she was dressed so smartly. A missed meeting, perhaps.

Once the Wi-Fi was restored, the crackling energy of desperation calmed. She returned wearing a pair of yoga pants, sandals, and a T-shirt that said *Coach Me* with a purse beneath it. She avoided eye contact, which was fine.

Carefully, as I sipped water, I tried to assess exactly what was going on. Small-town mom-and-pop shops like this fit the same pattern time after time. Inherited businesses, usually. This girl—Bethany, if that apron was right—was likely the owner-operator. Out to prove herself in the big bad entrepreneurial world with a quaint place she probably wanted to make into a bed-and-breakfast.

Which was way more work than she likely anticipated.

Judging by the aesthetic, her father, uncle, or grandfather had gifted it to her, or owned it first. A picture on the wall of a fiftysomething man in jeans, a ragged shirt, and the exact same baseball cap she was wearing now showed an uncanny resemblance. He held a fish on the porch of this shop. Probably the first day it opened. Maybe he caught that fish in the reservoir behind here.

That meant she was probably in debt from a mortgage on the place. If there was better cash flow, the decorations wouldn't suck so much, which meant she probably had little money coming in. In fact, I doubted she'd even thought of the decorations, which meant she was desperate.

Behind the register was a half-opened door, spilling light into a back room. Limited storage space meant their inventory moved quickly. She likely ran across the street to the grocery store for supplies often enough.

Chalkboard menu.

Smudged pastry display case.

A cash register from the eighties. Old enough to certainly be a pain.

The place looked more like an old antique store than a coffee shop. The only thing it had going for it was a chair in the back corner and an impressive assortment of coffee mugs on the wall.

A thrill zipped through me. I couldn't have planned this better if I'd researched for months.

She deftly avoided meeting my eyes, aided by the bill of the hat she wore to keep her black hair out of her face. She puttered around behind the counter, attempting to right whatever mayhem the guy that had stalked out of here had left behind. Every now and then her gaze flickered my way and she paused, but I always acted engrossed in my screen.

It wasn't a total lie, but I also didn't hate watching her work. Most people underestimated how much actions revealed personality. Her disorganization spoke worlds.

She had no idea what she was doing here.

I typed away, relieved to finally have access to the outside world again. A week getting started with renovations of Grandpa's cabin, while hiding from Mallory and her team, had been enough to make my skin crawl. Getting my hands dirty again felt good, but nothing felt better than Wi-Fi.

One thousand unread emails populated on my screen. *Not my problem right now.* Might be later, of course. But for now, I closed my eyes, drew in a deep breath, and let the feeling of freedom crawl through me. I navigated away from the inbox.

A text dinged on my phone just as a chat box popped up on the screen from a sales manager in Florida. Questions, questions, questions. They likely didn't get my memo. *Sorry,* I replied. *I'm on sabbatical for eight weeks. Direct all sales questions to José Martinez.*

Thirty other unread text messages awaited me as well. I ignored all of them. An email at the top of my inbox grabbed my eye. The subject said: *You're going down, Mav.*

Right below was another email from Mallory that said: *Burn in Dante's fiery inferno.*

With a grin, I clicked it.

. . .

*Mav,*

*Leave like this again, pig-face, and I will fire you instead of asking you to be my Chief Revenue Officer.*

*Only because you're my brother-in-law, have a mind like a whiz, and can guarantee my sales force won't fail am I allowing this little escapade to . . . wherever you are. Figure your life out, then come back to your promotion and the luxury of a higher pay grade.*

*I'll give you the company Bentley, but only if you haggle me for it.*

*And I plan on telling your mother what you've done, you hog. You'll burn if you don't come back.*

*—Mallory*

All my considerable control was the only thing that kept me from laughing.

Swine references aside, Mallory usually had a great deal of tact. Things must have been sufficiently bad after my unexpected leave of absence from her multimillion-dollar company. The need to take eight weeks off to disappear into family history and uncover some skeletons—mostly my own—surprised even me. Skeletons named *I'm tired of corporate culture* and *you can't pay me enough to be your CRO.*

Thanks to the Frolicking Moose Coffee Shop, I might never have to go back to corporate. Of course, I could just leave. Say *sayonara* and figure it out. But that felt worse. If I didn't take her offer, I'd need to move to something else. Something better.

With a gem like the Frolicking Moose, and its regrettably attractive owner, *Operation Maverick on the Loose* had just commenced.

Still, I owed Mallory a response. With a roll of my neck, I typed my reply.

*Hey Mal,*

*Sorry, can't hear you from over here. The connection is bad, and you're cutting out. Send my regards to Baxter, and tell Mom to save me some bacon.*

*Mav*

Mallory could stew on that. My brother Baxter could deal with the fallout of his rage-filled CEO wife. In the meantime, I had planning to do.

Not only did I have emails to actively ignore, a house to tear apart from the inside out, and beautiful mountain vistas to stare at, but now there was a certain coffee shop owner to research, smooth over, and sweet-talk into changing her own life.

All while she changed mine.

# Chapter Three

BETHANY

The sun was fading behind the mountains when I trudged upstairs. A watery palette rippled on the reservoir. The Frolicking Moose might be a collapsing shack, but it had killer views of the lake.

I collapsed onto my bed.

My eyes slammed shut, bloodshot and aching. Everything smelled like coffee, and I hated coffee. For several moments, I lay there, breathing in and out. Scenes from the day passed through my mind like ticker tape. Dad narrated in the background.

*That espresso machine is killer sometimes.*

*Steamer is fickle.*

*Who doesn't love a good frappuccino on a hot day?*

"Me," I whispered. "I don't."

*Bad day? Just think it out. Think it through.*

A smile twitched at the edges of my lips. Such a Dad thing to say. He said it about everything, whether I was stuck on homework, having a boy issue, or trying to figure out which college to attend.

*Think it out. Think it through.*

You could take the man out of the Army, but not the Army out of the man.

When my eyes opened, they stared at a picture of Dad and Pappa on the front porch, coffee cups in hand. Pappa saluted me with his usual three-finger greeting as I took the picture. He died the next day, never waking from his usual afternoon nap. That was five years ago.

Groggy with sleep, I pushed off the bed, kicked off my shoes, and stripped out of my clothes. I ditched them in a pile with the rest of the dirty clothes on the floor. A hot shower relaxed my tense muscles, allowing my thoughts to flow more freely.

Following Dad's advice, I thought it through.

- No employee, which meant more twelve-hour days.
- Shorter hours meant less money coming in.
- Lunch break shopping.
- The next credit card statement would be coming through again soon.
- Not a single soul that I really spoke to today.

Where had it all gone wrong?

By the time I finished, my postage stamp-sized bathroom had turned to steam. I emerged into my sticky-warm bedroom. It was always hot above the coffee shop. With my wet towel, I yanked my hair into a turban so it could dry and tried not to think about the unnerving quiet.

The sun sank beyond the distant mountains, coating the sky in burnt orange and carnation pink. I pulled the drapes, yanked on shorts and a tank top, and dragged a comb through my hair.

Signs of a messy life littered the room. Before Dad died eight months ago, it would have been immaculate. Dad always did military corners on his bed as soon as he woke up. Now neck-laces, dirty clothes, and old magazines cluttered the space.

The one-room bedroom held what was left of my life. My brighter, happier, less lonely existence had been lost in the months since Dad's untimely heart attack.

To distract myself from my depressing thoughts, I looked outside. My heart did a double take. Was that . . .?

Yes. Yes, it was.

The Viking had just stepped out of the grocery store and was scanning from left to right. He wore a black T-shirt and work khakis now.

Grateful for the anonymity of my upstairs window, I watched him cross the parking lot in the dusk. He was late twen-ties, possibly early thirties. Deep lines on his forehead meant he was a thinker, but he'd been easygoing despite my total mess this morning.

I spent so long studying him, lost in my thoughts, that I didn't realize he was staring right back at me. With a gasp, I jerked back and shoved the curtain closed. My heart slammed in my chest.

When I peeked out again, he'd disappeared.

Acting as if I didn't see the stack of bills on my desk that had arrived that afternoon, I pushed past the mess, tumbled onto the bed with my hair still wet, and fell into a restless sleep.

* * *

The wooden door to the Frolicking Moose Coffee Shop groaned open the next morning. With a quick kick, I propped it open to let cool morning air circulate inside. The OPEN sign flickered to life when I hit the switch behind the counter.

Still half-awake, I shuffled across the wooden floor that desperately needed a refinish and over to the drive-through window. A slight breeze whipped past me. The machines hummed a mellow greeting when I turned them on. After a thorough rinse that left espresso grounds bound into my skin, I'd been able to save the espresso machine from yet another espresso-doctor visit. Not to mention the two-hundred-dollar bill that would have choked off my food supply for the next four months.

My laptop sat on a nearby table, but I ignored it. No, there wouldn't be an email offer waiting for me. Namely, a scholarship to the online real-estate program I had been hoping to interview for yesterday. Getting my license would help me recover what dropping out of college had done to my life.

Really, what had I been thinking? With the Frolicking Moose this hot of a mess, I wasn't bound to recover from anything soon. And I wouldn't give this place up.

I yawned, heading for the bathroom and ignoring the voice of panic that constantly rang in my ears. Dishwasher to run. Inventory to tally. Cups to stock. I really should have prepped last night, but I'd been too tired.

Halfway to the bathroom, a little *scritch* near the back door caught my attention. I paused, turned an ear toward it, and waited. A shuffling sound followed.

Was that . . . a whisper?

Quiet voices, if they were voices at all, came through the door. I reached into my office, grabbing a baseball bat I kept propped against the wall, and slipped toward the back. It was 4:45 a.m. Fifteen minutes before the rush of people commuting an hour to Jackson City. No one should be outside.

I threw open the door.

Two pairs of human eyes stared at me, startled.

I jumped back, screamed, and lifted the bat. Two girls were huddled on the rickety porch, peering up at me in wide-eyed shock. I'd startled them, too. One of them grabbed the other, shoving her away to safety.

"Don't hurt us!"

Eternities seemed to pass as the voice registered in my brain, then traveled to my heart and almost stopped it. It happened the very moment I recognized the two faces. Those eyes.

Those emerald eyes.

I sucked in a sharp breath, the bat clattering to the ground behind me.

"Lizbeth?" I whispered. "Ellie?"

"Please," Lizbeth whispered, her coppery hair limp around a pale, thin face. "Please let us inside."

She was sixteen but looked closer to twelve right then. Her hair hadn't been washed in what looked like weeks, and smudges gave her sallow skin a dirty tinge. Her shoulders trembled as she stood in front of her little sister—no, *our* little sister—Ellie.

Ellie, with her raven-black hair, verdant eyes, and wiry frame, looked so much like me despite being only my half-sister. She would be eleven now, although she acted more like an adult.

In a daze, I stumbled back.

"Yes. Right. Of course. Come on."

Lizbeth whispered something to Ellie, who straightened. I'd never known Ellie to truly fear anything. Rage snapped like fire in her eyes, simmering into a slow-burning coal. Even when I'd seen her last at seven years old, on the second-worst day of my life, she hadn't been scared. No, she'd been angry.

Not much had changed.

Lizbeth put an arm around Ellie's shoulders and rushed past me into the shop. There wasn't far to go. Right next to the back door were the spiral stairs. The hallway that led to my office emptied right into the main coffee shop. Lizbeth shuffled off to the side, eyes darting around. I shut the door firmly behind us. Not until I locked it did Lizbeth relax. Even then, she reminded me of a frightened rabbit poised to skitter off.

"Can we talk?" she whispered.

"Of course."

"I . . . I didn't know if you'd . . ."

Her uncertainty stung, but it wasn't her fault. Lizbeth, Ellie, and I hadn't seen each other in years. Not since Mama died. Even now seeing them brought flashes of Mama back, because Ellie looked just like her. The three of us hadn't parted well after the service.

A thousand questions welled up in my mind, but I bit them all back. A healing split on Ellie's lower lip didn't need explanation. Nor did the slight discoloration around Lizbeth's left eye.

Shoving aside my shock, I said, "Are you hungry? Let me close the shop and get you something to eat. Then you can tell me everything."

* * *

Twenty minutes—and half the dry pastries in my display case—later, their appetite had finally slowed.

Ellie grimaced and held her stomach. Lizbeth hadn't attacked the food with the same zest and seemed to be in less pain. She stared at me over the rim of her green tea. I picked a cheese stick apart without eating it, satisfied by the way it splintered into fragile strings.

My gaze dropped to the bruise around her left eye. There were probably others. Mama had married Jim when I was seven, but Dad kept me away from him. Something undeniably ugly had always festered in his eyes.

It had clearly broken free.

"We're a good fit, doll," Mama had said after first introducing me to Jim. "You don't need love if you can find a good fit."

The numbers told the real story. Lizbeth was born seven months after their suspiciously quick wedding. It had never been clear whether Mama loved Jim or a roof over her head more. He was sullen and quiet, like a storm cloud. Maybe Mama's death four years ago had brought the hideous monster out.

"Jim?" I asked quietly.

A gentle breeze blew through the closed shop, stirring Lizbeth's dirty copper hair. They smelled like forest and sweat and body odor. An angry scratch marred Ellie's right cheek.

Lizbeth hesitated.

"What happened?"

Lizbeth and Ellie exchanged a glance. As usual, I couldn't read Ellie.

"Dad got worse after she died," Lizbeth said, her voice barely a whisper. "Not right away, but slowly. He just . . ."

"Lost it?"

Lizbeth nodded.

A rush of regret slipped through me. I hadn't been in contact much, but I hadn't deserted them, either. Christmas presents. Birthday cards. Occasional phone calls. Lizbeth had my number, and we'd text sometimes. That had slowly faded over the last year. Most of our contact had been obligatory.

"How often did he hit you?" I asked.

Lizbeth chewed on her bottom lip with a shrug of one far-too-skinny shoulder.

"Enough."

I slowly and carefully reached across the table. She let me touch her chin. I tilted her head back so I could see the bruise in the growing light of day.

My heart cracked.

"This has faded. It must have been worse."

She swallowed, the muscles in her throat working. Ellie sat next to her like a wooden statue, fixated on one point on the wall. I would have given the Frolicking Moose to know her thoughts right then.

"I don't have it that bad, to be honest," Lizbeth rushed to say. "I could have handled it, but . . . it's Ellie I was worried about."

Ellie's jaw tightened. Her nostrils flared. She didn't say a word.

Jim had always been more distant from Ellie. He hardly spoke to Lizbeth, but Ellie frustrated him constantly. Mom had always defended her, which had only isolated Ellie further.

"He was taking it out on you?" I asked Ellie. By some miracle, my voice remained controlled.

Ellie didn't answer, but her eyes met mine. The steel I saw there didn't surprise me. I'd seen it in Mama before. After the divorce. Scrounging for a job. When Jim muttered something rude under his breath about her body as she walked by.

Steel core.

Tears welled up in Lizbeth's eyes and rolled down her freckled cheek. "He was going to kill her, Bethie. He lost it one night. Just snapped. So we ran into the woods. He followed. So . . . we just kept going."

Her voice cracked. The sound of my childhood nickname carved a fissure deeper into my chest. *Bethie.* Just the way Mama used to say it.

If possible, Ellie tensed even more.

"He was so angry." Lizbeth's voice shook. "Throwing bottles. Screaming. I-I got her out of the barn, and we ran. We just ran. Ellie had ditched some clothes and shoes in a haystack a few weeks before, so we grabbed them and left. We never looked back."

"Why didn't you call me?"

"He hasn't paid the phone bill in months."

Another twinge of guilt stabbed me. No wonder I hadn't heard from her in a while. I *had* wondered. I just, stupidly, hadn't pursued it. Hadn't thought to, either, with the Frolicking Moose occupying all my time.

I too easily recalled the way Jim would scowl at Mama when she got dressed up to go out country dancing with us.

"He's just jealous, Bethie," Mama would say as she brushed

more mascara on. "Thinks I'm going to take you girls dancing and come home pregnant with another man's child, or something."

Lizbeth sank lower in the chair, frowning. "He's not a bad guy. He's just . . . he's going through a lot."

Ellie tensed when a car drove by. When it didn't stop, she relaxed.

"Home is four hours from here," I said, ignoring Lizbeth's sharp tone. "That's nearly two hundred miles. How did you get here?"

"Ellie is really good outside." Lizbeth rubbed her thin, pale arms. "We've been walking at night and trying to sleep during the day. She'd start fires if we needed it to stay warm at night. We hitchhiked a couple times, but we mostly just walked."

My eyes widened almost to the point of pain. "You hitch-hiked? Do you know how dangerous that is?"

Lizbeth shrugged. Ellie shot me a perturbed glare, and I backed down. Comparatively, perhaps not much scarier than facing their drunk father. Almost two hundred miles of mountains and high desert separated us from Jim. The thought of them crossing it alone made me sick to my stomach.

It must have been *really* bad.

"Did you remember how to get here?" I asked Lizbeth. Ellie had never been here before that she'd remember, but Lizbeth had, when she was ten and Mama got a bug to see me. She drove up without warning, just popping up at the house where I lived with Dad and Pappa. She and Lizbeth took me to dinner, then drove back home.

But now I wondered if there was more to that trip than met the eye. Had she been escaping Jim?

"Barely," Lizbeth said, pulling me out of my thoughts. "I knew the town name, but we had to figure it out by asking. I remembered the name of your dad's coffee shop from the pictures you sent at Christmas last year."

"How many days have you been gone?"

"A week."

Ellie reached out, grabbing the leftover half of a croissant on the plate that I'd loaded for them.

"I'm sorry," Lizbeth said, distress in her eyes. "We're dropping in here so unexpectedly. But I thought maybe your dad could help us. He was nice to me that one time we came. Or maybe you could help us hide for a little bit while this blows over or . . ."

I swallowed hard. "Dad can't help you. He died eight months ago."

Lizbeth's eyes widened, first with surprise, then possibly fear. Dad had been a large, intimidating man. Bigger than most, but kinder and softer than a butterfly. I suspected Lizbeth had always sensed something safe about him, even if he was just the father of her half-sister. Plus, Jim hated Dad. To the point of fear. Lizbeth had made a calculated decision in that brilliant mind of hers.

This girl was more than just books and science.

My throat ached. I wanted this conversation to be over with. Mostly because it proved just how awful a sister I had turned out to be. Amongst other things, like college student and coffee shop owner.

"You didn't say anything," Lizbeth said, hurt in her eyes. "Why didn't you tell us he died?"

"I know. I didn't say anything."

Ellie lifted one eyebrow.

"Of course I'll take you in," I said, eager to turn the subject. "It will be nice to have someone else around here."

"We won't stay," Lizbeth promised, resolute. "Dad might look here. We don't want to bring him to you. Just help us find *somewhere* to go until this blows over, or something. Maybe I can find a job and—"

"Support two people on the income of a sixteen-year-old who should be in high school?"

"I'm smart enough to figure it out."

The impetuous decision to leave Jim's house had saved Ellie's life, but to travel two hundred miles to a distant half-sister? Surely there was someone closer to them who could have helped.

Who could have called the cops, or something.

But then what?

A sudden tightening of her jaw told me that Lizbeth had already thought this out. Without me, they were headed straight to the foster system. The same system that had raised and destroyed Mama. If book-loving Lizbeth would rather brave two hundred miles of mountain wilderness on a chance my dad would help them out, it must be pretty bad at home.

Ignoring my rising panic about debt, bills, and credit card payments that would soon be turned over to a debt collector to harass me into the grave, I squeezed her cold, trembling hand.

"We'll figure everything out. First, you two need a hot shower, some fresh clothes, and a really, really long sleep in my comfortable bed. The portable A/C machine kind of sucks, but it's better than roasting to death. Sound good?"

Lizbeth sighed, gratefully transferring the position of leadership to me. She had always been a kind soul, born to speed through math equations, read books, and float on the idea of every romance she could find. Where Ellie had always thrived in rugged, unusual circumstances, Lizbeth preferred predictability.

"You did the right thing, Lizbeth."

Ellie stared at me through Mama's sooty lashes, her expression as hard as a diamond. Lizbeth paused, looking between the two of us.

"If Jim comes?" Lizbeth asked, voicing Ellie's unspoken question.

"He won't."

"If he does?"

"I'll kick him off my property and tell him to go back to the hole he was born in. Then I'll call the cops."

What a joy that would be.

The certainty in my tone seemed to calm Lizbeth. Ellie straightened, eyeing me, and fell in step behind Lizbeth as I led them into the hall and up the stairs.

*Chapter Four*

MAVERICK

Bethany was distracted today.

I sat at the same table, same spot, this time with a cup of coffee in my half-curled hand and a view of her puttering around the counter. An old pair of jeans and a tank top today. That old hat kept her hair in a ponytail away from her face, but it fell down her back like ebony ribbons.

While trying not to obviously watch her, I kept a running tally of the number of times she moved the milk gallon from one spot to another. Why didn't she just put it in the fridge? And what was with the wrinkle between her eyebrows?

*Distracted* didn't quite say it.

Something had happened between yesterday and now. The challenging spark that had ignited her pride, preventing her from taking my money yesterday, had dampened. She stopped, looked at the ceiling, and frowned.

Shifting uneasily, I realized I might have to wait on my proposal. If I posed my offer today, would she take it? So much of success in business contracts was about reading the person. Discerning what they needed and what they wanted. Business deals turned on saying the right thing at the right time. For all I knew, she hated this shop and didn't want to save it.

At which point, I would be screwed.

The shop was quieter today, as if it sensed her mood. Few sounds outside. An occasional car driving past. I couldn't help but wonder if she had high-traffic hours after the morning commute. With a reservoir like that, surely they had a peak in the summer.

*Business,* I reminded myself. *This is just business. It doesn't matter if she's having a bad day.*

The dry heat of the morning filled the shop, buffered only by the whisper of wind sliding in the drive-through window. Ignoring another sly glance sent my way, I reviewed what I knew from public records and soft inquiries around town.

So many people willing to talk in a small world like this.

*Bethany Beecham.*

*Twenty-three.*

*Owner for the last eight months.*

*Shop previously owned by her father, an avid fisherman, who died of a heart attack eight months ago.*

*Banks locally (assumed).*

*Mother is deceased.*

*Lives above the shop.*

*Dropped out of college.*

*Wants to pursue real estate (this was a rumor from the bartender—not sure of its origin).*

*Hates coffee.*

I stared at the screen for several minutes, letting my thoughts run.

Normally I had a good sense for deals like this. This time, I couldn't feel it out. Her careful avoidance of eye contact and her total absorption in whatever was distracting her today, kept the ground tentative. Besides, some of this couldn't be true. Who owned and ran a coffee shop if they hated coffee?

Thankfully, I liked the challenge.

Drawing in a breath, I decided to get the first step over with today. Putting it off would only create more uncertainty. A bad day was often a good time to pounce. With struggle came vulnerability, and with vulnerability often came an openness to change.

As I approached, she paused. Her gaze met mine. Her sparkling, aquamarine eyes startled me. For a second, she hesitated as I approached. Then she straightened, her chin tilted up, her shoulders back. Her eyes flickered to my sleeve of tattoos, then back to my face.

I smiled, but not too much. She didn't seem like the type to trust charm. I remained quiet. Breaking the air first gave her control. It helped, especially on bad days.

"Was your coffee okay?" she asked.

*Watery,* I thought. "It was perfect, thank you."

Her shoulders relaxed a bit. "Good. Can I help you with something?"

*Stop wearing those pants, for starters.*

"Do you have somewhere I could take a call? I have a business meeting with a member of my team, and I don't want it to be interrupted."

Her teeth bit into her lower lip for a second before she said, "Sure. I have an office you can use. It's a bit messy."

"I'm not afraid of messy."

*I'd better not be if we're going to do this together.*

"Down the hall, first door on the right." She gestured to a short hall only a few steps away. A wry smile appeared in a flash. "And no, it's not a closet. It's the office."

"Ah, thanks."

Her pulse picked up in her throat, but she didn't break eye contact with me. A new tension lived in her body that hadn't been there yesterday, despite the unmitigated disaster of a day. As if she looked away, she'd break.

Good.

I leaned on the counter with both hands, closing the distance between us. Throwing her a little off-balance was my only goal, but it backfired. Instead, I was thrown off track. She smelled like cotton. I couldn't think for half a breath. Hints of it lingered in the musty shop.

She immediately leaned back.

Ignoring the annoyance in her expression, I asked, "Can I make a deal with you?"

She blinked several times. "A deal?"

"Yes."

"About what?"

"I'm here to renovate my grandfather's cabin, but I have meetings to keep up with in the morning. The internet can't be installed for another couple of weeks."

*Or just one week.*

"And you want to work *here*?"

I pointed to her office. "I want to work there."

"That place would give a mole claustrophobia." She eyed my tall frame. "Will you even fit?"

"I'm sure it would be fine, thank you. I'll give you a hundred dollars a day."

By sheer experience, I kept my laissez-faire attitude about it. A hundred dollars was nothing. Coworking spaces in the city sometimes cost more than that, and without such attractive scenery. Besides, it didn't matter how much. What mattered was her reaction.

The final test.

Her gaze tapered, studying me. She looked up to the ceiling, then back at me with a wary mien.

*Good girl,* I wanted to say. *Don't trust me yet.*

"How many days?" she asked, folding her arms across her chest.

"Five days a week."

The math computed quickly in her mind. I could almost see the numbers adding up. If my estimations were right—and when weren't they?—that would double her revenue on slow days. A pittance for a place like this, with massive overhead.

The moment I saw her comprehend the amount, her brow grew heavy. "Why a hundred dollars a day?"

"Why not?"

"Because that's ridiculous."

"Why is it ridiculous?" I shot back. Nothing was as exciting as a counter. "I require a service that you can provide. I need a place with internet and a quiet room. You can give me that. It's the same business exchange as when you bring me coffee."

Her eyes widened. "It's not."

"I disagree."

"No. I won't make that deal."

"Why not?"

"I appreciate the offer, but it's too ridiculous."

"Really?"

She tilted her chin up. "Yes. You were here yesterday. Doesn't take a genius to see that this place is a hot mess about to start on fire. No one would offer two grand a month in rent for a four-square-foot office. C'mon. I'm not an idiot."

Oh, this girl. She was about a breath away from giving into this place. Maybe *she* would burn it to the ground. I could see the resentment in her eyes now, and that was good. Right where I wanted her.

"Regardless of your opinion"—I straightened, and she seemed relieved—"I still need an office. What would make this palatable to you?"

She hesitated for at least ten seconds. I let it ride, waiting without expectation or pressure. Only a rookie tried to fill the silence.

"Twenty-five bucks a day," she said with a piercing annoyance that would have cowed a lesser man. "Unlimited use before noon. If you need it after that, another twenty-five dollars. You can pay by credit card weekly, at the beginning of the week."

Quick deal-making meant she was fast on her feet, and her pride meant she wanted to earn her money, not just take it. Both admirable traits, but they were working against her in this environment.

With a smirk, I held out a hand. She accepted. I felt her touch all the way into my shoulders.

"You have a deal," I said.

She held out her other hand as I let hers go with unexpected reluctance.

"Great. Now give me your credit card."

# Chapter Five

BETHANY

"What is going on, Bethany?"

Jada met me at the back door of her office with a perplexed expression. She wore a tasteful knee-length black skirt and a bright-purple peasant top. Around her neck hung a stethoscope and a mess of beads. Despite her professional presentation, her shoes were a pair of ballet flats, double-reinforced for extra protection from standing on her feet all day. Her thick black hair was pulled back in a bun at her neck.

I stepped out of my clunky, post-college car with a heavy sigh, a small purse hanging off my shoulder.

"You sounded odd on the phone when you called," she continued. "I've been worried about you. Why did we have to wait until my staff was gone to meet? And who is this?"

"Ellie wouldn't come unless you were the only one here."

"Ellie?"

Lizbeth sat in the back seat, eyeing Jada warily. She'd donned one of my old caps and tied her hair back, hiding her beautiful fiery strands. She seemed entirely too small and vulnerable. Ellie lay under a blanket on the floor of the car. She'd refused to leave the attic until I promised her she could completely hide and Jada would be the only person we'd see.

"Something a bit unexpected came up," I said. "Do you have an exam room we can sneak into? I'll explain it all there."

Jada's curious expression dropped into concern as she gazed past me to Lizbeth, then back to me. Something seemed to click.

"Of course." Jada gestured toward her office. "Just back here."

Lizbeth's door opened. She undid her seat belt, murmured something to Ellie, and stepped out. Ellie followed; blanket pulled over her.

Jada caught my eye over their heads. I sent her a grim expression back and shook my head. She quickly led us toward the building.

Once inside, Lizbeth let out a breath of relief. Ellie peeked out from under the blanket as Jada strode into the back, but kept her face tucked into the folds. A few seconds later, I stood next to Lizbeth in a small clinic room that smelled like mothballs and a cotton-scented candle. Cartoon animals painted on the wall eased the sterile atmosphere.

When Jada shut the door behind us, Ellie stiffened. She stood against the wall, back straight as an arrow.

Jada stayed on the other side of the room, arms at her side, a warm smile on her face. Lizbeth returned it half-heartedly, but Ellie didn't emerge from her blanket. Although she didn't make it obvious, Jada was watching them closely. Having someone else see them filled me with relief. They weren't some apparition that dropped into my life so unexpectedly.

"I'm Jada, the doctor in this small town. It's good to meet the two of you."

Lizbeth mumbled something. Ellie stared at the wall.

Jada tilted her head to the side, nonplussed. To Lizbeth, she asked, "How old are you?"

"Sixteen."

"And how old are you?" she asked Ellie.

"Eleven," Lizbeth said. "She doesn't speak much."

"Can't or won't?"

"Won't."

"Well," Jada said, pulling in a deep breath as she studied Lizbeth's fading bruise. "Let's be honest with each other. You're not here for a regular checkup, are you? Somebody hurt you."

Jada cast Ellie a long glance, then turned back to Lizbeth. "Will you tell me what happened?" she asked gently.

Lizbeth recounted the same story she'd told me without wavering, still hesitating to throw full accountability on Jim. No doubt she had practiced retelling it on the long march here, deciding what to say ahead of time so each girl knew what to hide. That probably meant they were hiding something else. They'd always been close, but now they seemed to share a brain.

"Ellie might not let you see them," Lizbeth said, "but her ribs are hurt. There are a few bruises, and she had a hard time breathing. Seems to be getting better, though. We had to walk really slow at first."

The blanket remained immobile, even though Ellie was peeking out through a fold. But her eyes remained hidden.

"I'd like to take pictures of the injuries," Jada said to Lizbeth and me, her tone firm but still gentle. "The documentation will be beneficial to you and your sister later."

Lizbeth's nostrils flared. She looked at me in a panic. "For what?" she asked.

Jada calmly said, "To protect you in court so you can leave that house forever and go to a better home. Do you want that?"

Lizbeth said nothing, appearing torn.

Ellie stirred.

Jada turned to a clipboard she'd been scrawling notes on. "I'll make sure to write as much as I can in the reports so it would be clear to any jury what my findings are. The injuries speak for themselves."

Lizbeth's cheeks flared apple red. I put a hand on her shoulder. "Lizbeth, don't you want to get away?" I asked softly. "Isn't that why you came here?"

Her lower lip trembled. "I don't know. We just ran that night, and then we kept going. It . . . it seemed crazy to go back, then, with Ellie hurt. But to leave forever . . . "

Her words trailed away, leaving something unsaid.

Jada met my gaze. "Can I talk to you in the hall, Bethany?"

"Sure."

She gave Lizbeth another warm, reassuring smile. "We'll be right back."

* * *

"They're going to be physically fine. I can already tell that, if they truly traveled as far as you say they did. The scars that'll last are probably more emotional, and they'll run deep. Eventually, I'd like to see them in counseling, but for now, I'd focus on the most important thing: keeping them safe. That means one thing." Jada met me eye to eye. "You're going to have to make a decision."

"About keeping them?"

"You can't harbor them without telling their father. He may try to bring kidnapping charges against you."

"Him?" I cried. "He beat them."

"I know. And the photographs of the injuries will help the case against him, but just because you're their half-sister doesn't mean you can provide a better situation. Nor does it mean a judge would grant you custody. Jim can go to classes and prove himself under control and get them back. You need to decide what you're going to do."

"Jada, I'm not going to send them back."

"So, you're going to keep them? The coffee shop is failing even after you burned through your father's insurance money.

You can't sell real estate, run the coffee shop, and support these girls. They need school. Stability. A table to eat on every night. You have none of that."

"I have tables," I muttered, but the rest of my retort stalled in my throat. She was right. Half right, anyway. I had tables; they were just in the shop. The shop that was a failing mess and would potentially drag me into a pit of debt I had no way to swim out of.

Case in point—I'd forgotten to eat lunch. How would I keep *them* fed?

A rush of overwhelm slipped through me. Keeping myself afloat had been hit-or-miss since Dad died. I tightened my arms around my chest.

"If Ellie even had a whiff of suspicion that I would send them back, she'd run away," I said. "She may be young, but I think she'd rather die trying to scrape a life out in the mountains than go back to Jim. She's always been stubborn. And Lizbeth? She used to be soft as cotton. Now she's protecting him."

"They often protect their abusers."

"She's not made for this."

"She's doing a damn fine job," Jada said quietly. "Despite her loyalty to her father, she brought them here, didn't she? She may have saved her sister. Ellie may have been in for more than a kick in the ribs and a backhand to the face."

I winced, picturing it.

"What if I don't take them?"

"Then foster care is the next-best choice."

The words turned my stomach. "Foster care?" I hissed.

Jada put a hand on my arm. "I know it's not an option you like, but it's one you need to consider."

"The foster care system broke my mother."

"Or saved her. It depends on how you look at it. If she was in foster care, her home life must have been pretty ugly. Your father told me that Kat had mental-health issues that had never been addressed. You can't throw that on the foster system. Bethany, if you want them out of Jim's hands, and you can't do it yourself —something that no one would ask or expect of you—then there are really good families that can keep them safe."

"The nightmares—"

"There are always nightmares. But there are successes too. You just don't hear about them." Jada gave me a comforting squeeze on the arm. "Just think about it, all right?"

After a long, traitorous pause, I nodded. "I will."

"And think about talking to Kinoshi. He and I have done some family-law cases not unlike this together. He'd be good to talk to."

The thought of Kinoshi, a local lawyer, sent a shiver through me. A ripple of disbelief followed. How had things devolved to this so quickly?

"Are the three of you safe for now?" Jada asked.

"Yes."

"What if he comes?"

"I'm in the middle of town."

Her gaze tapered. "That doesn't make you safe. I know you can take care of yourself, but be aware that he will probably come looking for them. If this guy isn't stable, things could get ugly, and I don't like knowing you're alone at that shop with them."

My thoughts flitted to Mav. Not entirely alone. At least whenever he'd be there.

"Thanks, Jada. We'll take extra precautions."

"I'm always here for you," she said, lifting a long, skinny finger. "Always. But right now, you have a big decision to face. Start gathering the facts, and let me know if you need to talk about it. In the meantime, get them lots of fresh air. Keep them active and engaged. Kids grieve with their hands and feet. The more you give them to do, the less they'll need to lash out. Can you do that?"

I'd have to figure something out. They weren't toddlers. They could do things on their own. Maybe Lizbeth could help me barista, and Ellie could clean at night. A trip to the library would easily set Lizbeth up for weeks, but what about Ellie?

"We'll figure it out."

She smiled, and warmth and relief lingered in it. "Good. I like hearing that. Keep in touch, and send them my way this weekend. I need some help with the horses and in the barn. Ellie strikes me as the kind of girl who would get along great with my new colt."

* * *

We drove toward a lush sunset in near silence. The thin, pale line of Lizbeth's lips gave her away. No doubt she'd heard or listened to what Jada and I had said. If Ellie had heard, she gave no sign. I didn't want to hide the truth from Lizbeth. She deserved to know what was going on. But I didn't want to scare her, either.

Because I had no idea what I was going to do.

When I pulled into the back parking lot of the dark Frolicking Moose, my stomach sank. This catastrophe was always waiting. Always needing more than I could give.

Was parenting different?

Parenting abused kids?

Ellie climbed out and hurried to the back door with the blanket over her head. The only thing behind us was the endless expanse of the reservoir and Dad's favorite canoe.

"I, uh, forgot to get dinner," I said sheepishly. "How about the two of you watch a movie on my laptop upstairs while I go grab us something to eat?"

"Sure," Lizbeth said, quickly adding, "thanks. Let me know if I can help at all. I mean, to make it easier. I'm not even that hungry."

Her stomach growled.

I quirked an eyebrow at her.

She blushed. No doubt she was trying to make this easy, to be as small as possible, so they didn't disturb my life too much. Her quick smile, a little too forced, made me sick to my stomach. Before Lizbeth could go, I grabbed her wrist, stopping her.

She whipped around a little too fast, eyes wide. I released her immediately.

"Sorry," I said, "I . . . I didn't think that through."

"It's fine. I'm fine. You didn't do anything wrong."

Her rushed words made me want to rake my nails down Jim's face. How had Mama stayed married to him? "You heard me and Jada talking, didn't you?"

Lizbeth's eyes widened. She opened her mouth to deny it, but then stopped when I held up a hand and shook my head.

"Yes."

"You've done an amazing job so far, Lizbeth, keeping the both of you alive and getting here. You're also far more intelligent than I am. So, it wouldn't be very honest of me to lie to you and say everything was going to be a storybook from here on out."

Her expression fell, and for a moment, I thought I saw a flicker of something back there. Rage, maybe. The same steel that Ellie showed every moment. Lizbeth had it too—only it was way back there. Deep. Livid. Stewing.

"Are you going to keep us?" she whispered, slumping in the front seat.

"Do you want me to?"

Her brow furrowed. The war returned to her gaze. "I-I think so. I'm not sure."

"Do you want to return to Jim?"

"No. But . . ."

She said it so quickly, so softly, that for several moments I could only stare at her. "What's stopping you?" I asked.

Anguish filled her gaze. "Mama," she murmured.

Maybe Lizbeth felt some obligation to Jim. An allegiance or responsibility to take care of him, or something. Or maybe it was being drawn back to the only place Mama had ever existed for her. Severing Jim from her life could mean burying Mama all over again. I'd come to terms with Mama's death years ago, thanks to Dad, but Lizbeth hadn't had that support. Both of them seemed to still be reeling from her absence.

That only added to my fear.

"I don't know if I can give you what you deserve and need," I whispered, rushing to add, "I'm barely scraping by as it is. The coffee shop is . . . not doing well. Even before you came, I wasn't sure I was going to be able to keep it open. And there's the question of legality."

"I *won't* be split up from Ellie."

"I know. I just don't know that I can promise to take care of you the way you need. I can . . . I can barely keep groceries stocked for myself," I mumbled.

Jada's words ran through my mind.

*There are really good families that can keep them safe.*

Could *I* keep them safe? Run the coffee shop, get them to school, afford a place to live that wasn't a single-room studio above a store? What we had here could only be a very temporary bandage. The three of us living in a tiny room worked for now, but we'd soon need our own space. On some level, in Lizbeth's eyes, I could see that she understood.

"I'll work," she said hastily. "I'll do whatever. I can sleep on the floor and run the coffee shop. I'll even homeschool so you don't have to worry about driving me anywhere. I swear I can make it so I'm almost invisible and—"

I stopped her with a hand on her leg. "You deserve better than invisibility, Lizbeth. Nor would I ever ask that of you."

Lizbeth pulled in a deep breath. A hint of tears sparkled in her eyes. "Tell me before you tell Ellie, whatever you decide. I'll need time to make a plan that will keep her from running away."

Ellie peered through the glass door into the shop, the blanket still over her head.

Stated so matter-of-factly, the words felt like a knife through my stomach.

"Of course."

Lizbeth hesitated, then opened the car door and stepped out. "Thanks."

The gravel ground under her feet as she walked inside, Ellie disappearing through the doorway with her. Within moments, the lamp flicked on upstairs. I stared at the gentle glow of the light before throwing the car into reverse with a deep sigh.

At least I wouldn't be so lonely.

Chapter Six

## MAVERICK

When I strolled into the coffee shop the next morning, the smell of coffee beans greeted me.

Bethany stood behind the counter, hat-free. She looked at me, then the clock. Light barely tinged the horizon outside. Despite the wide-open door, I suspected she hadn't thought a customer would stroll in at 5:30 a.m.

"You're . . . up early," she said.

No yoga pants today. A navy summer dress rippled in an early breeze, waving around her curved hips. Her hair billowed around her shoulders when she moved, falling to the middle of her arm. She seemed to be counting something behind the register. Bright-red lipstick outlined a pair of lips I couldn't look away from.

"My team is on the East Coast," I said, forcibly shifting my attention. *Team* being the new virtual assistant who would help me get this business running. While he worked on the setup there, I'd figure everything out here. "We'll be getting started with meetings soon. Mind if I—"

I motioned toward the hole of an office I'd have to fold myself into.

She shrugged. "Go ahead. Do you want something to drink?"

"Black, two creams, no sugar." Halfway to the room, I stopped and looked back. "How are you today, by the way?"

The question hung in the air between us, along with my acute curiosity as to why she looked so surprised that I'd asked. The awkward stillness lasted for a breath before she swallowed and said, "Ah, fine. Thanks."

"Good."

"You?"

"Good. Slept on the deck last night. There's nothing quite like a mountain night in the summer."

She softened into a half-smile. "As long as it's warm, I would agree."

My gaze roved the counters behind her, then I made a sound in the back of my throat. The machines were old and not much to brag about. Maintenance must be tricky and cost a lot. She could highly benefit from an investment into better machines, but she'd be hard to convince of that.

With one last nod, I disappeared into her office and shut the door. She hadn't been kidding. There wasn't even room to slide the chair back, so my knees butted up against the . . . desk— more like a wooden board cut to fit the width of the space, then supported and nailed into place by other boards.

She'd cleared it off, though, leaving just enough room for my laptop and a few papers.

I had a feeling she'd be worth it.

# Chapter Seven

BETHANY

I stared at my office door, flabbergasted.

With a blink, I turned back to the coffee machine and drew in a deep breath. Was he really that nice of a guy? Nothing about his inquiry felt like a pick-up line. But such a sprawling man didn't strike me as the type to just be . . . kind.

Probably better that Maverick was holed up in the office so I didn't stare at him. Drooling, almost, but I didn't think he'd noticed that when he first sauntered in. As if he *knew* he looked like a Viking and didn't mind using it to his advantage.

Maybe he wanted something from me.

No. It wasn't like that, either. He'd seemed genuine when he'd asked about my day. Now I could just stare at the closed door and feel even crazier. Plus, everything was going to smell like pine in there, and my brain would never think again.

Thank you, attractive male dominance.

At least I'd worn lipstick.

I wondered what he saw when he looked at the shop. He certainly had studied it just now when he looked around. That wasn't the first time I'd noticed it. As if he knew what it all meant, when I wasn't even sure I did.

Did others see the same warmth and charm? Maybe it was a bit cluttered, but the place had a homey feel. Smelled like Dad. And sometimes like fish on a really hot day, but no one had ever complained. Besides, it was comfortable. Familiar. Like a constant hug from him.

That's all that mattered.

The sound of the bell drew me back to the shop, and I turned as someone came through the drive-through, relieved to throw my thoughts into *anything* but Maverick.

The morning rush congregated as usual, but this time I was prepared. My flustered days were firmly behind me now that I had enough milk and the machines were running. But I still couldn't stop yawning.

Even if the girls hadn't shown up, I probably wouldn't have gotten much sleep. The siren call of the real estate program still beckoned me, but the massive pile of debt always smacked it down. The stack of mail stared at me from the counter. I was far behind.

In more ways than one.

Sweet heaven, but I needed an employee who would stick around.

Shoving that thought aside, I stepped into the storage room to grab more lids. When I returned, Maverick stood at the counter, taking all the air as he peered out the drive-through window. He looked at me as if untangling his thoughts.

Making my tone nonchalant was no simple feat. "Hey. Meetings go well?"

"As well as can be expected. Do you mind if I ask you a question?"

The deep register of his voice was easygoing, but I still felt myself tense. I kept the counter between us. The intensity of his gaze weakened my knees.

"Sure."

"Do you have an operations manual?"

"A what?"

"An operations manual."

"What's that?"

A quick grin flashed across his face. "I'll take that as a no."

I glanced toward the back, mumbling the words *operations manual* under my breath. Dad kept a binder full of odds and ends in the storage room. Warranties. Random notes he took. Phone numbers scribbled with a name but no indication who the person was. That was Dad. He knew everyone, and everyone knew him, but give him a task with details and he was lost. The fact that I'd made it to eighteen was a literal miracle.

"I might," I drawled. "But if I do, I have no idea where it is."

He seemed to consider that. "Your employee who left the other day. How did you train him?"

"Myself. I showed him how to run everything. Real-time training." My shoulders straightened. "One-on-one."

*That's the sort of excellent service you get here,* I almost said, then recalled the dry scone and water bottle on the day we met and thought better of it.

"What would he have done if he had a question while you were gone?" he asked.

I blinked. The question didn't make sense because it had no grounding in reality. "I'm rarely gone during open hours."

His eyebrows rose. "You live here?"

"Upstairs."

He took that in smoothly, but wheels turned in his head. Should I have told him that? He didn't strike me as the creepy type. Not that I'd mind him prowling around more often. My cheeks heated, but his gaze had dropped to the stack of letters next to the cash register. I stepped toward them, but kept from shoving them out of sight by sheer willpower.

"Interesting," he murmured, with that same shrewd gaze. "And what would happen to this place if you were hospitalized?"

"Hospitalized? That's a bit macabre."

"Is it?"

Unnerved, I said, "It would remain closed."

"And your debt?"

"It would wait."

He lifted his brow. "Would it?"

"What is this?" I snapped. Considering that my father had died of a heart attack, perhaps I should have asked these questions already. But I hadn't because I was just trying to stay afloat enough to keep Dad's dream alive and find mine again. I eyed him with deep skepticism. "Are you an insurance salesman or something?"

He huffed a laugh. "Definitely not that. Who runs your accounts?"

"Like my bookkeeping?"

"Yes."

"Me."

"You do everything?"

I nodded proudly. "My dad taught me. Or I just figured it out. Mostly that."

My cheeks burned. Did that sound as juvenile to him as it did to me?

"Any reason for the third degree?" I asked as I tied my apron more firmly around my waist. I smoothed wrinkles that didn't exist. His gaze followed the movement, then skated away. The five o'clock shadow that he'd walked in here with the other day had grown into an early beard, filling the angled hollows of his cheeks. He looked darkly grizzled now.

Enough to set my stomach on fire.

"Yes, actually. There is a reason for my questions. I'm in Pineville because I'm considering a new business. It revolves mostly around taking failing brick-and-mortar stores and turning them into successes."

My spine tightened like a stack of dominoes with a string.

*Failing*? Okay, he wasn't wrong. But he didn't have to be so *right*, either.

"Oh?"

He flashed another quick smile, but something lingered beneath it. Something solid. Stern, but charming in itself. It reminded me of Dad. I didn't like that at *all*.

"We can both pretend that this place isn't on the brink of disaster. Or we can face the obvious situation for what it is."

My courage returned on swift feet. "You have some balls to walk in here and say that."

"Because it's true?"

"You don't know anything about my coffee shop."

"I can guess."

"Try me," I snapped.

One side of his lips lifted up in a smirk. "Fine," he murmured. "I will. You have credit card debt, and it's piling up. I'm willing to bet you're almost maxed out, but not quite. You make enough to satisfy the minimum payment, but the balance is starting to get to you. Soon, you won't be able to do even that."

My palms started to sweat, but I kept them balled up at my side. He continued easily, as if he'd glimpsed into my life with binoculars.

"You still have business overhead you have to deal with, like rent and supplies. You don't have an actual accounting system, so you can't tell me if you're hitting any growth, and I'd wager you wouldn't know what KPI stood for if I bet you on it."

My nostrils flared.

"On top of that, I'm also willing to bet that wasn't the first employee you've lost. You give them a crash course on the store and then leave them to it for a test run, but you have no system set up for them to make decisions. They fail every time. When it comes to supplies, you're guessing at what you need when you order inventory instead of doing regular audits and budget checks."

"Wrong," I said coldly. "We have a great system for new orders."

Didn't, because it had more holes than a sponge, but I couldn't drown here. My system was very much tilt-my-head-and-make-an-educated-guess.

He quirked an eyebrow but still seemed skeptical. "Point taken. One thing in your favor. In the end, you have almost no cash flow, you don't take home a paycheck, and you're barely scraping by. You live and breathe this business. You're starting to hate and resent it. Your own dreams and aspirations are getting sunk into this black hole, and you're starting to forget what even makes you happy. You're tethered, drowning, and have no idea how to get out. Is this sounding familiar?"

Oh, he made me want to hiss like a cat. If there was one thing I couldn't stand, it was bullying and pressure. In particular, when there were notes of truth in it. So many of them, too.

And . . . it wasn't exactly bullying, because he was totally, dead-on correct.

For several seconds, I stood there, debating how to handle my response. Then the bell on the door rang, announcing another customer. I glared at him.

"Please excuse me. I have a customer to attend to."

Millie Blaine sauntered up, wreathed in a bright smile. Her blonde curls bounced as she approached, the corkscrew curls bright with new highlights. Her lipstick was a bit too dark, but it made her eyes pop.

"Hey, Bethie! How are you doing?"

Relieved at the sight of a familiar face, I returned her smile. "Hey, Millie. The usual?"

"Mmm. Double shot today, please. I'm packed with hair appointments. Luckily, Devin's at home helping his father with a new truck job. Good Lord loves us."

Thankfully, Maverick faded into the office again. A long breath whooshed out of me when he shut the door. Millie silently tracked him until he disappeared, then turned to me with a squeal.

"Who is *that*?"

"Trouble," I muttered.

"Then trouble is gorgeous. Wait, why is he in your office?"

"He's renting it as a workspace."

Her nose scrunched. "That tiny thing?"

"That tiny thing."

She studied me with a shrewd gaze. "Uh-huh," she murmured. "And sparks are flying?"

"Millie, no! Geez. What are you . . . no. Nothing like that."

"Right. You haven't noticed that he's 1,000% male and the size of a fridge? Don't tell me you don't want to feel those arms around you, or haven't thought about it. That's a lie!" She pointed to me as soon as I opened my mouth. Her voice took on a wispy edge. "It would be like cuddling a Viking."

"Or a large piece of inflexible wood that thinks highly of itself."

She smirked.

I set her steaming cup in front of her with a dangerous glare. "This is not something I'm going to talk about. He's a paying customer of Dad's coffee shop, and that's it. I treat him with courtesy and respect, just like anyone else."

*Which is why I haven't punched him.*

"It's your store now," she said softly, a sad smile on her face as she took the cup. "It's not your dad's anymore."

"How's the family?" I asked, hearing the edge in my own voice.

"Fine." She sighed. "Mac's already butchered the cows we had on track for the summer, so he's picking up car work again. If we're not borrowing money from Peter to pay Paul, I don't know what we're doing." She glanced at her watch with a little cry. "Gotta go! Thanks, girl. You're a lifesaver."

After she left, Maverick's steady voice came from the office, a blur in the background. Probably in another meeting. I leaned against the counter with a long breath. Thinking was easier when I didn't have to *see* him.

*Life was never supposed to be fair,* Dad muttered in my head.

I made a mental note to riffle through the messy binder he'd left behind. Maybe there was an operations manual. The uneasy truth that maybe Maverick was right made me restless.

My eyes roved the shop, lingering on the old fishing knick-knacks decorating the far wall. Pictures of bass and trout and carp. Dad fishing in Alaska. Stupid signs like *I fish . . . therefore I am . . . not here*!

Homey. Cozy. Definitely Dad.

This didn't look like it was teetering on the edge of disaster.

Right?

The Frolicking Moose had been Dad's big retirement and dream. *A coffee shop and a bed-and-breakfast on the reservoir of a small mountain town, Bee,* he'd always said to me, sipping artisan coffee and looking out over the lake. *It's the life.*

He'd thrown everything into it after retiring from the military. Blueprints for the bed-and-breakfast expansion lay forgotten in the storage room, collecting dust. At the time, I thought him indomitable. Everything would happen because Dad *made* things happen.

Only now was I starting to see the truth.

He had been disorganized, at best. Drowning, at worst. He'd invested in things he didn't really need, like an awning, when the ice maker had been sputtering to death. I'd been forced to buy a run-down espresso machine that was unreliable on its best day.

Dad's booming laugh had hidden the truth. Everything had seemed fine. I'd called him the day before the heart attack. The last time I'd spoken to him in person, he'd left me with the biggest bear hug I'd ever felt. All my concerns about finishing college and settling into my real estate dream had felt much smaller. I *wished* that was all I was dealing with now.

Maybe that's what hurt the most. Seeing a side of Dad I hadn't known existed, left with a legacy I'd never wanted.

Had the coffee shop pushed him to that early grave?

Why had he hidden his debt from me?

Amongst the expenses was my college tuition. The mortgage. Some debt from years past. His insurance could only cover so much, and it was already gone.

Shaking that off, I found my determination again. This place would prosper. It would achieve all the dreams that he'd set for it, and then some. And then I'd crush it in the real estate market here with The Frolicking Moose as my very first sale.

As soon as I pulled it out of the mounting credit card debt, talked to the bank about the mortgage, and . . . figured out how to run this place without driving myself into the ground.

Like so many other problems, at least I could put Maverick off until tomorrow. The soft padding of four feet coming down the spiral stairs caught my attention. Just in time, too.

I had another quandary to face.

* * *

That night, I grabbed my laundry bag to head to the laundromat and then my second trip to the grocery store this week. Feeding young mouths was more intense than I'd thought. I stopped when the bag dropped to the ground, unexpectedly heavy.

Frowning, I stooped down and yanked it open.

An old plastic water bottle lay inside. It had already been used, but it was carefully refilled all the way to the top. Next to it was a collection of half-eaten pastries I'd given Ellie for breakfast. She must have stashed this all away here. Some doughnut packages and candy bars and protein bars I was sure had been stolen.

Amongst the food were old shoelaces, wire, and metal pointy things sanded to a sharp tip that she'd probably found outside.

Understanding dawned all at once.

Ellie had always been flighty. Half-feral as she roamed the woods and fields by Jim and Mama's house. They had open acreage for farming against a backdrop of forest, and Ellie had always lost herself in the outdoors.

But now she was trying to be ready again, just in case. She was always one step ahead of everyone.

Shaken, I stuffed the bag back where I'd found it and stared at my hands. If I didn't take the girls, Ellie would run. We might never find her again.

Grabbing my keys with a scowl, I headed out. Laundry could wait another day.

* * *

The wheels of my cart squeaked a lonely song as I snaked through the only grocery store in Pineville, my mind on Ellie. Everything here lay packed close together, as if they wanted to cram as much as possible into the rectangular space. Air conditioning blew on me from overhead vents as I drove past the fruit, grabbing a cantaloupe.

Then I wandered to the greeting card aisle and spent way too long laughing at a few stupid cards before I bought them. Sending cards had always been Pappa's thing, so I'd kept his list going in his honor. Birthdays. Deaths. Anniversaries. All of them inherited family friends, because all my other family had died, except Lizbeth and Ellie.

When I steered my cart back to the food, I realized I should have gotten a grocery list from Lizbeth. I had no idea what the girls liked. Or what I had in my bank account.

With a sigh, I tapped into my phone and logged into the banking app.

Ninety-seven dollars left.

"Yikes," I muttered. Boxes of cereal marched down the aisle in variegated colors. They were cheap enough. Could the girls live on cereal for a few weeks? Blech. No. Ninety-seven dollars should feed the three of us for a week. The real question was whether I could pry that much out of the coffee shop *next* week.

"I would go with Fruity O's, if that's the debate that's stalled you in the middle of the aisle."

A voice from behind made me spin around. Maverick stood there, a wry expression on his face, as if I hadn't glared him to death earlier in the day. I pushed my cart to the side, freeing the aisle, and silently waved a hand to indicate he could pass. He wore shorts, a prosthetic leg built for running more than obvious now. A slight sheen over his neck and a damp shirt meant he'd likely come from a run.

My stomach twirled.

"You're clearly still misguided if you're buying Fruity O's," I managed to say, tucking my phone into my back pocket. "Or any breakfast food."

"Not a fan of breakfast?"

My nose wrinkled. "I rarely eat before noon."

Forcing my shoulders back, I grabbed a box of plain Cheerios and quickly nabbed a Sugary Flakes after it. Ellie would go for those. Lizbeth ate almost anything. He eyed it, then me. His amusement made it hard for me not to roll my eyes. He had flecks of olive in his golden irises.

"If you're going to eat cereal," I said out of sheer nerves, "don't go for the sugary crap. Plain Cheerios is the way to go."

He lifted one eyebrow in interest. "Oh?"

"Sugar. Yuck."

"That is very un-American of you. No breakfast? No sugar? Who are you?"

A smile lit up his face. Very unfair of him. It was almost impossible to focus with something that gorgeous staring at me.

I shoved my cart down the aisle, trying to get away from the scent of pine and the urge to explain myself.

"I don't like sugary things," I said over my shoulder. "Sweet is not my jam."

He caught up to me with surprising speed.

"Then what do you like?" he asked, idly moving next to me as he perused the opposite shelf. Oatmeal. How very . . . bland. He tossed a round container of old-fashioned oats into the cart, followed by a jar of agave.

Intriguing.

"Guess," I said.

His lip twitched as he surveyed my cart. So far, I'd gathered only toilet paper, cards, cantaloupe, and cereal. Milk and eggs were next. Bread was always safe. The girls had to like pizza. I wracked my brain but couldn't recall anything special we'd eaten when I visited Mama. She'd always ordered out, sometimes making homemade burritos or breakfast for dinner.

"If it's not sweet that you like," he said, "I'll guess salty. Occasionally sour."

"Maybe," I drawled.

He fist-pumped. "Nailed it."

Unfortunately, spot-on, but he didn't need to know that. Chocolate wasn't my thing, either; something I'd always been grateful for. I had Mama's rounded hips that didn't need help. But sour straws? Those I could deal with all day, every day.

He grinned, drawing far too much attention to that perfect beard and set of firm lips. "I'm right," he said matter-of-factly. "You know I'm right. Again."

I ignored the tacked-on ending and kept going. The subtle jab there wasn't lost. I didn't try to correct him, afraid he'd bring it back up.

The dairy aisle loomed straight ahead, providing a perfect escape. While I tossed a half gallon of whole milk—we had limited fridge space—and some eggs inside, he grabbed shredded cheese and precooked, shelled hardboiled eggs. Containers of spinach, goat cheese, and an assortment of peppers filled the rest of his cart. He'd probably go for grilled, skinless chicken next.

Although he finished first, he lingered. "You?" I asked as he started cruising next to me. "Sweet or salty?"

"Sweet. It's my weakness."

"Only weakness?"

He laughed. We pushed our carts down the next aisle in tandem, moving slowly. I acted as if I were totally involved in which kind of cheese slices to get the girls, buying myself a few minutes to stop looking at him and let my heart slow down. He leaned against an open freezer to wait.

"Well," he drawled, "one could consider my prosthetic a weakness."

The tone of his voice was only slightly probing, as if he were testing something. Setting it out there to gauge my response. Dad had a different approach with his leg. He'd take it off and try to hit me with it sometimes. People often got weird around him, so he loved making them feel even more awkward. Then he'd break the tension with a laugh and the story of how it happened.

The memory made me smile.

"Depends on how you define *weakness*." I snatched a package of cookie dough—Lizbeth's favorite—from the case and tossed it inside. He studied it, then me, then straightened as I kept walking.

"Sugar is my ultimate weakness, but doughnuts are a close second."

"Same thing! You have to give me a surface one and a deep one."

"Have to?"

I hesitated. What I asked of him, I knew he'd ask of me. Maybe I wasn't brave enough for this conversation yet.

"Fine." I studied the sudden challenge in his gaze. "Sugar will suffice."

A slow smile spread across his lips. "You know I'm going to ask you the same question, don't you?"

"Yes."

"And you don't want to answer?"

I hesitated only a moment, then said, "No."

"Fair enough." His smile widened. "We'll call it even."

We continued down the aisle in silence, then turned toward the refrigerated section. I hesitated over frozen pizzas. They wouldn't fit in the freezer. Frowning, I kept going. He watched me, a little too studious, but said nothing. Finally, I set root beer in the cart for Ellie, my teeth worrying my lower lip. Was that even her favorite anymore? *How do you feed kids healthy stuff with only a dinky little microwave?*

Maverick leaned on his cart and peered out the front windows as he said, "You seem awfully nervous for a grocery store trip."

"Maybe you set people on edge."

He laughed, and it rolled long and deep. I hid my own smile.

"Actually"—I straightened—"I'm afraid you're going to take your leg off and beat me with it for being such an irresponsible coffee shop owner."

Another deep laugh, but I kept going.

No reason to let him know I liked the sound a little *too* much.

# Chapter Eight

MAVERICK

She'd walked around the grocery store like a lost puppy.

At first, she'd headed toward the produce, then turned away, brow furrowed, and wandered down an aisle or two before finally pitching some toilet paper in her cart and stopping in the middle of the cereal aisle.

Didn't take a genius to see her bank account as I walked up. Surprised me that she had at least ninety-seven dollars with how badly her business was failing. Still, color me intrigued as she spoke against sugar, then stacked her cart with it. She had to be shopping for someone else, even though I hadn't seen anyone else.

*Not your business, Mav,* I reminded myself. I steered toward the chicken breasts in the meat aisle. *Stay out of it and go back to Grandpa's place.*

But I didn't.

My cart just seemed to follow hers.

"Chicken breasts?" she asked, a smirk on those bright lips. Her thick, glossy black hair swung around her shoulders. It had been a while since I'd seen eyes that blue.

"Root beer?" I countered.

She blushed but didn't elaborate.

"So"—I leaned on the cart—"I gave you one weakness."

"Hardly," she scoffed. "I asked for it, thanks."

"Even better. So, what's one of yours?"

She hesitated, then let out a long breath. "My dad's motorcycle."

"Kind?"

She eyed me, then steered down the frozen fruit aisle, setting a smoothie mix in the cart.

"Triumph Bonneville."

"A cruising man." I tsked. "I like it. Bonnevilles are smooth. My dad rode one before—"

Her eyebrow perked up. "Before?"

"Before," I said with finality. She wasn't diving into her ghosts, so I wouldn't dive into mine. "How long have you been riding?"

"Eight months. But I first tried it when he bought it almost a year ago." She gave a tiny smile. "I love it."

"He bought it before he died, I'm assuming?"

Her eyes tapered, but no other change registered in her face. "Yes."

"I overheard your customer the other day." No reason for her to label me a stalker this early. Though it seemed I wasn't far off. "I'm sorry you lost him."

She softened almost entirely, like melted butter. Then she snapped back together and eyed me with her usual suspicion. Felt better to be on firmer ground, although I liked that gentle edge.

"How often do you ride it?" I asked, steering back to safe territory. We pushed through the freezer aisle again. She kept half her attention on the freezer doors as I grabbed a bag of frozen peas and kale.

"I used to ride it every day. I—" She cut herself off. I acted like I didn't notice and grabbed frozen blueberries. When she slipped behind me, her arm barely touched my back. I suppressed a shudder.

"When did you get your license?"

"This is more like an interrogation," she said with a wry smile, tossing a pint of vanilla into the cart. She kept moving.

Intriguing girl.

She wasn't shopping for her father, so who was she hiding?

*Doesn't matter, Mav,* I reminded myself. *She's giving you internet and a place to turn around so you can get out of here and start over.*

Because I didn't want to be CRO for Mallory.

I wanted to talk to Bethany.

"I have an Indian Scout that I drive to work every day," I said to distract myself from the silky threads of her hair falling across her neck.

"Oh?" Her voice lifted, and the genuine excitement that slipped into her smile hit me like a brick in the chest. "Not a Harley fan? That wins you points."

I didn't tell her I wanted all the points.

"How long have you had it?" she asked.

While I spoke about getting my first dirt bike at fourteen and stretched the easy topic out for a while, she relaxed. Navigating every aisle slowly, she opened up like a hesitant flower. I kept the chatter easy. Nonchalant.

"Never tried the Harley for more than a few hours at a time," she admitted. "Dad loved them but never bought one. Too rattly for me. I have a couple of trips mapped out, though. Four- and five-day rides through the mountains, mostly on dirt roads."

"Terrible idea for a Triumph."

She grinned. "I know. I'd rent a hybrid, or borrow from a friend."

"Harleys are loud and not ideal for long trips, depending on how you like the bike to handle. But as long as you're in the open air?" I shrugged, leaving the rest implied.

She grinned, her face illuminated. Picturing her riding on a motorcycle next to me did funny things to my stomach, and I wondered if I'd made a mistake after all. Of all the businesses to save, why did I pick hers?

I already knew the answer to that.

"Now it's my turn," she said. "I get to ask a question."

"Shoot."

I tried to stay casual as I eyed a package of jerky.

"Do your tattoos have any significance?"

My gaze dropped to my left arm. Her bottom lip blanched as she bit into it. As if she worried the question were too personal.

To set her at ease, I smiled. "Most of them are my nieces' and nephews' names, wrapped around some design work."

She smiled back, all velvet now.

"That's lovely to hear. You must have a big family."

"Huge. Well, relatively. Five brothers, four are married. The family reunions get a bit intense, but they're always fun."

"All of them have kids?"

"Just three, but it totals a whopping ten nieces and nephews."

"Definitely enough for a sleeve," she said, laughing. "I'm very jealous."

"You like utter chaos and tribalism between young children?"

"Better than the silence," she said quietly.

We ended at the same cash register run by a pimply high school kid. I gestured for her to slide in first. She unloaded her cart, grilling me on my family. She seemed fascinated. Shocked that I saw them so often.

Baxter and Mallory had built six brand-new houses in a wide cul-de-sac, then gifted one house to each member of my family. Some of my siblings lived there full time, near my parents. Some visited. I kept mine mostly furnished as a guesthouse and stayed there once every few months. The arrangement made for interesting Sunday dinners.

"One hundred fifteen dollars and forty-five cents," the cashier said, drawing her attention back. Bethany reached for her purse, then stopped.

"Sorry, how much?"

The kid looked up through glazed eyes. "One hundred fifteen dollars and forty-five cents."

She sucked in a sharp breath, looking through the items while he started to bag them. She riffled through the cash side of her wallet, finding only an extra dollar there. I was just reaching for my credit card to offer it when she shot me a dirty glare, produced another piece of plastic, and slid it over.

"Here."

I put my hand back on the grocery cart as if nothing had happened.

Bethany tapped her pink shoe, chewing her bottom lip, while the cashier ran the credit card through. Then she held her breath. Finally, the machine chugged out a receipt, and he handed the card back. She let out a long breath.

"Have a great evening," he muttered.

Bethany took the card, shoved it into her wallet, and loaded her groceries into the cart. She stood there awkwardly for a moment before she turned around.

"Thanks," she said, not quite meeting my eyes. "See you in the morning."

Before I could reply, she was gone.

* * *

"Do you know any lawyers that would take pro bono work?"

Her question came the next morning, breaking an hour-long span of silence. I blinked, looked away from my computer, and focused on her face. She wore her wavy hair down around her shoulders again today. That ratted old hat sat on top of her head, a bit too charming for my liking. Her eyes, as usual, peered out with unrepressed curiosity. No yoga pants, just shorts that made me want to die.

"Depends on the nature of the request," I said, turning back to the spreadsheet. Words changed in front of me as my assistant worked from the other side of the country. The shifting mosaic of words and letters would look like gibberish to anyone else, but to me they revealed the early rumblings of my idea.

If I could gently tip her over the edge and into it.

"Family law." She cocked her head to the side. "I guess?"

"I don't know any that are registered in this state."

Or cost less than $750 an hour.

She frowned. I couldn't imagine what she'd need a family-law attorney for, alone in her coffee shop. Seemingly alone in the world, anyway, if her fascination with my family last night was any indication. Something was amiss here. I hated a mystery I couldn't solve in under an hour.

"What kind of problem is it?" I asked.

Her eyes clouded for a moment. She studied me as intently as if we'd never spoken before. As if I hadn't been sitting in this exact spot in her coffee shop for the past several days, sometimes taking over her office, and always drinking her coffee.

"Ah . . . a problem."

"I have a friend you could speak with for general counsel, but he can't represent you here."

"Is it a paid consultation? I've called around, and most consultations require a fee."

"You wouldn't have to pay, no."

But I would.

She frowned, glancing outside, her gaze drawn to the east where the river spilled out of a canyon in frothy waves. Walls of granite and trees were visible from here. The mountains, so imposing, surrounded Pineville on all sides except the reservoir. Even that way, bluish peaks were visible in the distance, poking up like the jagged edge of a saw.

Ornery mountains. I liked them.

"Would you like to talk to someone?" I asked when the silence stretched over a minute long.

"No. I have someone I can talk to. Just don't . . . don't want to."

With a heavy sigh, she grabbed her phone, tapped out a number, and disappeared into her office. Trying to turn my thoughts away from her predicament, I returned to my spreadsheet. My thoughts had scattered.

Who could she be talking to?

Why did she need an attorney?

Telling myself it wasn't my business didn't help.

When she returned, her lips were pressed in a resolute line. I glanced at her out of the corner of my eye, but didn't ask. When her voice broke the quiet again, I looked up. She frowned at the machines along the counter. The strings that held her apron around her back had come loose, and the thing fell limply in front of her. Her black T-shirt declared *I found my first love at the Frolicking Moose* and showed a picture of a coffee cup beneath it.

She whirled around, icy eyes unreadable.

"I looked," she said slowly, "and I don't have an operations manual. But, you know . . . maybe I should."

With that, she spun on her heel, walked down the hallway, and disappeared up a set of spiral stairs. With intentional effort to suppress a grin, I turned back to my work. Two hours of drywall awaited me at Grandpa's, but first I needed to make a call that would keep my VA busy creating a logo and some graphic designs for the website.

Things progressed beautifully.

# Chapter Nine

BETHANY

Utterly infuriating.

Maverick, of course.

His pristine certainty. The unwavering confidence that couldn't *quite* be labeled as arrogance, but almost. The fact that he always had a point—and one that worked well—made me want to throw a coffee mug at his head. I stalked upstairs, annoyed with Maverick, although he'd done nothing wrong. Except be right, exist, and make points that poked holes in my fragile denial.

I stuffed that away and turned my thoughts back to the shop. The decision of whether to keep Ellie and Lizbeth couldn't be put off. I'd certainly done an admirable job of avoiding it the last couple of days, however. No matter how I looked at it, the fates of the girls and the coffee shop were entwined. Dad's dream had to live or die, and so did the girls' chances at a better life.

No, this wasn't just Dad's dream anymore. It was mine now. I'd inherited it. I couldn't fix a lot of things, like the fact that he'd never meet his grandchildren, see me work as a real estate agent, or walk me down the aisle of what would be a *very* chic wedding.

But I could let his dream of the Frolicking Moose Coffee Shop live on.

Lizbeth and Ellie were curled up on the bed. A book filled Lizbeth's hands, while Ellie watched a movie on my laptop. Ellie looked at me with glazed eyes, then turned back to the screen.

Lizbeth yawned. "Hey Bethany," she murmured, turning the page with a little sigh.

"Holding up okay?" I asked.

"Ellie's bored."

A lusty picture of a man and woman graced the front of Lizbeth's paperback. "Should you be reading that?" I asked.

Lizbeth waved a hand. "I skip the sex scenes. Sounds horrendous."

A laugh bubbled out of me, easing my tension. Ellie eyed me again, then returned to her movie. A survival show set in Alaska, of all places, with treacherously steep mountains and snow everywhere.

I sincerely hoped she wasn't taking notes.

My phone chimed, drawing my attention back to the text I'd sent in my office. First, I'd taken Jada's advice and called Kin—his full name was Kinoshi, taken from his Japanese parents—but he didn't answer, so I'd followed up with a text. His reply came in now.

*I can meet up tomorrow night. Let's hit Carlotta's and catch up. And yes, I can give you some legal advice. Dinner's on me.*

My stomach curled a little. Some of the sweet, meddling ladies in the town had been attempting to get me to date Kin forever. He was kind, from around here, and wouldn't get in the way of whatever I wanted to do with real estate, but he was also utterly . . . boring.

Outside, the sound of someone yelling floated through the window. Ellie darted over, abandoning the laptop on the bed.

"There's a boy that plays on the edge of the reservoir a lot," Lizbeth said as if she read my mind. "He looks like he's Ellie's age. She's been stalking him."

Ellie flipped her off.

"All right, eleven-year-old," I said, ruffling Ellie's hair. "No flipping the bird unless it's to Jim. And that boy is Devin. His mom is Millie. She owns the hair salon up here, and he's a great kid. You want to meet him?"

Ellie hesitated, not tearing her eyes away from Devin, then shook her head. She remained at her perch, looking out, chin stacked on her two hands. Lizbeth had already been reabsorbed into her book. I slipped into the bathroom, wound my hair into a high bun, splashed cold water on my face, and prepared myself to return downstairs.

"I can do this," I whispered, psyching myself up. "I can face him for another two hours with him sitting there, sucking up all the gravity in the room with his massive shoulders, and not crush on him."

Too late for that. I was way too lost in Crushland.

"Or feel deep shame over the fact that he almost offered to cover my grocery bill."

I winced at my own reflection.

The $35,000 limit on Dad's business credit card was just a couple hundred away from being totally maxed out. Scratch that. Eighty-five dollars from being maxed out now that I'd charged our groceries to it. Horror that Maverick had felt obligated to pay for my groceries sat like cold water in my veins. As if the other morning hadn't been embarrassing enough. Not being able to buy them food? What other expenses were there?

School supplies?

Clothes?

If I lost the Frolicking Moose, what then? It was all I had left except an almost-college degree and mountains of debt. Shoving that aside, I stepped back into the attic. I'd know better tonight, after dinner with Kin. Lizbeth had sunk so far back into her book that she didn't notice me return.

I paused in the doorway.

"If you change your mind, Ellie, let me know. Devin is really sweet and loves to be outside. And if you want to come downstairs and play some board games, feel free."

Ellie sank further into her sleuthing, and Lizbeth remained firmly entrenched in the arms of her romance. I slipped back down the spiral stairs, a quick retort ready for whatever Maverick would say.

But by the time I wandered back downstairs, he was gone.

* * *

Kin met me at the better of the only three places to eat in town: Carlotta's Italian Restaurant.

Jada had taken the girls to her place to give them a change of scenery. She'd feed them home-cooked food from her childhood like she always had for me. Grits and shrimp. Jambalaya. Gumbo. It filled the belly and the soul, and I wished I was there with them instead.

Annoyingly enough, the thought of meeting Maverick here at Carlotta's flittered through my mind and propelled me out the door. I shoved it away.

No need to stir that pot.

Candles glowed with an uncharacteristically romantic ambiance that made me uncomfortable. Surely Kin wouldn't think we were anything but friends? Kin, already seated in a booth, smiled and stood as I approached.

"So good to see you again, Bethany."

His sleek good looks, short dark hair, and kind eyes made him the catch of the town. Even though I didn't want to date him, it *was* good to see him. Stephanie, who owned the restaurant, hummed under her breath as she passed by. I inwardly cringed at her knowing look.

Sometimes, life in a small town really got on my nerves.

"Thanks for meeting me, Kin."

He put a hand on my arm and motioned to the booth with another. His touch felt distinctly routine, as if he did this with everyone. It had been a while since I'd touched anyone. With Dad gone, and the coffee shop keeping me busy, touch was a long-lost commodity. One I desperately missed. My mind wandered to Maverick again. What would those calloused hands feel like? That stubbled beard? I'd soak him up like a sponge.

I yanked my brain firmly back.

Kin had grown up in Pineville with his parents, but moved away to attend college a few states over. When he finished law school and passed the bar exam, he set up a practice in nearby Jackson City—only forty-five minutes away when driving through the canyon. He commuted back to Pineville every weekend to stay with his sick mother.

Tonight, he seemed fairly bright-eyed, which meant she must be doing well.

"How have you been?" he asked, unfolding a napkin on his suit pants. He wore a crisp white shirt, the sleeves rolled halfway to his elbows in a casual look that made this feel less like an official consultation. My tense shoulders relaxed further.

"Ah . . . busy?" I said.

Drowning. Trying not to scream. Terrified of debt. All applied.

"A good thing." He smiled, then motioned for Stephanie, who instantly appeared with menus in one hand and a cradle of buttery breadsticks in another. My stomach growled.

"For my favorites," she said with a purr, then disappeared. She didn't ask for our drink orders. She already knew I'd want sparkling water. Kin would take beer. The perk to living in a small town, as excruciating as it could be in many respects.

"You?" I asked, reaching for a breadstick. He leaned back, still affecting a professional demeanor.

"Delightfully busy. The practice is going well. I've had some intriguing cases, and I love the clients that I work with. Things are good right now."

"That's exciting, Kin. I'm happy for you."

The words *right now* lingered with something heavy. With his mom sick, there was no telling when all that could change for him. Still, work must be a stable spot. An escape. If he loved his work so much, then once his mother died, maybe throwing himself into long hours would be a relief. Although I couldn't imagine myself excited to work long hours at the coffee shop.

A bite of bread distracted me from the sudden bad taste in my mouth.

Movement out of the corner of my eye caught my attention, and I looked over to see a familiar pair of broad shoulders in the doorway. Maverick looked like another local with his dusty black beard. He wore a baseball hat and gave a warm smile to Stephanie as she bustled over.

I turned away, belly hot.

Of course he'd show up *here*.

"So." Kin laced his fingers in front of him. "I have a feeling this meeting isn't a friendly break-the-ice kind of thing. Is everything all right, Bethany?"

"No." I frowned. "Look, I don't want to take advantage of our friendship. I'm happy to pay for dinner, but I can't afford any legal consultation, and I'm in a bit of a tight spot."

"The coffee shop?" he asked, something in his voice making it sound like he'd been waiting for this conversation to happen.

"No, actually."

He leaned closer just as Maverick and Stephanie walked by. Butterflies stirred in my stomach at the scent of pine. Kin rested a heavy, warm hand on mine. His breath smelled like spearmint. "Bethany, we're friends. I'm happy to help you any way I can. Besides, I don't always charge for consultations, so you can let that go."

"Thanks, Kin."

"Everything okay?"

Thankfully, Stephanie led Maverick a little farther into the restaurant. I shrank lower in the seat, shifting to the side where Maverick couldn't see me.

"Yes, everything is okay. Well, not really. I think . . . ah, no. Can I ask you some questions about family law?"

"Please do."

"Thank you."

He listened while I recounted the story of Lizbeth and Ellie showing up on my doorstep. Until it started to tumble out, I didn't realize how much I needed to say the words. Kin, though he'd donned a calculating expression, listened with utmost attention. I needed it. I so desperately needed someone to tell me what to do. To be on my side. After Dad died, I'd lost my team.

I wanted one so badly it hurt.

No one in town had really known Mama. Her bright eyes and long hair still lived in my mind, an interesting dichotomy of love, uncertainty, and sheer desperation. Only Jada had officially met her when Mama drove out once to see me. Jada and Dad had been an unofficial couple. They twirled around their feelings, never committing, but never looking away, either. She'd known Mama, and had kindly reserved judgment.

Stephanie returned, setting down our drinks. She tried to catch my eye, her grin wider than ever, but I deftly avoided it by studying the menu. If Kin sensed the tension, he didn't say anything. I ordered something by memory, grateful for a momentary pause to collect my thoughts again. Repeating the story only made it sound crazier than before.

After a sip of his beer, Kin shook his head. He straightened when Stephanie moved out of eyeshot.

"Wow. Two half-sisters dropped in your lap like that is no small thing."

My brow furrowed. "I know."

"You did the right thing, taking them to Jada. The photographic proof and record of what they told her will go a long way. She and I have dealt with this before, so I know she documented correctly. It's a start."

"That's . . . good."

A short span of silence swelled between us. I didn't know what to say next. The feeling of Maverick's gaze distracted me every so often, but I didn't dare look. I'd lose my train of thought, and I'd finally gotten it back.

"The first thing I need to know is what *you* want," Kin said. "Do you want to try to get custody?"

I hated myself for hesitating.

Did I want them in my life? I selfishly wasn't sure. On one side, I couldn't say yes fast enough. Warm bodies in my house. People to talk to. Not being *so* alone. But they were like miniature versions of the best parts of Mama, and reminders of a painful past at the same time. Ellie didn't trust me. Lizbeth and I had competed for Mama's attention and affection, so I didn't think she really trusted me, either. Although, she must trust me on some level to have come to me.

No matter what I could have done to impress Mama, they'd have always won. She'd kept them.

This whole situation wasn't their fault, and any perceived competition with Lizbeth may have been in my head. But was keeping them the right thing to do? They weren't dolls. I couldn't offer them a home just so I didn't feel so mind-numbingly alone.

Ellie's stricken gaze and lack of speaking flashed through my mind. The real question was could I *help* them? Could I afford the clothes they needed? How much emotional help would they require? Lizbeth was sixteen. She'd be ready for college in two years, something I absolutely couldn't assist with financially. Ellie would be with me at least seven more years.

Then there was the matter of living arrangements. I lived above a coffee shop in a tiny, one-room area that barely fit the three of us. As a temporary thing, it was fine. But we couldn't stay there forever. I'd have to find a new place, and that required money. I shuddered thinking about it.

Amidst the spiral of my thoughts, a phone rang.

Kin fished in his pocket for it, mumbling something about a case. I told him to answer it, grateful for a chance to slow my thoughts.

Then I made the mistake of looking outside the booth. Maverick watched a baseball game at the bar. He looked back as if he sensed my attention. Something lingered in his gaze. Something curious.

Something . . . bold.

I sucked in a sharp breath, then scooted deeper into the booth, putting him out of my line of sight again. How had I let my attention drift over there? Making eye contact with him sent a buzz down my spine.

Seconds later, Kin wrapped up his call.

"Sorry," he said again. "I normally don't—"

"No problem at all. You're doing me a huge favor tonight. Anyway, let's assume I want full custody." I picked at a breadstick. "What would that entail?"

"Gather proof against their father, but you've already got some of that. Second, you need to prove that they'd be in a better situation here. Maybe access to school is better, school system is higher rated, etc."

He hesitated.

"And?"

"You'd have to prove that you could physically, financially, and emotionally support them."

My throat worked in a heavy swallow. "Assume I can do all of that. What if Jim comes back into the picture?"

"If he were to come forward, admit wrongdoing, get professional help, and attend the classes that the state offers, there's a chance he could get Ellie back. Lizbeth is old enough that most judges would allow her to choose."

"They wouldn't split up."

"Then Lizbeth would go back with Ellie. It's possible that some judges would grant you temporary custody while Jim works through whatever is going on." He frowned. "What *is* causing this, do you know?"

"A crappy personality?" I muttered. "He took Mama's death really hard. Lizbeth says he's drinking more. I'm not sure how long he's been physically hitting them. Alcohol plays some role, but they won't tell me much. There could be more going on."

"Then counseling would be ordered for him, as well as rehab and anger management."

For a long pause, we stared at each other.

"But I can't send them back, Kin," I whispered. "How could I?"

"They could always go into the foster system. And, if you couldn't support them and a judge ruled against you, they may."

My heart hurt just thinking about it. Despite Jada's optimism, foster care was the last thing I wanted. The girls didn't need another adult failing them. Mama had left. Jim. Even, in some sense, Dad.

"So, we could go through all of this and still lose them?"

"Technically . . . yes."

"Okay." I sucked in a sharp breath. "Let's say I fight for custody. Prove I can support them, and the girls want to stay with me. Would a judge grant it?"

Stephanie approached with chicken fettuccine for him and

lasagna for me. After our murmured thank-you's, she disappeared with a wink.

Maverick had moved to the bar, closer to the television screen, his back to me now. A half-drunk bottle of beer sat in front of him. How had I gravitated over again? Turning away from him, I picked up a fork and stabbed into the pasta.

"I think we could find a judge that would grant it," Kin said, picking the conversation back up as he twirled some fettuccine. "Of course, that depends on the judge, the time of day, and what kind of mood they're in. There are some that definitely favor family members gaining full custody, but others have known to be forgiving to parents who go through programs."

Talking about Jim had robbed some of my appetite, but I forced myself to try a bite. While encouraging, all of this simply meant one thing: I had to decide whether I could actually support the girls. Give them the stability, home, and support they needed in all areas of their lives. All while I felt like my own life was spinning in every wind that buffeted me.

I'd have to find a new place to live.

Get the Frolicking Moose running predictably.

Somehow afford attorney bills.

And give up my real estate dream for another year or ten.

"Thanks," I said to Kin, managing a smile. "I appreciate the help."

"What do you think you'll do?"

"I don't know, but this at least helps me figure out what it could look like. I felt totally blind before."

After small talk about his practice and well-wishes for his mom, we finished our meal. The anticlimactic meeting ended with little excitement. Kin gave me a hug before he offered to walk me to my car. He smelled like fading cologne.

"I need to stay and talk to someone," I said, "but thank you again."

I busied myself with my purse until Kin disappeared outside.

Once he was for sure gone, I buried my face in my hands and leaned against the table.

Tonight, I had to make a decision.

Either way.

There was a wild chance Jim would never look for the girls. That he'd simply let them fade away and disappear. But even *I* knew that wasn't likely. He'd know where to look once he exhausted all the local areas. In fact, barring a stroke of luck that had him drink himself to death one night, I knew he'd be here. In fact, I felt some surprise that he wasn't here already.

I had to be prepared.

Although I deeply didn't want to admit it, I couldn't deny it anymore. Maverick had been right. The shop was an utter disaster. Mounting debt. Missed mortgage payments. Old machines that didn't function correctly, and electrical circuitry that wasn't all that safe. Creating an operations manual was the *least* of what needed to be done.

Tears filled my eyes as I thought of Dad. An ache for him lived within me constantly, floating in the rage that he'd died in the first place. The disorienting feeling often crashed over me in waves. Tonight, I swam in deep waters.

I let out a long, whooshing breath.

*Control what you can,* Dad would have said. *Let the rest go.*

The girls needed me. Keeping them was the right thing to do, and I wanted to do it.

But could I?

## MAVERICK

When two minutes had passed after Bethany's date left, I had waited long enough. Whatever was said clearly hadn't been good. The guy didn't even walk her to her car.

Mallory was right. Chivalry was dead.

Bethany didn't even shift when I slid into the booth across from her, a thousand thoughts whirling through my mind. Who had that scrawny guy been? Why was she eating with him? Who orders fettuccine at this time of the week, anyway?

Realizing how irrational my thoughts sounded, I said, "You look like you could use a friend."

When she peeked through her fingers, the low lighting threw shadows on her face. Her skin was pale beneath blotchy, apple-red cheeks. Her eyes sparkled, clearly on the verge of tears. I worked to keep a neutral expression, though I couldn't help an irrational flood of anger.

Did that jerk proposition her?

"Could you really save my business?" she whispered.

Startled, I blinked. Her business? When she didn't back down from my scrutiny, I swallowed and said, "Yes."

Her eyes showed such soulful concern I couldn't even feel

elated at my win. This wasn't how I had predicted her acquiescence. In fact, I'd figured another disaster morning at the shop would eventually push her over the edge. But my speculation was wrong.

Whatever had pushed her to this, I could see the weight of it on her. My fingers itched to get started.

"I mean *really* save it?" She straightened. "Dad left me so much debt. I can't sell it because then I'll literally have nothing. No house, only a crappy car, a motorcycle, an unfinished college degree, and a dream of real estate. I can't buy food with any of that."

I leaned back. "Really save it."

"How long will it take?"

"How hard will you work?"

"Harder than you expect."

Despite having heard this before, I believed her. Most failing business owners were at their wits' end, but Bethany's desperation was palpable. Something else was driving her to this, and it wasn't just mountains of debt.

"Depending on the state of your financials, we could start turning a profit within three months."

"Consider them to be in the worst possible state you can imagine."

"That bad?"

"That bad. And I need it profitable in . . . one month."

I thought that over, calculating. A month? It would take that long to get the systems created and running, debt consolidated, and financials mapped out. Not to mention inventory, delivery, and repair work. She was trying to cram a six-month overhaul into thirty days.

Still, those blue eyes had me. I couldn't tell her no. Didn't want to tell her no. What did I love more than a business challenge?

Nothing.

Except maybe a frisky glare from her.

"We'll figure it out," I said, and that was the best I could do. "Let's start first thing in the morning, at seven, after the commuter rush. Be ready with whatever documentation you have on financials, operations, titles, leases, whatever. Bring it with you."

"Don't you have to work?"

"This is my work."

"But all the meetings?"

"Have been building what I'm about to do with you."

Her frown grew, and I wondered if she'd puzzled out that I'd been working for this moment since I stepped into the shop. I left the question unanswered between us. Right now, it didn't matter. All she needed was something solid in this sea of failure that she was floating in. I could give her that.

That didn't mean I should reach across the table and grab her arm, but I found it happening. I didn't stop it. Her arm was warm, firm, and the touch sent a shiver all the way to my work boots.

"We're going to fix this, Bethany. I promise. I have a process I've worked through. It's mostly proven, but not totally. At least not for small businesses like yours. If you're willing to work and take a chance, I'm willing to teach. Together, we'll get your company back on its feet."

"What will it cost?"

"Nothing except your feedback and cooperation and total transparency."

"Nothing?"

"Nothing."

Her lack of fight was another brutal blow. She really was that desperate. The woman hadn't even taken the change I'd left her when I bought the scone and water, but now she accepted free help.

Color me intrigued.

And a bit disappointed. Chasing her had been a great time.

She shivered, but stuck out her hand. When I accepted, that damn shiver skittered through me like a cruising firework.

"I'll see you in the morning," she murmured.

"See you then."

# Chapter Eleven

BETHANY

The coffee shop lay in near silence when I returned from a long motorcycle ride to clear my head. The implications of taking the girls had far-reaching effects. Ones I was certain I couldn't even comprehend now.

One thought stood out above all the static: I wanted them.

They were my family. My only connection to someone, and I desperately wanted them to be safe. Mom would want it. Dad would have taken them in half a second and threatened his shotgun on anyone who tried to stop him. Even though they were the children of the man Mama had chosen after him.

Jada had dropped the girls back off at some point. Shopping bags littered the attic floor. Lizbeth lay asleep in my bed, a book on her chest, snoring softly. Her burnished copper hair spilled across the pillow in the moonlight when I shuffled inside. Ellie sat at the window, bathed in starlight. She wore one of my shirts that was several sizes too big. Jada had texted me a picture of some pajamas they'd bought her. Why wouldn't she wear those?

I stopped, arrested by the similarity to Mama. That stubborn tilt of her chin. The graceful arch of her nose. Ellie was already a wild beauty. She'd be a handful as a teenager even without her looks. They would only make it harder for her. Even worse because she couldn't care less about things like that.

Her gaze flickered to me when I advanced into the room, then returned back outside. I stood next to her, peering out. Someone sat in a canoe on the lake, a light hanging from a pole on the side. Devin. Still out fishing.

With a sigh, I sat next to Ellie, pressed my back against the wall, and tilted my head up. The unusual quiet and darkness was a soothing balm, and I sank into it for several minutes. She didn't say a word, and Maverick's reverberating voice played on repeat in my mind.

"She cried for you."

Ellie's whispered words shocked me. I sucked in a sharp breath as her bright-blue eyes locked on mine. They were the first words I'd heard from her in years.

"Mama?"

She nodded. Her hands gripped the windowsill until her knuckles turned white.

A sinking feeling collapsed in my chest. "I cried for her too."

Ellie studied me, then carefully crouched down. She sat with her back to the wall, but far out of reach. "You're going to give us up, aren't you?"

"Do you want me to?"

Her silence lasted for so long that I turned to look at her. She peered at me with luminous eyes. Then she blinked and looked away. Her knees came up against her chest. She didn't answer.

"I'm going to keep you, if you'll have me. Tonight, I met with a lawyer to figure out how to make it happen. You're safe now, Ellie."

"You can't promise that."

"I can," I countered. "I *am*. We may not have a lot of space. We may have some things to figure out. And we may not always get along, but I can promise you that you will *always* be safe with me."

A sense of rightness flooded my entire body. I'd keep them. I'd keep them and fight for them and make sure Jim never laid a hand on them again. No matter what. No matter *how*. If I had to leave the state with them, I would.

I'd figure it out.

She swallowed. "If you kept us," she whispered, "I would stay."

"Do you promise?"

She nodded.

"You won't run away in the middle of the night?"

Her nostrils flared, but she nodded. "I promise."

"You won't hide supplies?"

"That's just being smart."

"No hiding supplies. No plans to run."

Her voice was stark. "I always have plans."

"Not anymore."

For a long moment, there was total silence. Then she let out a long breath. "I promise."

"Thank you."

With that, she scrambled onto her bed—a blow-up mattress with a pile of blankets on top. The answer was more than just willingness. For her, it was a sign of peace. Behind every door that lay on the path ahead, I feared that Ellie would just up and leave. Retreat to the mountains to try to live by herself. Or disappear the moment Jim showed up.

Her compromise was exactly what I'd needed without even knowing it.

I remained there for several minutes, the chilly breeze brushing over me from the open window. The quiet *clink clink* of Devin's lamp rang from the canoe below. For a moment, I thought I felt Mama. Her touch on my arm. A whisper of her voice.

Then it faded.

I fell asleep on the floor next to Ellie, sliding deeply into the languorous waves for the first time in weeks.

# Chapter Twelve

## MAVERICK

While I looked forward to going over Bethany's business with a fine-tooth comb, I knew from the moment I woke up that the day would be an intense one.

Making people face all the places they'd failed was never easy. Most businesses took a nosedive because people didn't want to see their problems, so they let them keep growing. In Bethany's case, this wasn't her fault. But there was still a *lot* of ugly.

While I'd braced myself for defensiveness on her part—she didn't strike me as the teary, hysterical type—I hadn't expected to walk into the coffee shop to see three girls staring at me.

Bethany wore a dress that brushed her knees and a pair of strappy sandals. Her hair, pulled away from her face, still swept her shoulders. One of girls, a redhead, held a cup of coffee. A fortune cookie on the front of it said, *Your life is about to change. Order more coffee.* She extended it to me, lips pursed into a tempered smile.

Her voice was lyrical. "Bethie said you like it black, two sugars."

She set it on my usual table, which was filled with piles of paper, several binders, and an open laptop. The girl retreated to another table by a stack of books. Behind the counter stood another young girl. Raven hair like Bethany, but her eyes were more seafoam than glacial blue. Her gaze darted to my prosthetic then back to my face without a flicker.

Bethany could have been her sister.

"Maverick," Bethany said with a smile laced with . . . something. "I'd like you to meet Lizbeth and Ellie, my half-sisters." She motioned to the two girls with a sweep of her arm. "They wanted to meet the man who's going to guarantee them a new home. I figured it would make sense for you to understand the urgency behind what we're doing."

I paused, halfway to the table.

Wait, what?

An awkward pause filled the room, instantly kicking my instincts to life.

"Nice to meet you," I said, slipping into my best attempt at smoothing the situation into something more comfortable. Nerves made for terrible deals. When I looked back at Bethany, eyebrows raised in silent question, she almost smiled.

"Do explain," I murmured, on guard already.

"Lizbeth, Ellie, and I share our mama. Their father is a pig and deserves to be shot, but since I can't legally do that, I'm keeping them. We want to do everything we can to prove to a judge that the three of us can live together in better conditions than at Jim's home, where they aren't safe."

The bartender at the restaurant had mentioned that Bethany's date last night had been a local lawyer. The puzzle pieces slid together slowly.

The family-law attorney.

Pro bono work.

Worries about cash flow and the business.

Sugar in her grocery cart.

Half-sisters.

"I see," I said. It all made sense now.

Bethany stepped out from behind the counter wearing her usual faded black apron with pockets in the front. She tucked her hands into the pockets, her teeth worrying her bottom lip. It was her only tell.

"Maybe you see a little of it," she murmured, "but not entirely. Their bruises have faded for now, but if Jim gets ahold of them again, they won't."

My fists clenched at my sides. A little fire had ignited in Ellie's tempestuous gaze, but she hadn't moved a bit. Lizbeth peered at me from the top of a book, her long legs sprawled over the side of her chair, as if she wanted to shield herself from the world but didn't want to miss this moment.

I held Bethany's gaze in wordless question. Bethany nodded, her jaw tight. All right, then. Stakes were higher. Abusive father of young girls. Challenge accepted. Nothing would feel better than taking this bastard down.

"I brought out everything that I have on the coffee shop." She waved a hand toward the cluttered table. "Any paperwork Dad left when he died. Books. Receipts. Whatever. I think there are delivery logs there too. I haven't really kept track since I took over."

The flippant *whatever* made my skin crawl. No wonder this place was such a hot mess. No part of the numbers of any brick-and-mortar business could be *whatever*. This clutter, while entirely unnecessary with the right organizational system, could hide a gem.

Could. We'd see.

Her nose wrinkled. "Owning a business is a lot of paperwork."

"You don't own a business yet," I said quietly. "You've been operating one, but until you can walk away without fear of debt, you don't truly own it. The bank owns it. You're running it. There's a difference between keeping plates in the air and sculpting, executing, and realizing a vision."

That same annoyance I'd seen the first time we spoke about this flared up in her gaze. "I disagree," she croaked. "But for the sake of efficiency, we'll go with that. I'm *running* this business."

No, it was running her, but now wasn't the time for that clarification.

A few things clicked for me in that moment. Bethany was taking a huge risk bringing these girls into her life, and even though I didn't have any of the details, I could tell they weren't sister-close yet.

Not only was the risk significant, but her business was about to bottom out. Her only chance to prove herself able to provide for these girls was likely just about to crash in a final blaze of financial debt and lackluster glory.

If she truly lived upstairs, that meant losing the Frolicking Moose really did mean she'd lose everything. So would the girls. Someone at the gas station had mentioned that Bethany had walked away from college after her father died, which meant she had no real chance of saving herself or them without this firepit.

But there was something in her eyes that told me she wasn't ready to walk out of the flames yet. Impressive as hell. As long as she'd try, I would too.

And then she would win.

Setting aside the unnerving desire to maim the man who'd harmed either of these girls, I nodded to the table.

"Then let's get started."

# Chapter Thirteen

BETHANY

"This is bad," I whispered, "isn't it?"

A muscle in Maverick's cheek twitched as he stared at the mass of papers in front of us. The disaster that the Frolicking Moose hid was so much bigger than I'd really wanted to know. It seemed easier to not think about it.

Until it wasn't.

Recent credit card statements told only part of the story. There were invoices due on supplies. Some insurance for the building that was just about up, and three mortgage payments I hadn't paid. Not to mention the line of credit with the bank that was just about gone. Still didn't even cover the credit card debt, either.

"It's . . . not great," he finally said. He glanced up briefly through thick eyelashes before turning back to his computer. Why did men get the most gorgeous eye fans?

"Worse than you thought?"

His lips thinned.

A spreadsheet filled the screen as he scrubbed a hand over his now-full beard. Lizbeth watched like a hawk from a nearby chair. Ellie sat in the hallway where she could see the front parking lot and dash away whenever a new customer appeared. She moved like a cat.

A lump filled my throat. There were still hospital bills and funeral expenses to pay off, too, but I didn't tell him that. Maybe they'd disappear. Maybe I had an unknown relative about to die. Maverick leaned back in the chair, scrubbing a hand over his eyes. We'd been sitting here for three hours.

"Let's take a break from numbers and focus on processes." He stretched his long, corded arms overhead. Out of the corner of my eye, I appreciated the elongation of his torso. How did shoulders get that wide, anyway?

"Sure."

"Mind if we go behind the counter?"

"Not at all."

I jumped to my feet, relieved to be away from the financial prison Dad had built. Of course, he never would have done any of this if he'd known. Known how short his time would be. Known he'd be leaving me with a disaster . . . and then some.

"Would you like the official tour?" I asked. "It's not much, but then you can see what machines we have and what we can offer." My nose wrinkled. "Assets, would you call them?"

A quick smile lit up his face.

"Assets, indeed."

Ellie watched us from the hallway, tossing a bouncy ball back and forth between her hands. Quickly, I described the different machines, the fridge, the storage in the back, the cleaning supplies, the broken ice machine that didn't make ice, but at least kept it cold, and the cash register. It didn't take long. He took it all in smoothly, seeming none the worse for wear despite our hours of misery.

Finally, we stopped. He stood with his arms crossed. I kept my eyes on his face, then realized that wouldn't help, and looked at the spot behind his right shoulder.

"You mentioned not having an operations manual before,"

he said. "So, how did you teach your employee to work the machines?"

I shrugged. "Just . . . taught them. Showed them how. Want me to teach you?"

My voice perked up a bit, unintentionally, like this was a game. In truth, I loved talking to people. Overseeing a task from beginning to end and creating a product. Only I wanted this on a bigger scale. Houses instead of cappuccinos. Lifestyle and decor instead of coffee and pastries.

And, if I were being totally honest with myself, I wanted him to see me in a moment of doing something well. My life in front of him had been one failure after another. Not that it should have mattered.

But it did.

Maverick lifted an eyebrow.

"Yes," he drawled. His tone suggested he was testing me. He leaned back against the counter, eyes bright. "I would love to learn your espresso machine, but I'm a terrible visual learner. Before I can be hands-on, I need to see it written down so I can process it."

I frowned. "Then this is going to be a difficult working relationship."

He shrugged. "You own this place, right? You take responsibility for all aspects of it. You've hired me, so now you have to deal with the situation."

Another test.

"Yes, I suppose that's true . . . but maybe I just needed to have better questions in the interview process."

He tilted his head back and laughed, a deep, throaty sound. Lizbeth perked up. Ellie stopped throwing the ball to pay attention.

I tried to ignore the sparks shooting all the way down my spine and into my toes.

"Nice try." He leaned back. "If I'm better studying in words first, it's in the best interest of your company to provide that. Otherwise, I may burn myself and hold you accountable, saying I didn't have appropriate training suited to my needs."

"That's a risk regardless of training," I shot back like a power-debater. "And you'll have to do it, eventually. That is the purpose of the job."

"But if I don't feel adequately prepared, that means my safety is in question."

Heat rose in my cheeks. Maybe I wasn't the linguistic powerhouse I imagined myself to be. He had me there.

"If you haven't provided training in a way I can understand, and I get burned or worse, you're responsible for covering my medical bills."

My eyes widened. "Shut up!"

"You're the owner."

"But what if I showed you how? It's not my fault if you mess up."

"Do you have documentation that you showed me?" He leaned a little closer. I stopped breathing so I didn't get distracted by his smell. "Can you prove your training process? Do you have something written down in case I need to troubleshoot, or in the event of an emergency?"

The blood drained from my cheeks, leaving me cold. I had never considered this. Why couldn't people just . . . *work*?

"I see," I murmured.

"It may seem boring, but it's absolutely essential that you have an operations manual and a training program dictating every aspect of running your shop. It's the only way you'll ever be able to leave it, turn this into an investment, and do whatever else it is you want to do."

Like sell houses.

His words stung in all the wrong places, because how could I even deny he was right? When he presented the facts like that, they seemed indisputable. Even if it wasn't really that easy. I fidgeted. What business was it of his, anyway?

Oh, yeah. Definitely his business now. He wasn't saving the Frolicking Moose or the girls. He was saving me from myself. I'd promised to work harder than he expected, so I forced down the bitter pill of pride that had lodged deep in my throat.

"Okay." I blew out a long breath. "You're right. I need to figure this out. How do I start an operations manual? I'm ready to get started, but I don't . . . I don't know how to do that."

He grinned, and his deep voice rolled like thunder. "That is easier than you think, and takes longer than you think. But if you have help, it can be efficient."

Lizbeth straightened, shoving her romance novel into the space between the cushion and the chair. "Are you writing a book?" she asked.

Maverick sized her up. "Yes, but it's no romance."

"That's fine."

He turned, half-facing her. She tilted her head back, accepting his study. "Do you have nonfiction experience?" he asked.

Lizbeth thrilled to the attention. "I read everything."

"Can you type fast?"

"Seventy-five words per minute."

"You interested in helping?"

She shot me a look, then nodded. "Yes, I am."

Maverick looked at me but pointed at her. "You have an assistant. While I get this spreadsheet figured out and your financial situation put into real numbers, the two of you will get started."

Dread, maybe anticipation, built inside me. I'd never had a team. Going into this with people felt . . . freeing. Maybe it wouldn't be so bad. How hard could it be to write down the things I did every day? A breeze. Maverick looked toward the hallway, but Ellie had disappeared.

He slipped into business mode now, all hints of devilish testing fading. Even his serious face made my heart flutter.

"You're going to teach Lizbeth everything about this company as if she were a new employee. I mean *everything*. How to run the credit card machine step-by-step, complete with all the ways it can go wrong. How to make a cappuccino. How to write on the chalkboard."

I scoffed. "She knows how to write on a chalkboard."

He lifted his eyebrows. "But does she know how *you* want her to do it? This is your store. Your rules. You tell her where to find the chalk, how to plan out what the menu will say, and how to use colors. You can be general if you want, but it still has to be stated."

My lips rounded into an *O*.

Why did I have a feeling we were about to start something so big I'd never recover?

"If you do it, Lizbeth will write it down. Lizbeth, grab Bethany's computer. Open up a document, and get ready to type as fast as you can. First thing, Bethany, is to make a list of all the things you do in a given day, from the time you open to the time you close. Then we're going to make an operations manual."

* * *

"No. Espresso beans are different from coffee beans. We need to explain that . . . somewhere."

"Craaaap," Lizbeth growled, her voice echoing in the hollow space that her arms made as she rested her forehead on them. "This is going to take forever. Literally."

I stood behind the counter, staring at the cash register with a lost expression. How *had* I survived this long? Just dictating all the things that I did in a day had been hard enough—I was a surprisingly busy woman. But then tackling even one task and detailing all the ways it could go wrong made my brain hurt. From there, I still had to walk Lizbeth through each step. Even my hair hurt at this point.

It was only four thirty.

"Take a break," I said, rubbing my temples. "My mind is mush."

Lizbeth shoved away from the table with a groan.

In between helping the occasional customer, reviewing what Lizbeth had written, and compiling a separate list of other tasks I'd have to explain, I felt like my skull couldn't contain all my racing thoughts.

Maverick had poured over my financial situation, calling banks, credit card companies, even one of my suppliers. Around noon, he'd looked at the clock, shoved his computer in his bag, and said he'd be back with a completed report later.

"Keep going," he called over his shoulder as he left.

In truth, it'd been easier to work without him around stealing all the air. Jerking my attention his way whenever he called someone with that deep voice of his. The most wonderful distraction. Lizbeth had snapped her fingers in front of my face more than once.

My stomach twisted. "Where's Ellie?" I asked, glancing around.

Lizbeth shrugged, eyeing the hallway. "She was playing with a feather and a fishhook a while ago."

"What? Where did she get a fishhook?"

Lizbeth yawned. "She's always finding weird stuff outside. You should have seen her box of treasures at home. I can't believe she parted with it. She was so in love with that thing. I think she hid it in the barn."

I opened the drive-through window and looked outside. Sure enough, Ellie was out there, blanket over her like a tent, crouched down. Although I couldn't be sure, she was either looking for something on the ground or spying on Devin again.

Maybe both. He wasn't in the canoe this time. He stood in the reeds near the reservoir, studying the mountains. She wouldn't wander far, at least.

"Would you like me to make dinner?" Lizbeth asked as she slid off her chair, stretching her dainty, pale arms toward the ceiling. Sometimes I had a hard time seeing her as sixteen. She seemed more like a young nineteen or twenty.

"We can throw something together." I waved a hand. "There's stuff upstairs."

"I'll do it," she said quickly.

"You don't—"

"I want to."

I opened my mouth, but stopped. If doing some work made her feel a little more comfortable, I wouldn't prevent her. Maybe it's how she'd survived with Jim. "All right."

Lizbeth hummed under her breath as she moved toward the spiral staircase, long hair shimmering like fire. She carried her open book in front of her, gliding expertly without seeing anything but the words on the page. Maybe both girls had fallen into their own retreats—books or the outdoors—to escape.

A text pinged my phone. I picked it up to see an unknown number.

*Meet me at the bar tonight, if you can. I'd rather review the numbers without the girls there to hear.*

Had to be from Maverick. He must have pulled my number from the financial stuff. A hot weight dropped all the way into my stomach. Needing to talk at the bar couldn't mean anything good. Not at all. With a heavy sigh, I texted, *What time?*

His response was almost immediate.

. . .

*7:00. See you then.*

Grimacing, I shoved my phone into my pocket. My stomach tingled with nerves. I wanted to hide. Too bad it wasn't a date. I frowned.

Maybe *I* needed a romance novel.

When I peered back outside, Ellie had stood up, the blanket draped over her head and shoulders like a nun's habit. This time, her head poked out. She was staring at Devin—who had slowly started walking away, his back to her—like a lost child.

# Chapter Fourteen

## MAVERICK

Bethany looked like she'd walked to her own funeral that night.

Under the anemic bar lights, her face had paled. Not likely the torture of recounting operating procedures hour after hour —although that wasn't fun, either.

Maybe it hadn't been the right move to text her hours before we spoke, but Ellie and Lizbeth didn't need to hear this. Besides, I liked the idea of getting her to myself. She was far more fun when I could actually rile her up.

Unfortunately, this part of the job would really suck. Emotional support had never been my strong suit, but I'd have to figure it out. If I could do it with Bethany, I could do it with other store owners.

Based on what I'd seen, things weren't good with the Frolicking Moose. In fact, this shop was already half-drowned and taking on more water. They were just this side of total debt annihilation. If the girls' chances were between Bethany or the foster system . . .

I let that thought go.

"Hey Mav," she said over the too-loud country music.

I liked the easy way my name rolled off her tongue.

She eyed me warily as she slid onto a stool next to mine. She wore the same dress but had brightened up her lipstick and slipped a light jacket on.

Though I softened my expression with a quick smile, it didn't seem to ease her tension much.

I lifted a hand for the bartender, signaling for one more.

"Hey."

She grimaced. "That bad?"

"Maybe."

Once the beer arrived, she took a giant swig, then set it down and met my gaze with a long inhale.

"Tell me."

"You first."

Her eyes widened. "Me?"

"Listen, if you really want me to help you, I need the whole story. Not the least of which is the fact that there could be a very angry man invading your life any day now, and I don't like that."

"You don't have to like it."

I fought not to roll my eyes.

"Don't you think you need to be worried about some guy barreling into the coffee shop with a gun? I'm worried you and the girls aren't safe. You have to include me in *all* of this."

I tapped on a pile of papers enclosed in a folder to illustrate my point. Her expression clouded.

"All of it meaning the Frolicking Moose?"

"And Jim, yes."

She didn't seem surprised. Bethany was sharp. The idea that Jim could come after them would have occurred to her. Although she'd turned a blind eye to her financials too long, I could tell she'd thought this inevitable ending out. That gave me a little comfort, but I still didn't like this situation.

Not at all.

"The whole story," she murmured. As if mentally deciding something, she nodded once. "Fine, but not here."

She'd lived here long enough that everyone knew her, if the sheer number of greetings and friendly catcalls when she walked in meant anything.

"Fair enough. Let's take this to my place."

With one last uncertain glance, she agreed. I grabbed my coat and followed her out the front door, relieved to get her somewhere I could have her to myself.

# Chapter Fifteen

## BETHANY

The sun had just started setting by the time we made it to his grandfather's cabin.

I knew the area as soon as Maverick turned off the highway to wind through roads that led deeper into the mountains. The truck climbed effortlessly up steep, dirt hills until we leveled out on a small driveway that fed off from a one-track residential road. The driveway curved over a forested slope before stopping at a hidden house that took my breath away.

The seat belt hissed as it slid across my chest.

"This," I breathed, is your grandpa's cabin? This looks like a luxury home."

He cracked a half-smile. "Yeah, but it's not as glamorous on the inside. It only looks this good on the outside because the contractors just finished the wood siding."

I followed him through the dusky evening. He led me to a door along the side of a three-car garage below the house. Above it, a sprawling deck jutted out, elevated above the treetops on the steep mountain below. My breath caught at the sweeping panorama view.

"It's the most beautiful house I've seen near Pineville."

Considering how often I'd stalked all the real estate sites over the last five years, that was saying something.

"It is, but there's a lot to be done. Electrical rewiring. Laying down some tile in the kitchen, installing new countertops and carpet, reworking the wooden floors and the brick around the chimney. He built it big, but not modern."

"Is this why you're here?"

He didn't glance up, but his expression grew thoughtful. "For the most part. My grandfather died and left it to me in his will. He knew I liked this sort of work, I think. I have good memories from here."

A flurry in my stomach caught me by surprise. The fact that Maverick had family here, and had visited before, meant we might have run into each other in the past. And, though this felt like a *long* stretch, maybe he could be here to stay. Because that was a wagon ride I'd jump on.

His vague response left me with even more questions. But I let most of them go. For now.

"Who was your grandfather?"

"Wayne Davies."

"Oh! I knew him, but not well. He'd play golf with my dad. Sometimes he'd come get coffee in the morning, but he seemed to like his isolation."

Maverick smiled and opened the door into the house. "He loved golf and silence."

The warmth in his gaze and the hint of a dimple on his left cheek forced me to look away or make a fool of myself. I steered the conversation back to safer ground as we stepped inside. "You're doing the renovations yourself, aren't you?"

He nodded, meeting my gaze with a wry look. "A lot of them. That surprise you?"

"Not really."

He lifted one eyebrow, and I took it as a silent question.

"You seem like the hands-on type." Though it went far

deeper than that. If Maverick thought I'd assumed he wouldn't do all the work because of his leg, he was dead wrong. Dad had always proven that having a prosthetic leg didn't stop him.

"I am."

"Well." I turned back to my perusal of the interior. "It's breathtaking."

Thanks to the height of the main A-frame, the house peered over all the trees that draped like a skirt down the mountain. In the distance, the reservoir glimmered in the dim light, reflecting the rising moon. The far-off mountains looked like jagged black teeth. Aside from tools, wooden planks, and plastic sheeting, there were no hints of life in the house. No knickknacks or errant shoes. Not even a dirty dish.

We wandered through the kitchen and onto the patio.

"Grandpa had good taste," he murmured, leaning against the railing, "that's for sure."

I managed a smile, preferring the view of Maverick to the mountains. Not that the mountains weren't breathtaking, but I'd grown up with them. He was something else altogether.

"He had better-than-good taste," I said. "This place will be a dream when you finish."

"Will it?"

His query seemed genuine as he glanced around.

"Not your style?" I asked.

He shook his head. "A little too much for me."

"You prefer a shack?"

"A tent would do," he quipped, but there was an edge to his tone. "Something small and uncluttered."

"Uncluttered?"

He shrugged. "I don't like *things*. My family says I'm a minimalist."

Interesting.

"Clutter can be distracting," I said, studying the vista instead of the sooty eyelashes that hid his mysterious caramel eyes. "I can appreciate a little minimalism. But maybe not tent-level. I'm assuming that you don't plan to stay here?"

"No."

The simple word, spoken without emotion or wavering, made something inside me crack. But why should it? He owed me nothing. I knew almost nothing about him. This was just a crush that I'd let get a little too much steam. It had felt wonderful not to be so alone.

Still, best nip this growing attraction in the bud now.

To preserve myself, I switched to safer topics. "The Frolicking Moose story. You ready to hear this?"

"Lay it on me."

For the next ten minutes, I told him about the coffee shop. About Dad retiring from his work in Jackson City and wanting something grounded. His plans for adding a bed-and-breakfast —that brought an adorable little smirk to Mav's handsome face —and how much he loved fishing. I breezed over the heart attack and the funeral and went straight to the day after the funeral, when I picked the shop up.

When my dreams for real estate really started to tank, and everything pulled me under.

"I can't remember much, to be honest. My memories of the early days when I was trying to figure everything out are hazy."

Wrapped in grief. Fuzzy, the way humidity and heat warp the horizon. All I could clearly recall was stumbling around, a knot in my chest and tears at the ready. Dad's picture in my pocket. Coffee spilled on the floor and me not remembering how it got there.

Constant loneliness in my chest.

"And Lizbeth and Ellie? What's the story there?"

My lips pressed together. For a moment, I'd forgotten about my inherited parenting duties, and the reminder brought a sudden chill.

"Not really that pertinent. Suffice it to say, Jim will eventually look for them here. I don't know when that will be. I don't think he'll make a scene in public. Despite all evidence to the contrary, he doesn't normally make a big deal out of things. At least, not with people around."

As if he saw something dark in me, he straightened.

"Come inside." He gave a little jerk of his head. A night breeze had descended, stirring goosebumps on my arm when he touched the small of my back. "Let me show you what I mapped out for the Frolicking Moose. Great name, by the way. Who came up with it?"

I laughed, relieved to turn the spotlight away from me. "That was 100% my dad."

"A frolicker?"

We moved inside, and he flicked on the light. At least some of the electricity was working, then.

"A total dork. You'd never know he was a colonel when you met him outside of work."

He perked up like a cat. "Army, huh?"

"You too?"

He winked. "Something like that."

His laptop sat at a kitchen island complete with brand-new counters that still had a protective layer across the top. He headed to the fridge first. I watched him go, wondering if he was being evasive on purpose.

"No beer," he said over his shoulder, "but I have water. Want one?"

"Sounds good."

Seconds later, he stood next to me, his arm brushing mine. The brief contact sent a dizzy thrill all the way into the pit of my stomach. I breathed through my mouth to avoid the scent of pine while he navigated his computer. There wasn't even a document on his desktop. No sign of clutter there, either, as he pulled up several spreadsheets. His arm didn't move.

I didn't retreat, either.

The first spreadsheet displayed an array of numbers and calculations that made my head spin. "Please tell me you're going to explain that."

"My pleasure. This is a complexity I love. Believe it or not, numbers are minimalists."

He leaned over the counter, the muscles of his back pulling. I kept my gaze trained on the friendly glow of the computer screen. He ran through a couple of phrases that went in and out of my head. *Lacking key performance indicators* and *inefficient lead systems.*

Finally, I put my hand on his shoulder. He immediately stopped talking. I pulled back, unable to tell what the blank expression on his face meant. Perhaps I shouldn't have done that. Maverick was nothing if not professional, and I'd broken some kind of boundary.

"Can you just tell me the bottom line?" I asked, leaning back to put a little space between us. "All of this is too much for me to track right now while I'm worried about what you're going to say. I don't know those terms or what they mean. I just want to know."

He looked at me. "Too much information?"

I nodded.

"That's good to know, thanks. I'll need your help telling me what part of this process does or doesn't work. Bottom line? You have two months before you'll be forced out."

The words took the wind right out of me. I stood there, staring at him. In my head, I could only see Lizbeth and Ellie marching away from me with a social worker from the state. Dad's dreams burnt to cinders.

And me, alone in the wreckage.

The Frolicking Moose and my sisters were officially all I had left. If I lost one, I'd lose the other. I forced myself to stare the monster right in the face.

"That bad?" I whispered, strangled.

"Unfortunately," he said slowly, "yes, it is. But that isn't the same thing as hopeless. Bethany, I think we have a chance at salvaging this. I just don't know if it will be in time. We don't know what could happen with their father and . . . it's a variable I'm not sure how to consider."

Concern haunted his eyes. I forced myself to take a deep breath.

"But there's a chance?"

"Yes."

"Then what do I do, besides what we're already doing now?"

He stared at me for a moment, then motioned to the computer with a little nod. "First, you speak to your representative at the bank. We may buy you a few more months if we can show him what you're doing."

"Steven." I sighed. "Great. Well . . . now's a good time to take up religion, if you haven't already. We're going to need it."

He studied me but didn't ask me to elaborate. "Tonight, you and I are going to go over a plan that we'll put into place while you do the operations manual and straighten the business out. You'll take this plan to Steven, full disclosure, and show him everything you're doing."

"Why?"

"If they see that you're trying something, that you have a data-backed plan, not to mention a killer business consultant, they may extend some payment grace. We're going to strip this debt away a little at a time by plugging all the little holes in your company."

"Through the operations manual?"

"Partly, but other places too. Inventory, for one. You have products that hardly sell at all that you keep stocking."

"Oh."

He meant Dad's specialty coffees, probably. Or his favorite scone that I just couldn't stop ordering, even though they were a close relative to hockey pucks. He was right. I could get rid of that kind of stuff, but I'd never thought about it before. It was just what I *did* in the shop.

"There are other places you're losing money. Employees aren't, thankfully, an issue now. That will help. Once we get that squared away, we're going to get more people in your shop and increase your profit. If you can get some grace from the bank, we can cover the minimum payment on the mortgage checks and really focus on throwing that credit card debt down so you're not getting raked over with interest. Given time and a steady plan, this is doable."

He spoke firmly, confidently. The even cadence of his words, so assured, calmed my rising hysteria. The details jumbled in my brain. This mess was inherited. Sure, I hadn't exactly been steering it correctly, but when I took over, Dad's debt had already been past scary. I'd managed those minimum payments but missed a few mortgage payments in the meantime, and the debt had gone straight to *atrocious*.

"Okay," I said when I realized he was waiting for me to say something.

"Okay?"

"I can do this. I'll text Steven now and meet up with him tomorrow."

"Good. It's a start. In the meantime, we'll keep the operations manual going. That'll help us find the money leaks, as well as establish your documentation so you're ready for help when it comes."

"It makes sense."

He paused, studying me. "It does make sense, but it seems like there's something bothering you."

For the love . . . he had to be beautiful *and* perceptive? My gaze dropped to my fidgeting fingers. How did I explain how stupid I felt? How ridiculous this entire thing had become?

"What is it?" He nudged me with an elbow. "Now is not the time to hold back. If you want my help, you have to be all in."

There was no wavering in his tone. Nothing that screamed *safety* in most regards, but I felt safe enough to not hold back. Dad had been the same way in emotionally charged situations.

*Keep it to facts, then feel it once you understand it, Bee.*

"I just . . . I feel really stupid. Like I should have known this. Like this is all my fault and I could have prevented it." I peered at him through my eyelashes. "Does that sound insane?"

To my surprise, his expression softened. "You took Entrepreneur 101 in college, did you?"

"No, I guess not."

"They don't teach you this in a formal way when you inherit a disaster." He shrugged. "No one expects you to step into a new role and naturally know everything. This mess was handed to you. You were given a dumpster fire, and now we're just trying to keep your dumpster."

Unable to help myself, I burst out laughing. The image of the Frolicking Moose as a dumpster wasn't drastically far off. He relaxed, chuckling and rolling his shoulders.

"You were Army, too, weren't you?" I asked. "You were being facetious, but I can tell."

He didn't seem startled by the question. Nothing seemed to surprise him. His deep voice rolled like a river when he said, "Yeah."

"MOS?" I asked, trying to decide what kind of job I could picture him having.

"Infantry captain."

"Usual story?" I gestured to his leg, expecting shadows and reticence. At the very least, a hesitation to speak about what happened. Neither came.

"If IED is the usual story, yes."

"How long have you been out?"

"Ten years."

"Medically discharged?"

He nodded.

I reached into my back pocket, pulling out a torn, tattered, slightly rounded picture of me and Dad that I carried with me everywhere. Having it eased the ache that made it hard to get out of bed. I lived in Dad's world, but I still carried him with me.

The picture showed the two of us in front of the Frolicking Moose, just after he'd bought it. I'd just graduated high school—was still wearing my cap and gown, in fact. I was kissing his cheek while he gave the camera a thumbs-up. He wore his favorite board shorts, and his prosthetic leg was apparent.

The moment Maverick's eyes registered it, his expression changed. I grinned with one side of my lips when his eyes met mine. Something in them had shifted. A darkening, like uncertainty.

"IED?" he asked.

"When I was twelve."

The memories were bitter and terrifying. I'd been staying with Mama on my weeklong spring break instead of with Pappa, who came to live with me whenever Dad deployed. When the news arrived, Mama had been pale. Shaking. Something in her eyes had been terrified.

I didn't sleep for days.

"He called as soon as he could after it happened," I said, my voice suddenly thick, "but it was days after that I found out. Pappa knew but didn't tell me. I felt like I aged ten years waiting to hear if he'd die. He had infections and complications, and was in Germany for . . . forever."

The words tumbled off my lips with a sigh. I could still feel Pappa's leathery arm wrap around my shoulder when he finally came to pick me up from Mama's. He'd pulled me into his lean body that smelled like tobacco and hay, and I felt instant comfort and relief. Jim lingered in the house, hidden in the shadows. Mama had hugged Pappa with tears in her eyes that I'd never understood.

*He'll be fine, kid,* Pappa had said, holding me tight. *He loves you too much to die, you know. And even if he did die, you'll always have me.*

I blinked out of the memory with a deep breath. But, of course, Pappa died. Mama died. Time had been peeling away all the people I cared about.

Maverick watched me intently.

"Eventually, Dad made it back," I continued, "and we found a new normal. He got out. Started trying different careers but could never settle. Pappa lived with us while Dad flew around, going to various appointments. Within a year and a half, he was back to his usual dorky self, just with one leg instead of two. Sometimes he'd pretend to hit me with it. Was worried I'd be embarrassed to be seen with him."

Mav half-smiled, still looking at the photo. "Thanks," he said, meeting my gaze. "Thanks for sharing that with me."

But he meant so much more—I could read it in his eyes. Like whatever professional ice lay between us had cracked. Nothing drastic.

But a definite crack.

"I'll text Steven tomorrow." I cleared my throat and glanced at his computer to avoid his intense expression. "But there's so much here I don't understand. Will you go with me? I'll . . . I'll feel better if I'm not trying to tackle this meeting on my own."

He smiled. This time, it reached his eyes.

"I will. Have a seat. You may not understand now, but you will. We're going to walk through all of this together."

# Chapter Sixteen

## MAVERICK

"Act confident in the process," I told Bethany as we strode into the bank together the next afternoon. "It will go a long way."

Five hours of work lay behind us. While Bethany and Lizbeth wrote down a few more processes for the operations manual—ordering coffee through an online portal for starters—and Ellie read a Boy Scout guidebook, I'd poured over a spreadsheet template that detailed every aspect of the process I'd set up. Then I'd sent a copy to my VA, who would make a system out of it for the next company I helped.

Bethany wasn't the only one creating a plan. If this company could work and allow me the freedom to move, I had my own manual to make. Moving every three to four weeks wouldn't be easy, but it would be easier than roots. Relationships, while cuddly, were a breeding ground of issues and expectations.

And expectations really sucked the *f-u-n* out of life.

Already, holes in my business approach were apparent. I'd scoured too much financial data yesterday and needed to make a skeleton structure for future clients. It had wasted my time and overwhelmed her. Bethany had been right; I'd given too much information.

I also had to remember to use different vocabulary—another system to develop.

Not having an instant grip on this idea frustrated me. Until I executed it well, it was just an *idea*. Bethany would have to prove me out. It might never prove out, of course. Then I'd go to Mallory, fully prepared to throw myself into CRO and wait for the semi-truck of corporate life to plow me over again.

Molding a company all by myself, however, felt like a dream. No layers of corporation to move through, or teams to assign to the work *I* wanted to execute.

Mallory looked farther away every day.

"What if I mess this up?" Bethany whispered, pulling me out of my thoughts. As if afraid Steven would hear us from inside the brick building. A dry wind scuttled past us, stirring her hair, which she'd worn down. The smell of fresh cotton filled my nose. Lipstick brightened her face, eternally drawing my eyes to her perfectly sculpted lips. I pulled my gaze away from her legs.

For being raised by a single father, she certainly had a shining feminine appearance.

"He's either going to help, or he's not," I said, striving to stay nonchalant. "You do the best you can. It always works out."

Nerves never served. While there were controllable aspects to every negotiation, over time, I'd learned that you couldn't control what came before your meeting. A late morning. Spilled coffee. A crappy post on social media. Often, those little things had the greatest impact on negotiations. They were totally out of your control.

A skeptical expression crossed her face, then disappeared. She drew in a deep breath. "Okay."

Her unusual, quick trust impressed the hell out of me.

I reached for the door into the bank before she could, nudging her inside with a tilt of my head. My hand touched the small of her back as she passed. I instantly regretted it when an unexpected smile stretched across her face. I felt it all the way to my gut.

"Thanks," she said, and slipped inside.

At least she wasn't wearing yoga pants today, but that lipstick sure wasn't doing me any favors either.

While the receptionist walked into Steven's office, Bethany's forehead crinkled. "Should I tell him about the girls?"

A question I'd debated in my head last night. In a small town like this, gossip spread like wildfire, and that could potentially harm the girls later. But the truth built trust. In the end, this was about me teaching her how to read the situation. Even though I wanted to fix this for her, she had to do it herself.

That wasn't easy. But, if I knew anything, it was how to work a negotiation.

"Feel it out. You'll know if it's the right thing."

She opened her mouth to protest, saw something in my face, and closed it again. "Right. You're going for this mysterious leader type of thing, aren't you?"

I laughed.

A few minutes later, an office door opened. A man with salt-and-pepper hair, a sharp nose, and rigid features stepped halfway out. He took us both in with one glance and disappeared back inside.

"Go ahead," the receptionist said with a little smile. "That means he's ready for you."

This would be interesting.

Bethany stopped just outside the office, closed her eyes, drew in a deep breath, and straightened her shoulders. Then she walked inside, head held high, heels lightly tapping on the wooden floor. I followed, more eager than ever.

Steven, head of the Bank of Pineville, stared at me from across a glossy mahogany desk. Warm sunlight blasted from floor-to-ceiling windows that looked out on the nearby mountains. I met his scrutinizing gaze with a nod.

"Who're you?" he asked, rising.

"This is Maverick," she said. "He's a business consultant that I'm working with. He's here to help me with the Frolicking Moose."

One of Steven's dusty eyebrows rose, but he said nothing. Bethany settled into a chair across from his desk but sat on the edge, her hands resting on her thighs. I made myself comfortable, trying to read Steven's tics.

"So." He finally looked at Bethany. "You're in trouble."

"Good to see you, too, Steven. It's been a while. How's Margaret?"

"It's been seven months and fourteen days. I'm fine. Margaret appreciated the birthday card you sent last week, by the way. You look healthy, and your coffee shop is on its last gasping breath. Does that cover everything?"

Bethany's jaw tightened. "Not in the slightest."

Atta girl.

"You can't be here to beg for more grace. There is no more grace, Bethany. It's time. Time to accept the inevitable. The Frolicking Moose is dying. Kill it. Sell it. Let it go. Whatever you can do to restore some of your credit before it takes you to the grave as well. Pardon my pun."

My fingers twitched with a sudden, undeniable surge of annoyance. Who made a miserable death joke like that less than a year after someone lost their father? I could handle this guy in three sentences.

Maybe sitting on this side of things wouldn't be as easy as I thought. Although I had a feeling I was too emotionally invested in this one. It wouldn't be like this going forward. I made a mental note to forward a rule list to my VA.

*Accept no clients I can't stop looking at.*

*Accept no clients whose smell makes me want to stay in their business outside normal hours.*

*Accept no clients that look like Bethany in yoga pants.*

Bethany spoke up while I detailed in my head exactly what I'd say.

"I have a plan." Her tone rang with confidence. "A good one. I came to tell you about it as a show of faith. I know that our line of credit is out. That the mortgage has three back payments due, and that you know about the credit card."

He lifted his brow in acknowledgment. Bethany reached into her purse, pulled out a stack of papers, and slammed them onto Steven's desk with a dramatic flourish.

"I came to talk."

* * *

Never in my Army years or while scaling the corporate ladder had I felt so proud of someone.

Thirty minutes later, Bethany stood next to Steven behind his desk, a strategic display of papers in front of him. The graphs, spreadsheets, and calculations were all familiar to me by now. Steven regarded them like a man of money.

Like *maybe* she had a breath of hope.

Bethany had warmed into the back-and-forth. I sat back, slightly bored. Maybe she didn't need me at all.

"I know this is going to work." She tapped a finger on the paper that detailed my projected profit-and-loss for four months from now. "How could it not?"

Well, a thousand ways, but no need to interject them. He would see them as well as I could. Steven looked at me with shrewd intent as he peered over the top of his thin, black-rimmed glasses. For several seconds, we said nothing.

"It's something." Steven leaned back in his chair, waving a hand toward the paperwork. "It's lovely what you've done. Really. But that plan could take months. Your father promised me the same thing. Bethany, it's not *you* that's failing. It's the shop. The store. The property is bloody cursed. Not even the strongest plan could work there. Nothing ever has."

Her lips tightened. "With all due respect," she murmured, "no one has ever been *me*, either."

The struggle to keep from clapping was real.

Steven stared at her, then burst out laughing. "Fair confidence, dear Bethany. I love seeing that in a woman. But confidence doesn't pay over three hundred thousand dollars of debt, if you include the mortgage."

Now *I* was ready to get involved.

Bethany spoke before I could open my mouth. "What if I could cover the overdue payments on the mortgage and guarantee to leave the line of credit alone?"

I tried not to stare at her and give him reason for suspicion, but my brain immediately flipped.

Wait, what?

Such a sassy remark could only mean she had an undisclosed asset, and I didn't like that at all. Unexpected assets in a negotiation meant she hadn't been fully transparent with me. Did that bother me because I was her consultant, or because it was Bethany?

Steven steepled his hands in front of him like a mad scientist. "Go on," he murmured.

"Let's say I could front . . . ten thousand. That would cover the last three months and this month's mortgage payment. At the very least, square us up."

Steven's nose wrinkled. "How?"

*Yeah*, I wanted to say. *How?* She'd definitely left something out on purpose. A tangled web, this one.

She swallowed hard, her throat working. "The bike."

His eyes widened. "Your father's motorcycle."

"Yes."

"I know the one." He immediately straightened. "I tried to talk him out of it, but he said it was a Christmas miracle he'd found it and that the gods of Christmas didn't mess around, so you didn't want to anger them."

The corners of my lips twitched. I was sad I'd never meet her dad.

"I still have it."

"What can you get for it?"

"At least ten thousand. Dad bought it new in December, so it's not yet a year old. He rarely drove it this winter. I've only put a few hundred miles on it so far. If I can do that, will you allow me some extra grace in the upcoming months . . . if it's needed?"

For the first time, a flicker of humanity showed in Steven's face. "Are you really ready to give that up for this shop? You may be sinking all this money into something doomed to fail, and giving up parts of your father with it, Bethany."

She hesitated for half a breath.

"Yes."

"Then . . . yes. I'll take that as a measure of good faith. Or desperation. It at least proves how serious you are, if nothing else. You still have interest on the line of credit, and some fees on the back payments, but we can waive those for a later date. You truly believe this will work?"

"Yes."

All business now, he nodded. "Great. Get me the money, and we can talk about dropping your payments by five hundred dollars, extending your credit due date by a year, and giving you an additional six months to prove the changes will work."

"Thank you." She infused just the right amount of grace with confidence. "I appreciate the flexibility."

He waved a hand. "Shoot me a monthly email report so I can track things as they happen, and then we'll discuss payments as they come. You have a lot to prove."

# Chapter Seventeen

## BETHANY

Exactly ten steps outside the bank, I squealed, spun, and threw my arms around Maverick. He caught me with calloused hands, preventing us both from falling.

Seconds later, I realized my massive mistake. His body. My arms. His grip. Heat swelled between us like a nuclear explosion. Forcing myself to push away and create distance, I shot him a grin, sliding my aviators over my eyes as if I did this every day.

As if I wasn't absolutely starving for a protective touch.

"We did it!" I cried, sounding only half-strangled.

He blinked, no doubt recovering from the shock of finding a client in his arms. Couldn't have been too traumatized, because he managed a smile. "No, *you* did it."

"That was . . ."

My hands shook, even though the rush had evaporated within minutes of explaining Maverick's plan. No, *our* plan. I'd made suggestions last night that he'd immediately adopted. It almost felt within my fingertips. Entirely possible. At the very least, I knew what to *do* to make this more likely.

And then?

Real estate license.

"Now," Maverick said, stuffing his hands in the pockets of his khakis, "you have to sell the bike."

My elation bottomed out like a quick discount on Rue La La.

"Oh. Right."

I bobbled a bit on my heels as we headed toward his truck. He reached out to steady me, but I ignored the proffered hand. A ball had risen up in my throat, blocking my ability to thank him for the kind gesture. At that moment, the realization slammed into me: taking the girls meant giving up more of Dad. I wasn't ready for this.

But I kind of had to be.

A somber feeling washed over us as we climbed into the truck. My life already felt out of my control. Now it was a runaway train on fire. Didn't matter if I wanted to mourn Dad a bit longer. The girls needed me here and now.

Thankfully, the Frolicking Moose was just down the road. Technically, I could have walked, but I was already tired of wearing heels.

Could you force grief processing?

Did I have a for sale sign?

Why did Maverick smell so good?

Why were my thoughts all over the place?

"Penny for your thoughts," Maverick said in a subdued tone as we sat in the truck, not going anywhere. Heat from the rising sun already made it too warm, but I welcomed the burn.

"I just . . . Steven is right. Isn't he? I do have to give up pieces of my dad."

He nodded, seeming to process that. I set my hands in my lap with a sigh.

"I guess there isn't much of a choice. I just . . . I wish I didn't have to. The bike is more than just a piece of my dad. It's . . . *my* thing. The only way I have of really getting away from this stupid coffee shop. We bonded over motorcycles. I try to ride it every evening before I go to bed, just to . . . *feel* something, you know?"

Maverick's brow furrowed. "A little, yes."

Sighing, I looked back outside. I should stop rambling. He was a business consultant, not a therapist, and he certainly hadn't asked for this. Sometimes I wished I wasn't quite so open about how I felt.

*An open book, Bee,* Dad always said. *You always have been.*

Blinking back a hot rush of tears, I swallowed the emotion and said, "Thanks for coming with me. It meant a lot to have you in there."

He shrugged. "You carried that whole thing yourself."

"It's nice to have someone in the room for me, though."

The admission came out quieter than I expected, and cost a little more courage than I thought it would. Loneliness had forced my hand in a lot of ways. Taught me to reach out to friends. Showed me the sheer power of a broken heart. Made me pick myself up by my bootstraps and try again the next day. Day after day after day. But it had never been a warm companion there just for me.

Having him at my side meant more than he'd ever know. Even if he would just leave in the end.

My heart ached again, and I longed to freshen my lipstick and cruise real estate listings for a few hours. There were several gorgeous homes I'd been salivating over, watching to see the market and their progress in it. So much to learn just by study-ing, really.

Instead, I'd go back and write more processes down. Figure out where things were broken and attempt to fix them. Allow Lizbeth to create an organizational structure for the storage room based off a Pinterest board she'd been showing me, and hope Ellie got rid of that ridiculous blanket.

Talk about the opposite of minimalism. For the first time since his unexpected arrival, I regretted saying *yes* to Maverick.

Because now I knew I'd have to say goodbye to him too. That stung a bit too much.

"Would you mind taking me back?" I asked.

He hesitated, mouth open as if he wanted to say something. Then he nodded. "Sure."

The truck started with a roar, and we pulled away in silence.

* * *

Two days later, my heart threatened to give out.

Watching a total stranger circle Dad's bike with an assessing eye made me want to snap at him. *Stop touching it!*

Instead, I stood back, arms tight at my side. Dad might not have taken care of the coffee shop, but he sure took care of his bike. A detailed binder of every oil change, repair, and update lay on the table outside the Frolicking Moose.

Lizbeth, with a stack of new romance novels we'd gleaned from the library the previous evening, hunkered in her chair in the shop, a fan blowing on her. Ellie ran in and out the back door, searching the weeds near the reservoir. Every now and then her head would pop up, watching the back of the hair salon where Devin often appeared. She was scrounging for something, but kept her search a mystery.

Maverick worked inside, standing in my postage stamp of an office while he spoke with someone on a teleconference call. Every now and then, his deep, rolling voice would laugh. I could only pick up a few words here and there.

*Templates. Indicators. Rate of return. Mallory.*

My head, unfortunately, focused on the word *Mallory*. Who was Mallory? Why did he sound so amused when he spoke about her?

Why on *earth* did I care?

"Looks good," the man said with a grunt, pulling me out of my thoughts. Blinking, I shook my head and adjusted my aviator sunglasses. Today, I'd worn a shade of bright-pink lipstick. The one I broke out when I meant business but didn't want to dive too deep. More of a caution sign. Uncertainty mixed with poise. Or so I liked to think. I imagined I looked more like a fractured wall ready to crumble.

I waved a hand at the binder, my throat tight. "Everything is in there, if you want to look through it. Any repair work was done in town by Kareem, just down the road. My father bought it new in December. It has a long clutch, but you'll get used to it."

The guy looked up through bushy salt-and-pepper eyebrows. "You ride it?"

My nostrils flared. "All the time."

He grunted.

"If you want to try it, just leave me with a driver's license and you can take it up and down the road here."

A few minutes later, he drove off. I watched him go, grateful for a trial run that forced me to watch it leave. The engine puttered beautifully. Tears filled my eyes, but I blinked them back. Now wasn't the time. Later, I'd call Jada. Or I'd stop by her house and dissolve into a hot mess.

Wait. No, I wouldn't. Because Lizbeth and Ellie would see, and ask why, and have one more thing to feel bad about.

One day, I'd feel all this.

Just not today.

"Did your Prince Charming just ride off into the sunset?"

Maverick stood in the shade of the porch just behind me. He leaned against the doorjamb, entirely too at ease for my comfort. If he had to be business savvy, did he have to be so rugged? Who *was* he, anyway, to stand on my stoop like that?

"He's seventy-one, has assless chaps, and is ready to marry me in Vegas," I said with forced levity. "As soon as he fills up with gas, he's going to swing by and pick me up to drive me into the sunset."

"Huh."

"What? Didn't see me as the eloping type?"

"No, didn't see you as a ride-on-the-back type."

At Maverick's feet lay the *For Sale* sign that I'd removed when the guy had climbed on. I stared at it, then let out the thought that kept circling in my head. Maverick would understand. He'd been there, in the room with Steven. He drove motorcycles. He listened.

"I guess it seems fitting that Dad should have to pay for the mess he landed me in," I said, not without some emotion.

"Fitting," he murmured, "but not fair."

Tears filled my eyes again. An unexpected, warm hand on my shoulder made me suck in a sharp breath. I could feel him behind me. The long planes of his chest. The strength of his hand weighing on me. He exuded heat, and not an unwelcome heat, either.

Would he think me totally crazy if I tucked myself against him and curled into a ball? Because that sounded like the best idea.

"Do you want to talk about it?" he asked.

The roar of the engine coming back down the road cut off my response. I shook my head and croaked, "Not yet."

He didn't move, so I stayed close to him as the stranger returned. Like gravity, Maverick kept me centered through the next couple of moments.

The man slipped off Dad's bike, removed his helmet, and said, "I'll take it. I'll meet you at the bank in twenty minutes."

# Chapter Eighteen

## MAVERICK

She played a tough game, but Bethany was Jell-O under that cracked exterior.

The Frolicking Moose lay in almost total silence while she dealt with the sale of the bike, chin held high and jaw firm. Lizbeth had retreated upstairs with an airy wave and a yawn after finishing another book. Ellie tromped around outside, talking to herself. Every now and then, she paused outside the office as if to see if I was still there. She still hadn't said a word to me, but I couldn't help feeling that she wanted me there. Just in case.

I stared at my spreadsheet, wondering.

Part of me couldn't help but admire Bethany's vulnerable tenacity. The girl wore her entire heart on her face. The other part of me regretted not buying the bike, hiding it, then giving it back when things smoothed out. I'd done it before. Bought my employee's car right before he was going to lose it, then gave a low, interest-free loan until he got back on his feet. Did it for one of Father's friends when he almost lost his house after his wife died from cancer.

But I had a feeling Bethany wouldn't have taken it. Nor was it my job to save her.

Damn, but I wanted to.

Just as I updated my assistant on a few tasks for scouting out failing businesses in a small town in South Dakota, the front door opened. Seconds later, Bethany stepped behind the counter. Her fluttery summer dress shifted in the breeze. I shoved my computer in my bag, slung it over my shoulder, and stepped into the coffee shop. Her eyes were red and puffy, but her face clear. Lipstick fresh. A quick cry on the way back, no doubt.

She stared at the cash register, eyes glittering.

"It's done," she announced. Her voice wavered. "I have some safety on the mortgage, at least."

"You did a hard thing today."

She met my gaze. For several long seconds, neither of us said a word. She didn't duck away or try to hide her grief. She stood there. In it. Owning that monster with regal strength and grace. A monster I didn't dare approach. Maybe the monster I was running from.

I'd never seen anyone so devastated and so lovely in the same breath. The tears in her eyes sparkled like sunshine on the lake.

I'd never done that.

Sometimes, I didn't even think about it. Like Bethany, it haunted me too.

"Yeah," she whispered. "And it's like . . . like he's gone all over again."

In two steps, I had her in my arms. She tucked her head under my chin and released a tiny sob. Her hands gripped the back of my shirt in tight fists. She robbed my breath with her raw grief. When I put a hand on her head, stroking her hair, she calmed. My agitation settled with hers until I didn't know who was comforting who.

She finally pulled away, a charming mixture of sheepish relief. "Thanks," she whispered. She wiped at her tears with her fingers. "I, uh . . . it's been a while since anyone has hugged me."

I smiled and wished I could do far more than that. Unable to stop myself, I tucked a piece of hair behind her ear. The tips of my fingers lingered on her jawline.

"You're strength, Bethany. Strength."

Before I could cross another line, and with the sound of my father's voice ringing in my head, I turned away. Like a coward, I left before my heart slammed right out of my chest and told her everything I'd hidden away.

# Chapter Nineteen

❦

BETHANY

My heart lay in a tangled heap, a hurricane of emotion for the rest of that week.

Why had I thrown myself into Maverick's arms again?

Was I really so starved for touch?

Well, yes. Absolutely yes. I'd split from my last boyfriend well over a year ago, and aside from an occasional hug from Jada, I felt like a woman in a desert.

But why had he left so quickly?

Professional boundaries, probably. At least *he* had some. Clearly, I didn't. We maintained careful distance over the following days. The work continued, and so did the tingling in the pit of my stomach every time he said my name. But I kept a careful amount of space between us. Distance was the only safety.

Because the last thing I needed was to get used to his touch. Work aside, Maverick kept himself a mystery. Would he leave once he fixed up his grandfather's house? If he did, where would he go? Was this his career, or was there more?

And who the crap was Mallory?

When I wasn't stewing over my unfortunate crush on the

Viking, my thoughts alternated between Dad and the coffee shop. Sometimes, I could think of Dad and laugh. Sometimes, I felt nothing. When I did feel my grief, it crashed like a wave. All-encompassing. Terrifying. As if it *wanted* to drown me.

The low rumble of Maverick in my office filled the background, far easier on the ears than any radio. It had a soothing effect on the whole shop. I found myself excited to see him in the mornings. Eager to hear him start a call so I could turn down the radio and just hear *him*.

"Mama loved pepperoni, especially with stuffed crust."

Lizbeth stared at the pizza I'd picked up for lunch from Carlotta's, a wistful expression on her face. Ellie looked up, her gaze haunted. I leaned back against the counter.

"I know. She imparted that love to me."

"Me too."

Lizbeth locked eyes with me for a second, then turned back to her pizza. Ellie stayed glued to Lizbeth's other side, chewing.

Grateful to *not* be cataloguing ways to troubleshoot the cash register if credit card charges didn't go through, I snagged a second slice. People fail, but pepperoni and melted cheese do not.

"Do you remember"—I tore off another bite—"when Mama took us swimming in that pond not far from your house? I was fourteen, so you would have been seven."

A smile appeared on Lizbeth's lips. "You had leeches stuck to your legs," she said. "Ellie thought it was really cool, so she kept pulling them off, and you were yelling at her to quit. Mama couldn't stop laughing."

Despite the vivid memory of those suckers on my leg, I giggled. Tears had run down Mama's cheeks from laughing so hard.

"You were only two, Ellie, so you may not remember," said Lizbeth.

Ellie frowned.

"Mama was never afraid of bugs," I said. "She would kill any spider, cockroach, whatever."

"She set them free sometimes," Lizbeth said. "I think she vented her inner wild child through Ellie. Mama is the reason Ellie loves being outside so much."

For a moment, Ellie melted into an eleven-year-old puddle. Her bright eyes darkened, and her expression fell. Mama had been everything to Ellie. Lizbeth had always had friends and books and dreams and other things to focus on. But Ellie?

Her whole world had been Mama. Mama and the woods.

Ellie straightened, cocked her head, and scuttled behind the counter. She slipped into the dim pantry without a word. She'd made a sort of bed out of massive bags of coffee beans back there that couldn't be comfortable, but she seemed happy with it. Lizbeth and I ignored her erratic behavior. It had grown to feel so normal that I didn't really notice anymore.

My thoughts swirled on Mama and Ellie for a moment before a jangle at the door caught my attention. I glanced up as Millie Blaine walked into the coffee shop, her blonde hair billowing in curls around her shoulders. The unmistakable scent of hairspray followed her in.

"Please tell me you have *all* the caffeine," she said.

"For you, I have *all* the caffeine."

Millie replied with a gleaming-white smile.

Devin trailed in, grinning shyly at me. I brightened. Ellie had been spying on him since the girls arrived ten days ago. Maybe this would be my chance to get rid of that nasty old blanket. Then again, there was no forcing Ellie into anything she wasn't ready for. If she wanted to meet him, she'd probably just introduce herself.

A head of dark hair poked out from the pantry right then, as if she could sense his presence.

"Get me my usual," Millie said, "but this time as large as you can. I have eight cuts and a highlight today, so it's going to be nonstop."

"I'm on it. Hey, Dev. How are you?"

He tucked his hands into his pockets. His chocolate eyes stared back at me.

"He needs some sugar too." Millie dug into her large purse. "Mac is fixing a tractor today, so Devin came to fish while I work. If you need any help around here, let him know. He's already bored, even though it's summer."

"I see you out there fishing," I said to Devin with a warm smile as I rummaged in a drawer for his favorite hot chocolate mix. In the summer, he took hot chocolate on the rocks. "You must love it."

Ellie stirred. She remained in the shadows, crouched like a cat on the balls of her feet.

"Yeah, I love fishing."

"My dad used to fish out there."

The light in Devin's eyes immediately faded. Millie put a hand on his shoulder and said to me, "Your father used to fish with Devin all the time. They would sit on the back porch and tie lures together. He misses his fishing buddy. Said he wants to go into the military like your dad. He told him to go with the Marines."

My heart caught as if a string had just been pulled through it. "Oh. I didn't know that, Dev. I'm sorry."

"He was teaching me fly-fishing," Devin mumbled.

"You know, I hadn't thought of it before now, but I think he has all kinds of tackle and stuff in the attic. Would you like to have it?"

"Really?"

The joy returned to his expression in a heartbeat. I felt immediately better. Without Dad at my side, the fun of fishing had died for me. Slippery, cold fish were gross, but I could deal because Dad loved it so much. The joy had gone out with his death. Devin clearly still loved it.

He turned to his mom.

"Mom, maybe he has my lure! I might have left it in his box on accident."

"Devin has a lucky lure," Millie said as I grabbed an empty cup to fill with ice. "We haven't been able to find it for months now, and his fishing has drastically suffered as a result."

Ellie rummaged around in the pantry and knocked something over—an empty cardboard box filled with trinkets. She stood, strode out in her bare feet, and walked right up to Devin. Her hair swung in locks around her face as she extended a fist.

Devin regarded her, looked at his Mom, then back to Ellie. She opened her clasped hand to reveal several lures and fishhooks.

"Where did you find those?" I asked.

"Hey!" Devin cried. "That's it! That's my lucky lure."

"I found it outside," Ellie said quietly, as if this wasn't the second time I'd heard her speak. As if it was so easy for her to do so when she wanted to. "It was in the reeds, tangled around a piece of bark."

"Near the big rock?"

"About thirty paces to the west of that."

He grinned. "Thanks. Will you show me where? There might be others."

She nodded, grabbed his hand, and tugged him out the back door. I stared, wide-eyed in shock. Lizbeth shrugged when I turned to her in question. Had Ellie actually *touched* him?

Millie peered down the now-empty hall, then turned back to me. "Who," she asked, "was that?"

Lizbeth peered at me from over the top of her book but went back to reading as if the world hadn't just shifted. As if Ellie hadn't acted totally normal and without fear for the first time in what must have been years.

"That is my half-sister," I said, overcoming my shock. "Her name is Ellie. She's eleven. Our sister Lizbeth is right behind you. They're here to stay."

Lizbeth waved a hand, eyes glued to a romance about bakeries and magic.

"From your mom?" Millie asked.

I nodded.

Millie gazed out the drive-through window, toward where Ellie and Devin were combing through the weeds. He had his lure in hand. Mud already coated Ellie's legs up to the knee. Her long hair trailed into the water as she bent low.

"She seems . . ." Millie's gaze tapered, then brightened. "Like she'll be wonderful for Devin. He's had a hard time since your father died. Summer means he's either working in the garage with his dad or stuck with me since his friends are all gone or busy."

Devin crouched in the water and reached for something as it swam by. Ellie laughed when he squirted her on accident.

"I have a feeling you're right," I said, filled with unabashed relief.

Maybe we had a fighting chance after all.

* * *

"No, you can't reverse the steps, or the machine won't work. I think. I've never tried," I said, lips pursed as I regarded the espresso machine.

Lizbeth grinned maniacally. "Let's try it."

I swatted her hand away and jabbed a finger toward the laptop. "Just take some more notes. We can clean this process up later."

The espresso machine had been tricky to learn, but I'd forced myself through it as best I could when Dad first died. Vaguely recalling his actions from when we'd hung out in the shop on my visits had helped. Trying to picture the behemoth through Lizbeth's eyes now made it easier to break it down into smaller steps. She'd never operated it before, which forced me to remember all the little details.

Like how to flush it, for one.

*Step back,* Maverick had said, *and imagine you're seeing this process for the first time. What can you say, and where can you start, to make this successful for your employee?*

Lizbeth sighed and leaned over the counter to study what we had already done. The sheer number of things I did to run the shop every day boggled my mind. Documenting them had simultaneously exhausted and validated me.

Lizbeth, who thrilled to the organization and fell more in love with the shop every day, tapped away at the computer. She read aloud what we'd just written, verified processes, and asked questions. Maverick sat at the table, a running ledger of numbers on his computer. Most days he wore a pair of glasses that made him even more attractive.

If such a thing was possible.

"We still haven't discussed the close-down routine," I muttered. It had been a week since we started this process, and every day we found more to do. More to clean up.

Numbers to run.

I suppressed a groan. This process *also* brought to light my own weaknesses with glaring intensity. Just this morning, I'd run out of whole milk and had to send Lizbeth across the road to the grocery store to buy more. Half the time, I spent more mental space trying to create a definitive process, then follow and test it. Maybe I didn't make cappuccinos the best way. Was there another way?

My inventory? A laughingstock.

No *wonder* Anthony quit in a fiery huff. I kind of didn't blame him. I should send him a card. Did they even make sorry-I-fired-you-because-I-suck-as-a-boss kind of cards?

"Put drive-through customer service on the list too," I said. "Maverick will want a process for dealing with difficult customers."

"Affirmative," Maverick called from the office in a deep, amused growl. I listened, savoring every second with a fluttering stomach.

"Can I take a break?" Lizbeth asked, eyes hopeful. A new stack of romance books waited in her usual corner. We'd been at this for over two hours. I had to remind myself that it wasn't her job to run this place, even though she wanted to help. She was still a teenager and deserved some semblance of a summer.

She'd likely just spend it with her romance novels, but at least she'd be happy.

"Of course."

With a squeal, she retreated, grabbed her stack of books, set them on the floor, and curled into the chair. Ellie was messing around in the pantry with a few fishing lures I'd given to her and Devin. The two heathens had been running wild outside since they'd met, usually wading in the lake. She impatiently waited for him every morning now. He hadn't shown up yet, but it didn't stop her from casting a glare at the door every five seconds.

"Sandwiches for lunch, Ellie?" I asked.

She nodded, her tongue stuck out one side of her mouth.

Outside, a car door slammed. I glanced up to see a willowy figure with red hair and freckled skin standing there, squinting. My heart dropped all the way to my stomach.

Jim.

He headed toward the door. Our moment had finally come.

"Lizbeth, upstairs. Now," I said quietly. "Ellie, you too."

Something in my voice must have clued her in, because Lizbeth didn't even look. She pitched her book to the floor and scrambled out of the chair. I slid out from behind the counter to block the view of the hallway just as Ellie stood. All color drained from her face when she saw Jim.

She leaped over the counter.

Lizbeth grabbed her arm and hurried her into the hallway behind me. My stomach flipped as Jim reached for the handle, yanking the door open. The girls' feet quietly padded up the steps. The upstairs door locked behind them just as Jim walked inside.

My upper lip curled into a sneer at first, but I turned it into a surprised half-smile that probably looked feral. Thankfully, today I'd gone with red lipstick. Power red, thinking I'd need it to get through this stupid manual. Plus a pair of flats that went a little too perfectly with this dress.

I was ready for this.

"Jim?"

Jim stopped just inside, his beady eyes darting around the shop. Those eyes were a deep hazel and surprisingly clear. He had Lizbeth's fair complexion and red hair. The locks were lank and choppy, as if he'd attacked them with a pair of rusty kitchen scissors in the dark. Knowing him, he probably had. Too bad he hadn't stabbed his eye in the process. A ragged pair of jeans with holes in the knees and a shoe with a missing shoelace completed his ensemble.

"Bethany. Never thought I'd see you again."

*Never wanted to,* I thought.

We stood there for a moment, at an impasse.

"This is . . . unexpected," I said. "I haven't heard from you since Mama died."

He frowned, valleys furrowing in his forehead. "Been busy."

It took all my willpower to gesture to the chalkboard, as if he were any other customer. I strolled behind the counter. "Can I get you a drink? On the house."

"No." He shoved a hand in his pocket, eyes on me as he advanced into the room. I imagined him barreling toward the girls, whiskey on his breath, and stood my ground. My chin tilted up. His gaze flickered with uncertainty.

"What brings you here?" I asked.

"The girls."

I frowned. "The girls?"

"They here?"

"Here?" I echoed again, resting my hands on the counter so he didn't see them trembling. "Why would they be here?"

He studied me. His own hands shook. Withdrawal, probably. With any luck, he'd leave, get drunk, and crash his car on the way back.

He could burn for hours for all I cared.

"They ran off a while ago."

I feigned surprise.

"That wild idiot Ellie probably put it in Lizbeth's head to play a prank on me, and they haven't come back. People are starting to ask."

This time I didn't hold my anger back. They'd been gone for weeks. He probably only came *because* people were asking.

"You've lost them?"

"No! They ran off. Not like I could stop them."

"As their father."

His scowl deepened.

I let out an exasperated breath. "They're *girls*, Jim!" I cried.

A shadow moved out of the corner of my eye, near the hall. I sensed Maverick's presence as he slipped out of the office. Jim didn't appear to notice.

Jim's jaw twitched. "Are they here or not?"

"You know we weren't all that close. If they did run away, they sure didn't come to me."

He glanced at the stack of romances on the floor. "Those aren't Lizbeth's, then?"

"Mine."

"Sure." He scoffed. "Your daddy struck me as the real

romantic type when he kicked your mama out after his deployment."

My nostrils flared. "That's not how it happened, and you know it."

"Give me the girls."

"They aren't here," I hissed.

"Yet," he added softly, his intent gaze still boring into mine.

"If they die out there, that's on you."

He stepped forward. "I never did like you."

"The feeling was mutual, I assure you."

"Kat talked about you way too much." Disgust filled his eyes. "All the time. Bethany, Bethany, Bethany. Lizbeth hated you, too, you know. Fought with a ghost for her mama's love."

His vinegary breath turned my stomach sour. Some of what he said was true. Mama had a hard time controlling her moods. She acted totally enamored with someone, or something, one moment. The next? They were forgotten. Sometimes, that happened to her daughters.

The bells on the door rang behind him, admitting a familiar flash of sandy hair.

"Hey, Miss Bethany," Devin called, "is—"

"Everything is upstairs that you'll need to get started, Dev," I called loudly without taking my eyes off Jim. "Please go upstairs and get started right away."

Devin paused, assessed the situation, and immediately headed down the hall. His feet banged up the stairs. Seconds later, the upper door opened and closed.

"I know you have them," Jim muttered. "Those are books that Lizbeth loves, and Ellie would know enough to get them here."

"If I had them, I would never give them back to you."

"Never is a long time."

"Especially in prison."

He hesitated, studying me. He questioned whether I'd do it

—I could see it in his eyes. He didn't believe I'd take them or rat him out. My careful distance from them over the years certainly gave him reason to doubt. I'd never truly fit in at that house. With my lipstick, my attachment to my dad, and my plans to break into *real* money one day.

"Then let's make this easy on everyone," he said. "Keep them, but get them back before school starts, or we're going to have problems. I'll tell the neighbors they're visiting their sister for the summer, the way I suspected."

He knew.

Maybe we'd gotten careless, or maybe it was clear they had no one else that Lizbeth would trust, and Ellie would tolerate. Either way, there was no secret now. He knew the girls were here.

Still, I retorted, "How do I know I shouldn't call the cops and report them dead?"

He growled and advanced on me, but a firm hand on his shoulder stopped him. Seconds later, a broad back blocked my view of Jim. I let out a long, steady breath of relief.

"Time for you to go," Maverick growled.

One easy shove, and Jim stumbled back against one of the tables like a slinky. For a second, I thought he'd retaliate. But a quick survey of Maverick's shoulders seemed to give him pause. Eventually, he righted himself, peering around Maverick.

"I'll be back," he hissed.

Maverick advanced a step, and Jim shuffled back with a petulant glare. He threw open the door and stalked back to his truck. Once he started driving away, I hurried around the counter and strode to the window. I wanted to watch him leave. His truck disappeared with a belch of inky smoke.

My body trembled as if it wanted to shake all my organs loose. Maverick walked up behind me. I could feel his chest at my back, only a breath away.

"You all right, Bethany?"

I don't know what made me do it. What made me lose all

sense of reason. Resilience had been woven into the fabric of my life. I'd weathered Dad losing his leg. Pappa's funeral. Mama's funeral. Had endured the loss of Dad all by myself.

But in that moment, my strength disappeared.

I spun and pressed into him, wrapping my arms around his back. I buried my face in his chest and tried to close any space between us.

As if I had that liberty.

"No," I whispered.

His heavy arm wrapped around my shoulders. "He's gone," he murmured. "You're safe."

For that moment, I believed it. Because both of his arms came around me, hugging me closer. My head fit into his shoulder, brushing the bottom of his jaw, like a puzzle. He put a hand on my neck and stroked his thumb back and forth in an oddly soothing gesture.

The heady scent of pine calmed me. For now, Jim was gone. Maybe he'd stay away, maybe he wouldn't. But for now, we'd bought some time.

*School,* he'd said. *Get them back before school starts.*

* * *

"Girls?"

The attic door flew open the moment I tapped it. Lizbeth stood there, shaking. Tears streaked her face. She clutched her favorite romance novel to her chest, a well-loved thing that she'd hauled all the way here in the back pocket of her jeans like a comfort blanket. *Love's True Whisper.* Its edges were curled, the spine torn, half the cover missing.

"Is he gone?"

"Gone." I put a hand on her face. "Gone for the rest of the summer."

She relaxed. Tears filled her eyes again before she threw her arms around me with a sob. I held her for a moment, feeling her thin body shake against mine the way I'd clung to Maverick. My entire body still burned with the feel of him, the smell of pine heady.

"Just seeing him." She shuddered. "I . . . feel so much. I thought I could go back but . . . I can't, Bethie. I can't go back."

"I'm sorry, Lizbeth."

Behind her, the room lay empty. When she pulled away, I advanced in a panic. "Where's Ellie?"

Lizbeth gestured to the closet door, which I pulled open. A dark lump sat on the ground. I reached down, pulling the ratty black blanket up to find Devin and Ellie next to each other. He had his arm around her, lips pulled into a frown. She shook, her teeth chattering and her gaze averted.

I crouched down.

"He's gone, Ellie. He already left. Maverick is downstairs to make sure that he stays away."

She blinked, seeming years away. Then her gaze registered again, hardening. "You said he wouldn't come!" she cried.

"I said, 'I wouldn't let him take you.'"

Her nostrils flared as she turned away. "He doesn't want me."

Any reply stuck in my throat, because I couldn't deny it. He certainly hadn't spoken kindly of her; his venom oddly targeted her direction. But no little girl should ever feel that way about her father.

"He doesn't know much but his own pain right now."

"He'll come back."

"Maybe." His threat echoed in my ears. "But it won't matter, because we'll be able to prove that I can keep you, and you'll never have to see him again. At the very least, we have until the end of the summer. He promised me."

Devin tightened his arm around her. She looked so young, so scared, clinging to him. The storm in her eyes deepened until

Devin whispered in her ear. Her tense arms relaxed, and she nodded.

Devin looked at me. "Can I take her on the reservoir in my canoe?"

Immediately, I understood. Jim hated the water more than anything. Had a deathly fear of lakes since he nearly drowned as a little boy. I wondered if Ellie had told him. Likely, she had some kind of profile on all her enemies.

Which no eleven-year-old should have.

"Of course. Just don't go out too far."

They scrambled down the stairs and out the door. Lizbeth and I watched from the window as they sped into the canoe. Within seconds, they were on the lake, Ellie crouching under the blanket.

Lizbeth toyed with the end of her paperback, rubbing her fingers along a portion of the cover that had torn off. Her tears had dried. I wondered what it had been like for her to sit here, waiting in the quiet, alone. No matter how much I tried to protect them, I couldn't save them from everything.

Would I be able to live with that?

I set a hand on her shoulder. "You okay, Lizbeth?"

She drew in a deep breath. "Yeah, I'm okay."

"Really?"

Her welling eyes met mine, and she shook her head. "No. I . . . I don't ever want to see him again, but . . . but I still feel sad. Some . . . some part of me *does* want to see him. I mean, he's my dad. We weren't really close, but he was still there, and there were some good times . . . and I'm so confused."

"You might be confused for a while."

"Yeah."

"But you don't have to be scared. He knows you're here. He said he'd leave you alone until school started." Panic flared in her expression, but I shook my head. "That gives us time to prove you can live here, all right? You're going to be all right."

"I'm sorry."

"For what?"

"For coming. For shoving us into your life. I really thought your dad was here and that we could just stay for a few days until things blew over."

"You don't have to apologize, Lizbeth. Coming here was the right thing to do."

She paused, then said, "I know about the motorcycle. About the debt. I know it's not likely you can dig yourself out of debt to prove you can keep us."

"What? How do you know?"

A guilty expression crossed her face. "I've been reviewing Maverick's spreadsheets. His accounting is sound. Statistically, you *do* have a shot at pulling it all together, but it's not a great shot. So . . . I guess . . . thanks. For giving up everything for us."

"You're worth it," I said quietly.

Tears filled her eyes again. I folded her into my arms and let her shake softly against me as she cried. Her thin body trembled, gripping me hard.

I had two more months to turn this place around and secure their life with me.

I had to believe we could do it.

# Chapter Twenty

MAVERICK

This wasn't good.

Not. Good.

Bethany fit into my arms like my body had built itself to accommodate her. Holding her against me had left me weak as a kitten. No deployment, surgery, board meeting, or sales presentation had ever taken my courage in the same way.

My feelings for Bethany had long ago crossed the professional line. Watching her stand up to Jim, saucy blue eyes narrowed like cold firecrackers, sent a thrill through me. Pride, too. She was all vulnerability and rage in the same breath.

She could take care of herself. She *had* taken care of herself. But I didn't want her to have to do it alone. No, I wanted to step in. That's how I knew that this had gotten out of hand. While I would have stepped in to protect any client, I wouldn't have held them for that long. Imagined their soft lips on mine. Or forced myself to leave hours past closing.

I wanted to prove to Bethany that she wasn't alone. That the burdens weren't hers to bear. But how wrong would that be? In a few weeks, I would be gone.

And she would be alone.

I sat in my truck and stared at Grandpa's house with a mental sigh.

Only a few weeks lay between me and completion on this project. A few weeks to prove my business idea, sell the house for some initial capital—not that I needed it, but it would help—and tell Mallory, *Thanks, but no thanks. I don't want to be your CRO.*

If I could walk away. Not just from Mallory, but from Bethany, too.

The way things looked?

I stepped out and slammed the door behind me, the smell of her hair still burning my nose.

# Chapter Twenty-One

BETHANY

That night, I stared at an empty binder.

Maverick said the new operations manual would be the beginning of the new Frolicking Moose, and I believed him. It was the place where we made coffee-tinged magic happen. Where profitability put more money into my bank account, and that money brought me a certificate to support my sisters and sell real estate.

But executing that new coffee shop required energy and time that the girls had been taking up.

Daily trips to the library, grocery runs, meal coordination, and the stress of living with two other people who suddenly saw me as a mother figure. Ellie still didn't even seem sure that she liked me, which made it hard to force her to sweep and do her laundry. Two weeks of living with them had made it abundantly clear that neither of them had really been taught how to clean.

Putting together this stupid operations manual had forced me to see exactly what was going on in the shop. To intimately face the failure of Dad's attention to detail. To stare down every speck and spot to which I'd been turning a blind, overwhelmed eye.

For every process I knew about the shop, more questions popped up that I was clueless about. Maverick combed through Dad's paperwork to get clues when we didn't know answers. Called vendors. Even contacted Dad's most loyal customers. And he constantly had decisions for me to make. All of that meant the operations manual had inched forward like a broken slug.

But now it loomed in front of me.

Everything I wanted seemed to lie on the other side of this. We couldn't truly improve until we'd swept our way through every part of this store, put in an efficient process, and documented it.

My brain hurt just thinking about it.

Jim's expression ran through my mind, tugging at an already-weak system. The wariness of his gaze. The utter lack of caring. I couldn't decide which was worse: that he'd left the girls willingly for the summer, or that he'd figured me out so quickly.

This wasn't just a goal. This was their lives. This was Ellie and Lizbeth facing down the ugly Jim monster.

Court rooms.

Custody battles.

It was about more than just winning. We had to destroy his ability to ever get them back. And I had to do it before the end of the summer, a mere two months away.

With Ellie and Lizbeth upstairs reading Ellie's favorite horror story out loud, I opened my computer. The shop was closed and quiet. I'd changed into a loose pair of sweatpants, flip-flops, and an old college T-shirt. My hair perched on top of my head in a messy bun. I liked the feel of Dad's stuff around me as I pulled up the operations manual documents. With one last, determined look at the machines behind the counter, I pulled up my first document.

Time to get truly serious.

When I started to type, a desperate punch of energy hit me.

All the things I needed to figure out came together slowly. Emptying my thoughts onto the page made it much easier to think this operations manual through.

- Organized procedures
- Efficient decisions
- Don't crowd the workspace if more than one person is working.
- Need a cleaning section.
- Ooh, can't mix two of those chemicals—BAD BAD.
- Work culture
- Smile with every new customer?
- We're here to bring the joy and the caffeine. (Could be a T-shirt logo.)
- How to deal with an angry client
- Validate
- Team has each other's backs
- **Do not accuse or throw coffee no matter what happens, FULL STOP.**
- What to do when the Wi-Fi goes down
- Or the power
- Who to call if the furnace dies
- Make a list of all contacts for maintenance? A maintenance flow chart!
- **Maintenance flow chart**
- Espresso guy
- Wi-Fi company
- Furnace guy
- T-shirt person
- Coffee bean company
- Things to write procedures for:
- Length of brewing time
- How to restock the creamer

- What kinds of milk to buy and when
- Cleaning out the fridge

For the next two hours, the systems of running a coffee shop poured out of me. Night descended fully. Traffic outside slowed. I scrounged in the fridge for a diet pop, then sipped it to make it last while I typed, and typed, and typed.

Sometime around midnight, I hopped myself up on two servings of iced chai. At one point, I made a cup of coffee, taking notes on every single step. Snapped pictures of the espresso machine and uploaded them. Created a chart with details on different types of roasts and how they tasted based on what Dad used to say. (No way was I going to drink them.)

One o'clock in the morning closed in.

In the midst of everything, I drafted an even longer list of ways to clean the shop up and increase our profits. Stop stocking those gross scones, for one, and introduce cupcakes. Just because I didn't like sugar didn't mean I shouldn't sell it. This was America. Everyone else liked sugar way *too* much.

Eventually, I moved to the biggest table at the front of the store to allow myself space to stretch out. My fingers ached. A cup of green tea kept me up, though my eyes burned like sandpaper.

Two o'clock came and went.

Somewhere around 3:15, my bleary eyes felt like I'd been blowing smoke in them for days. I'd have to be up soon to prep the store for the morning commuters. I thought of an hourlong nap but turned back to my computer with a jaw-popping yawn. Only a few procedures away from finishing.

It would be a yoga pants and comfy bra kind of day.

* * *

The feeling of a heavy hand on my shoulder startled me from a dream. Dancing coffee beans had been trying to throw broken pieces of a coffee mug at me. They'd laughed whenever I fought back, and then turned into money. The moment I'd touched the money, it disappeared.

"Bethany?"

Groggy, I straightened.

Dim, overhead lights felt painfully bright to my eyes. Those definitely weren't my attic bedroom lights. Understanding dawned slowly. I'd fallen asleep working at my computer. I jerked fully awake with a gasp.

"Whoa there," came a deep rumble. "Everything okay?"

Maverick crouched next to the table. The world was still dark, the shop quiet. A faint blush lingered on the distant horizon. The clock said 4:15. It would be full light soon enough, and I was already fifteen minutes late for prepping.

"Fine." My voice croaked. "I'm . . . I'm fine."

The puzzle pieces slowly slid together. Vaguely, I remembered a long, long blink that must have turned into a nap.

Maverick slipped into the chair next to me, one arm across the back of my chair. He wore a metal running leg. Sweat glistened in a light sheen over his face and neck. I forced myself to look away, assaulted by butterflies. The man looked like a Viking god *without* eyes brightened by a run. Now he was otherworldly.

He motioned toward my laptop with a wry tilt of his head.

"Working late or up early?"

I pushed the hair out of my eyes. "Both."

My thoughts lay heavy and sluggish. It would be a bear of a day trying to stay awake.

He put a hand on the back of my neck. The comforting warmth sent an electric zip under my skin, melting me into a puddle. I turned to face him. All the hours of caffeine, fueled by desperation, crashed around me. I'd finished a hard thing.

But now the terror had settled in.

"Mav," I whispered. "I don't know if I can do this."

His inquisitive expression softened.

"It's going to be all right, Bethany. Everything will get done. We'll turn this place around so you have profit and can pay your debts at the same time."

"It's so much."

"You're not just talking about the shop."

"No. It's more than just the shop. Of course, I'll throw my all into saving the girls from their father. I'll do whatever it takes to prove they belong here. But then what? Then I have to mother them. I have to be something I'm not. Something I've never seen before. Mama . . . she tried, but . . . she couldn't. At least not well." A half-sob choked me. "She messed all of us up. What if I do the same thing?"

Until I'd spoken the words, I'd had no idea the fears were even there. They'd been dammed back by my determination to finish this stupid manual. I buried my face in my hands.

"Sounds like you had a tough relationship with her," he murmured. He hadn't moved his hand off my neck, and I was glad. It centered me. No makeup. Hopped up on caffeine and drowning in sweats. He was a saint for not running as far as his prosthetic would take him.

"Mama and I were . . . complicated."

Maverick's expression softened. His breathing evened out. He waited, gaze soft with curiosity when I let my hands fall. His thumb rubbed a circle on my skin, setting it aflame.

"My parents divorced when I was seven. I lived with Mama at first, but mostly because she filed while he was on a deployment. She took me and ran without a word."

He winced. I bit my bottom lip, grounded by the pressure, and silently agreed. It had been a cowardly thing to do. Their marriage hadn't been abusive or lackluster. Dad had tried hard, but Mama had itchy feet. She'd never really thought she'd stay when she married him, but she wanted to see if she had it in her.

She didn't.

"Life with her was just . . . too unstable. She flailed around, trying to figure out what was next. Find something. Her emotions swung on a pendulum. We lived out of her car, occasionally stopping at seedy hotels. She'd disappear at night and come back in the morning without explanation. Then we'd leave for another small town.

"It wasn't healthy for me, and I missed Dad. So, one day, while she was out, I found a payphone and called Pappa. Dad's father. I just . . . I missed them. I wanted to know if Dad was still safe on the deployment or would be home soon. Pappa sounded so scared, so relieved to hear my voice. I remember thinking that something was wrong.

"From there, I promised to keep calling and at least let them know I was okay. He asked me where I was, but I didn't know. He told me to tell him what was around me. I remember reading license plates and hotel names and a restaurant. That's when I realized Mama had lied. She'd told me Dad wanted me to go with her for a while. But she hadn't told him anything. Just emptied the bank account and disappeared, having her lawyer send the divorce papers to him on deployment."

Maverick whistled low under his breath.

"Tell me about it," I muttered. "I didn't realize it at the time, but Pappa was trying to track me down. Dad came home early to find me when they realized I was just . . . gone. One day, Dad showed up while I was sleeping in the car, alone."

My voice felt far away as I recalled that night. The memories blurred, smudging like a dark blue sky seen through filthy car windows.

The seat had smelled like rubbing alcohol and cigarette ashes, even though Mama didn't smoke. Vaguely, I recalled her raven-black hair as it spilled over her shoulders. Her thin nose, broad smile, always tinged with something like terror. She'd loved me so much she almost couldn't handle it.

"What happened?" Maverick asked.

"Dad showed up like some kind of knight. He pulled me out of the car and hugged me for probably ten minutes. I didn't realize it then, but he was crying. So . . . relieved, I think."

Maverick's thumb paused, then resumed, moving in a slow, comforting circle.

"I can't imagine the terror he felt, not knowing where you were," he murmured.

"Me either. We waited for Mama to come back. He didn't let go of me the whole time. I was so relieved to see him, I cried for almost an hour. It was five hours later, at five in the morning, when she returned. They fought. Mama screamed, but she didn't stop him from taking me. I think she wanted me to go, but she didn't want to admit it."

Maverick watched me carefully now, showing nothing but genuine interest. Perhaps a little surprise. My mind churned for a moment. Did I *want* him to know all of this? No.

But maybe, yes.

Because who else did?

No one alive. Because my team had died.

"How did you feel?" he asked.

"Sad, but relieved. Dad didn't leave my sight for a week. I wouldn't get in any car for over a month. I desperately missed Mama. Sometimes I woke up crying at night. At the same time, I never wanted to see her again. For some reason, the thought of her just made me angry and sad."

The battle of emotions in my little body had almost torn me apart. Missing Mom, but wishing for Dad. It was like I had no place to belong for a while. Floating in an in-between, trying to find purchase. Eventually, I settled into a routine with Dad, and then he became my world.

Maverick leaned back, his fingers resting along the vertebrae at the top of my spine. My skin tingled all the way down my back.

"Your mom recovered enough to marry Jim, it sounds like."

"Yes. Then had Lizbeth a few months later."

He quirked one eyebrow in question.

I shrugged. "No, Mama didn't love Jim. Jim gave her a safe place and steady food. She kept things running in the house while he worked the fields. She didn't seem bothered by the hints of darkness in him."

Maverick tightened his fingers, pressing them into my skin. But it didn't hurt. It felt more like a possessive caress.

"Did he ever hurt you when you visited?"

"No."

His subtle grip relaxed.

"He never said much, not even to Lizbeth or Ellie. Lizbeth always tried. Ellie ignored him. He ignored her. Mama made up for everything Jim wasn't. She was like a spirit with nowhere to wander." Unable to stop now, I launched into the heart of the matter. "I was so jealous of Lizbeth and Ellie. They had her all the time in person. She laughed with them. Was carefree with them. When I had lived with her, everything had been so stressful. Minute to minute. Terrifying."

"Sounds like she was doing the best she could."

His compassion tugged at my heart. Only after her death was I better able to understand that. Her parents had died, and she had no siblings. There was a druggie aunt somewhere in Florida and a distant uncle who had cut ties and moved across the country. Neither came to her funeral.

"She did," I said softly.

"What happened with your dad and his heart attack?" he finally asked, his expression puzzled, as if he wanted to put something together.

"I came home for a weekend visit from college last fall, and he was sitting outside in the canoe, hunched over. When I got to his side, he could barely breathe. I called an ambulance. A helicopter came to take him to the hospital in Jackson City. He died in the middle of the ride."

"You clearly adored your father." A hint of a smile appeared on his face. "Considering what you're doing for his legacy."

Tears welled up in my eyes. Mama I could talk about all day. I'd resigned myself to her death years ago. But Dad?

I still couldn't yield.

"Life was so much better with Dad and Pappa. Between the two of them, I had stability and safety. They were my team. I think . . . I think I've been chasing it ever since," I added quietly.

He tilted his head back, looking outside. The span of silence allowed me to collect my frazzled, scattered thoughts. For half a second, this all felt like a huge mistake. He hadn't asked for this. He was my business mentor. A coach. Sometimes, he felt more like a boss . . . but most of the time he felt like my friend. I'd just vomited my past all over him like a sick toddler.

That was a friend thing, right?

Maverick's hand turned into an arm, and before I knew what was happening, he'd pulled me into him. All space between us evaporated, and so did the air in my lungs. The feeling of his body against mine was the first steady anchor I'd felt in the last eight months. I quickly curled into the proffered warmth with a sniffle, tucking my head under his chin.

"Bethany, I . . ." He trailed off, unable to complete his thought. His loss of words soothed my prickly heart.

"I know."

"This seems daunting." He tightened his hold, which was already encompassing. "Straightening up this business and taking on two girls who need you, but it's not more than you can handle. And you aren't alone. You have a team again. This is all going to work. I promise. I can see it in my mind, and I've never lost when I've bet on my own ideas. We'll make sure you can prove yourself to a judge before the end of summer."

I forced myself to lean back and meet his gaze. He meant it—

I could tell. His certainty, the logical way he approached each problem, convinced me. My body sank shamelessly closer to him.

"You really believe that."

"Really."

My eyes dropped to his lips. The next thing I knew was the searing heat of his lips on mine. All the blood left my body, replaced with fire. Maverick's grip tightened on my arms, crushing me against him. My heart beat an uncertain, eager staccato.

He tore away. "Bethany—"

I closed my eyes. Stupid. Stupid. Stupid. Never kiss a business consultant! "I'm sorry, I—"

A hand slid up the side of my face until he palmed my cheek with a calloused hand. Seconds later, another kiss stole my breath. This one was soft. Gentle. Perhaps a little wary. It trapped me on this side of magic. I leaned into him until there was no more space in my head.

Nothing but him.

His fingers ran through my hair, rubbing my scalp. The scent of pine filled the air. I wanted to swim in it. In him. To pull this Viking's arms around me and sink into an eternity. He pulled away slowly, our foreheads pressed together.

"Don't apologize." He ran a thumb over my cheekbone. "Not for that. Not for what you told me. But I don't want you to think I'm taking advantage of you in a vulnerable moment."

My eyes opened and locked on his. As surely as he sat before me, I knew I'd regret this later. When I couldn't stop staring at him. When he went back to business mode.

When he left.

But for the love, I couldn't think about it. Couldn't see anything but him in that moment. Hear anything but the deep rumble of his early-morning voice. Couldn't help but die a little in the light of his golden eyes. Absorb every molecule of heat from his touch. Like a woman locked in ice, about to meet fire.

"*Are* you taking advantage of a vulnerable moment?" I whispered.

"Not on purpose." His breath caressed my cheek with a slight smile. Sweet mint, as potent as his kiss. "I've wanted it for a while."

"Me too. But what do we do now?"

His lips parted, but no sound came out. "I don't know," he finally said.

My heart bounced around my rib cage like it wanted to fly free. If I strapped him down, would he just disappear? Was it even fair of me to ask this question so soon? We were supposed to be two professionals saving a store. Not two hearts trying to save each other.

"Why don't we just . . . let it be whatever it is for now," I said, pressing my hand to his chest. A shiver moved through him.

He frowned. "What do you mean?"

"No . . . rules. No . . ."

"Expectations?"

"Not yet."

Of course, I'd build expectations. I'd already fallen hard for him. Already longed to breathe him in and never let him go. But it would be worse to hold him at arm's length and never know what we could have had. Broken hearts mended. I knew that by experience.

He was a minimalist. An emotional runner. Commitment, on some level, seemed to frighten him. Why else would he run away from whatever he'd left?

In order to have him, I had to put away all expectations.

"Bethany, I *will* leave. I won't stay here and—"

"I know."

"You know?"

"Yes."

"And you still want to let this be?"

I swallowed. "Yes."

"There's no way to stop yourself from creating unconscious expectations, and that's a breeding ground for pain and disappointment. This doesn't sound wise."

"I know."

He pulled back to study me. "Then why are you doing this? I don't want to hurt you. To get attached and then leave? It's . . . heartless."

A thundercloud overtook my mind. I scooted back a little. What if I had read this all wrong from the beginning?

"Are you not interested?"

His hands tightened around my arms. "Of course I'm interested. But I'm not looking for commitment. What if you feel something and . . . and I break your heart?"

"Then that will be my problem. It will suck if you leave, but not as much as never knowing, right?"

Not as much as never having this. Besides, people had been loving and leaving me my whole life. This was a world I knew very well.

Maverick's troubled expression only deepened. "Maybe," he finally said. "No expectations? I leave whenever I leave, and you won't hate me for it?"

I nodded once, dizzy with the movement. One day, I would hate *myself* for this. But right now, I couldn't see that day. I saw only this one.

"You're worth it," I whispered.

All the space between us vanished as he kissed me senseless again. I left behind the loneliness of my life to fade into the unexpected heat of his kiss.

No matter how much it would hurt later, it was already worth it.

Right now.

# Chapter Twenty-Two

## MAVERICK

After a kiss that would sear itself in my memory for the rest of my life, Bethany wrapped her arms around me and snuggled into my chest. She remained there, tucked shamelessly against me, as the night faded into morning. Cars drove past. A few people peered inside the closed store. She held me so tight, I thought she'd crawl inside me if I let her.

Wrapping my arms around her felt natural. I held her longer than was appropriate, because none of this was truly appropriate. Why would she set herself up for heartbreak? Let a visceral exchange of emotion happen when there was an expiration date on *us*?

She was either very brave, or very stupid.

While I worried about her, relief also flooded me. I *wanted* her to crawl into me. Wanted it in a way that made me feel things I hadn't felt for any woman ever. Protectiveness. Uncertainty. Unequivocal attraction. Things that stirred my chest and gut. I didn't like it. I'd officially stuck myself in this spot by agreeing to her audacious request.

Rock, meet hard place.

Mallory was right. Love ain't easy.

When Bethany pulled away, hazy from fatigue, I pushed a strand of hair out of her face. Even though this was wrong, my arms stayed locked around her. Willing and reckless or not, her heartbreak would be my fault.

"Jim isn't going to come back for a while," I said. "You bought some time yesterday, so we'll figure this out together, all right?"

Her fear faded. She seemed to regain her strength and solidity. The moment she pulled away, I felt regret, but let her go. She fit, and no one had ever fit.

She tilted her head back and smiled softly, utter adoration in her gaze.

How could she be so openly vulnerable? What kind of courage did it take to *feel* without restraint like this? I stared at her in a mixture of terror and awe. Even my own father's death hadn't inspired this level of honesty and emotion in me.

Years in the corporate sector had introduced me to world leaders. Billionaires. Millionaires. Fools and geniuses. Only Bethany made me marvel.

Those lips moved barely an inch from mine. Her smoky gaze, clouded with bottled adrenaline, captured me. Her kiss revealed a part of her that everybody caught glimpses of, but I wanted totally. Passion. A compulsive nature. An undeniable loyalty to whatever felt right in that moment. I wanted to draw the truth out of her and make it mine, like the swapping of souls.

She closed her eyes and pressed her forehead to mine.

"Thank you, Maverick."

I held her closer, totally unable to speak.

* * *

Bethany attacked the rest of that day with undeniable energy.

Even Lizbeth watched her, one eyebrow quirked, from over

the top of her book. Bethany had found her stride again. Even tired, this woman was unstoppable.

While she stuffed pages of something into a binder and muttered a list of things left to do under her breath, I made notes in a spreadsheet and tried to keep my mind focused. My assistant was waiting for me to review three modules he'd put together. For the life of me, I kept rereading the same line.

Bethany's bright eyes intruded on my mind. Soft lips. The heat in my belly flared again and again when I thought about that kiss.

I shouldn't have done it.

Could not have stopped it.

Definitely wouldn't take it back.

Today, she didn't even try to hide her distraction. Every now and then she'd stop, stare into the distance, look up at me, and grin. My stomach felt like I'd been on a roller coaster all day.

I didn't need to be at the shop this long. The module approval could be done tomorrow, and I'd mostly been staring at my inbox. But I couldn't seem to stop watching her move about her life. The little things fascinated me the most. When she wore the baseball hat, then took it off. Then lost it and spent a few minutes searching, only to realize she'd stuffed it in her apron pocket.

Or the way she reflexively reached for her lipstick. Didn't always use it, but held it when she felt a moment of uncertainty.

Her conversations with Lizbeth. Quick smiles for everyone. The way she lit up around people.

Finally, around noon, she tossed a wet towel into the sink and headed my way. She'd changed into a turquoise summer dress and white flip-flops. A binder landed in front of me with a heavy *thud*. I jerked out of inappropriate thoughts. Bethany stood next to the table, a hand on her cocked, curved hip.

"Is this what I think it is?" I drawled.

"Potentially. It's hard to know what's in your mind, Mav.

Lizbeth is scouring Pinterest for a 'really cute design that matches the general decor.' Because, 'Bethany, don't be a cave-man. It all must *match*.'"

Lizbeth, across the room, snorted.

I laughed and peeled it open to see the first page.

## THE FROLICKING MOOSE OPERATIONS MANUAL

The next page revealed a neatly typed table of contents, with the Frolicking Moose logo on the top of the page and a blocky, western font that matched.

Organized words filled every page. Proofread, no typos, in order, and with helpful markings to indicate when one standard operating procedure referred to another one. She must have finished writing it last night and printed it out this morning.

"I have an online version and this one, just in case the internet is down or the barista can't get to my computer. Lizbeth has volunteered to be in charge of monthly update audits, which makes both of us ridiculously happy because, frankly, the word *audit* makes me want to scream."

Pride swelled within me as I ran my eyes over page after page. She'd not only managed it, but she'd done *well*. Beyond what I'd ever imagined. In fact, she'd given me a great gift.

She'd shown me that it was possible.

Although I'd improved Mallory's business landscape through her sales force, a small business was an entirely different animal. The validation of my business instincts was almost as powerful as the change in her. I needed to know that this could work, and she was proving me out.

Defensive, uncertain Bethany was a confident owner in her own right. She didn't even realize the intensity of her own instincts yet.

"Amazing." The paper whispered as I flipped through the binder. "You did it, Bethany."

Her eyes shone. "I know! I can be taught." She reached into her purse and slid an envelope across the table to me. Color pinked her cheeks in a lovely way. "Here. This is for you."

I quirked an eyebrow. "A card?"

"It's . . . it's really not much. Open it later," she added hastily.

"Sure."

I tossed the card farther onto the table, out of reach, and her shoulders relaxed.

"Now, I don't know what's next," she said.

"Profitability, for one. You've identified a whole list of issues and started fixing them. Now we get more people into your store, test your process, and increase how much money you make."

Her face paled slightly. "Oh, is that all?"

I grinned and sprawled an arm across the back of the chair next to me. "That's all."

"Stability, too, for the girls."

"And for you."

Her nose wrinkled. "Right."

I laughed at the momentary expression of horror on her face. "What? You don't want stability?"

"It's not that. It's just . . . it feels like a lot."

"Success *is* a lot. But you'll handle it well, because you have a path now, and it's working. Just don't sabotage it. Keep going. Do what works. Success feels so good."

Hoping to get her closer, I pulled up a spreadsheet.

"Here, have a seat. Let's look at a few things here."

She settled next to me. A shudder skated over my skin when her arm touched mine. She reached down, our fingers intertwined beneath the table, out of Lizbeth's sight. I pulled in a deep breath to rally my thoughts.

While we reviewed the reports that she would generate every month, along with some ideas for getting people into her store, I tried to focus. She asked questions, and I typed them into a document as feedback to send to my assistant, but I couldn't remember any of them a second later.

"Tomorrow." I leaned back and scrubbed a hand over my eyes. "We'll talk about foot traffic strategies. This was a good start today, particularly since you finished the manual."

My fatigue had little to do with my early morning and everything to do with the fact that I couldn't sleep with her on my mind. Which had led to the run that ended in a brain-numbing kiss.

"Right." She fought off her own yawn. "Tomorrow."

Lizbeth had retreated upstairs to get a new book and hadn't resurfaced. "I overheard that Lizbeth is going to hang out with Jada tonight," I said.

Bethany blinked, her eyes bloodshot. "Jada has an extensive library. They're planning on making dinner and then reading together in the same room."

"Wild."

She laughed.

"What about Ellie?"

"Sleeping at Devin's house. I can't get them to split up."

"Good for her. She needs someone her age on her side."

A sense of relief seemed to emanate from Bethany whenever Ellie and Devin's unexpected friendship came up.

"I was going to ask you to dinner tonight," I said in a poor attempt to sound nonchalant. "But you look tired as hell."

Her eyebrows lifted in a wan smile. "I wouldn't be much of a date."

"I seriously doubt that."

Bethany paused, studying me. When her gaze dropped to my lips, it took a considerable amount of control not to kiss her.

"Maybe you should ask," she murmured. "I might say yes."

"And fall asleep over your soup? I think it's best if you just go to bed."

"Well, what did you have in mind?"

"Dinner at The Upstairs Cellar in Jackson City."

Her eyebrows rose. "Fancy."

"Is it?"

"Yes. Very. Didn't you look at the menu?"

"No."

She laughed. "Well, it's at least a hundred dollars a plate."

"That's fine."

Bethany blinked. "Fine?"

I laughed. "Are you surprised?"

"A little."

My gaze tapered. "How poor do you think I am?"

"Not sure. You never talk about yourself, and there's nothing at your grandpa's house except tools."

"My minimalism has nothing to do with taking you on a fantastic date that you deserve."

She nudged me with her shoulder. "Are you one of those billionaires that has no house and hoards lots of money while you travel the world?"

I tilted my head back and laughed. "Definitely not that. I just thought you might like something . . . special and fun and *not* Carlotta's."

Her lips pressed together as she fought off a yawn.

"We can reschedule."

"But I want to hang out with you," she said.

"We still have a few weeks."

Her brow furrowed, and silence fell between us. For the guy who couldn't wait to get away, *weeks* sounded far too short all of a sudden.

"Ask me, Maverick."

"Fine. Want to eat some takeout and pass out on my couch

while we watch movies?" I dropped my voice, and she shivered. "I promise no funny business."

Those perfect lips quirked. "Too bad. That could have been the funnest part. I accept your offer. I'll head over after I drop off Lizbeth."

## BETHANY

Buttery light spilled onto the forest floor, warming the cooling air as I pulled up at Maverick's house. Crickets sang in the background as I ascended the stairs, wearing a cozy pair of yoga pants and an oversized shirt underneath my jacket.

Maverick opened the door and laughed. "I'm glad you followed orders."

He wore a pair of jogging pants and a plain white shirt that fit his broad shoulders a little too well. I wanted to run my hands along his arms but settled for dreaming of it instead. A box of pizza sat on the counter behind him.

"Come on in." He tilted his head. "Can't wait for you."

"For me to what?"

"For you."

Seconds later, my body pressed against his. His rock-hard thighs lined mine. His hands were in my hair, his arms around my back. He dipped me into a kiss, forcing me to surrender my weight to him. I hovered in his arms, paralyzed by the tilt of his lips against mine, until he straightened. The broken kiss lingered on my lips like a whisper.

His boyish grin melted me. "For that."

He wound our fingers together and pulled me farther into the house. I stumbled after him and tried to pull myself back together, unable to peel the smile off my face.

*Totally* worth it.

The skeleton interior had amped up significantly. New granite counters sparkled beneath a protective film. Wooden stools lined the bar, covered in plastic. A faint hint of wood stain lingered in the air, and the walls seemed far brighter. An updated light fixture made of elk antlers dangled overhead. No furniture yet.

On the table sat my card, propped open. Nerves twisted in my stomach. I hadn't said anything blatantly obvious in the card about how I felt, but I hadn't been reserved, either.

"It's really amazing." I slipped a hand over one of the counters, sawdust gritty on my palm. "I'm impressed. This will be such a lovely home. How will you part with it?"

He shrugged.

"Oh. Right. This isn't your style."

He grinned and flipped the pizza box open, shoving it toward me. "Grab a slice. We'll eat in here, then I have some movies picked out. And no, it's not my style. But it's *someone's* style. And that's who will buy it."

Grateful to get some food in my belly after forgetting to eat lunch, I grabbed a slice of what appeared to be all-meat-man pizza and sank my teeth into it. Delicious, crisp crust exploded in my mouth. Maverick went for his own slice.

"Then what is your house style?" I asked, eyeing an open cupboard that still needed repair. He'd replaced the black cupboard doors with all-wood ones, giving it a more rustic, gentle feel. Near the dining area to the left, another elk-antler chandelier sat on the floor, awaiting placement. This one sprawled to at least ten points. It would be a talking piece all its own.

Swallowing, he said, "I prefer . . . subtle freedom."

"*Subtle* freedom?" That piqued my attention. I chewed, nearly melting into the delicious cheese. His response sounded a lot like noncommitment. "What does that mean?"

"I'm not big on the spotlight. I don't like attention, and I'd rather fly under the radar. I think my house should reflect that."

"Minimalism at work?"

"Definitely. I rented that truck and arrived with only a bag."

Such a revelation seemed so at odds with how he always presented himself. Charismatic. Confident. Even caring. I recalled the way he'd vowed to save my company without knowing much about it. Even now, he leaned against the counter with an arrogant little smirk I wanted to kiss away.

"And freedom?" I twirled a piece of cheese around the tip of my finger, dizzy with him standing this close. The entire house smelled like pine, drenching me in memories of our kiss.

"Staying in one place has always been hard for me." He frowned. Grooves formed in his brow. "That's why the military appealed. I prefer movement. Freedom. You know . . . change."

He shifted his weight but held my gaze. A challenge lived there, and I didn't know what it meant. But it surely meant something, and so had that kiss. Together, it was an ugly arithmetic. My thoughts moved so fast they strangled themselves. He studied me carefully, and I felt both of us take a metaphorical breath.

Falling for that ridiculous voice and those strong shoulders was a little too easy. Maybe this hadn't been my best idea.

I forced a smile and said, "Sounds like a bachelor's life."

# MAVERICK

*Stupid,* I thought the moment Bethany dropped her gaze. *That was really stupid to say.*

It wasn't often that a situation caught me by surprise, and certainly not a surprise of my own idiotic making. Tonight, Bethany with her bright-blue eyes and dark hair, looking tired but eager, stirred me up. Maybe it was her handwritten card.

*Thanks for swooping in to change our lives. I'll always remember you. And this. You're one of a kind, Mav.*

My defenses had been built for corporate executives and sales leaders. There was a reason I could run a sales meeting with undeniable charm and force, because I knew that world. I'd earned it. Fought for it. And while I'd done that, moments like these had fallen to the side. I could negotiate a multimillion-dollar company deal, but I didn't know how to tell Bethany that I wasn't sure I wanted to leave her.

I wasn't ready for an open-hearted mountain girl trying to

save the world for her half-sisters. She'd all but extended her vulnerable, beating heart.

"Sorry," I heard myself say. "I'm a bit blunt."

Her eyes widened as they met mine. She blinked, then relaxed.

"A little."

"I just meant that . . ." Setting aside the pizza, I leaned onto my hands, meeting her increasingly concerned gaze. "My parents were married in name only for much of my life. They had long been out of love, and obligation held them together. Because of that, they sort of . . . lost respect for each other. Their lives ran parallel and never intersected."

"Oh," she murmured, as if that explained it all.

She didn't even know the half of it.

"When I was twelve, my father was surfing during a family vacation in California. He fell hard. The board came up and nailed his back. Thanks to my older brother being right there, Dad didn't drown. But he broke his back."

"Was he paralyzed?"

As if the injury could transfer, I put a hand on my back, reliving the horror of it all over again.

"He lost all function from the waist down. Luckily, all five of us boys were old enough that we didn't need him to chase us around the house in diapers, so my mom went back to work. Dad became bitter, and angry, and determined that none of his sons would ever be incompetent, the way he felt."

Which is why he was gone now. But no need to go that deep.

"I'm sorry about that."

"Me too."

The fading sunset had nothing on the natural glow coming from Bethany's eyes as she stared at me like a quiet, intrigued statue. Her clothes looked snug and comfortable, like she'd curl up around me on the couch all day. Something I wanted more than anything right then.

Should have requested she wear a dirty potato sack.

Her hair swept her shoulders in silky black waves. I wanted to wrap my fingers around them and tug her lips back to mine. Maybe then she wouldn't affect me. But she would, which is why I'd left a counter between us.

"So, you're afraid of long-term commitment that could end like your parents' relationship?" she asked.

*No. I'm afraid of disappointing you,* I thought. *Because I was always a disappointment to Dad.*

My gaze dropped to the counter.

"Something like that."

Commitment seemed so blasé compared to what really lingered in my head. The truth wouldn't encourage her to put up with me. If she had any sense, she'd leave now before pizza turned into a movie, that turned into cuddling, that turned into a depth of emotion I couldn't even tap into right now.

She quirked her lips in thought. The silence lasted for several moments before she gave me a wry smile.

"You could always stay." A wistful tone had overtaken her voice. "Stay in tiny little Pineville with me and my three big attachments, where you'll always be good enough, no matter what."

Something thick clogged my throat. I cleared it. "Now it's my turn to ask a deep question," I said, straightening.

Her brow lifted. "Oh?"

"Why didn't you tell me that your father was an amputee? Few people know this world even half as well as you do if you've lived with someone who lost a leg."

A strand of hair fell into her eyes. "My dad hated it when his prosthetic became a topic of conversation. Aside from a few little things, it didn't really stop him from doing what he wanted. He used to wear shorts all the time just to prove it." Her lips twitched into a sad grin. "He was larger-than-life that way."

"He sounds like a guy I would have liked to have a beer with."

She slid easily into details about her dad, which brought out the light in her even more. My exact plan.

The tension from lack of sleep faded quickly as she spoke, weaving a story with her animated hands. Her adoration was apparent in her voice. Darkness settled on the cabin, and stars glimmered through the windows. The night symphony started up, but I only had eyes for her.

Away from the shop, she seemed to bloom in the moonlight. She, Bethany, with whom I had two professional arrangements —she was both my client and the owner of my working space. She had three big attachments herself. Talk about a world rife with disappointment.

I set those thoughts aside.

She'd said it herself—no expectations. We could allow this to be what it was.

No matter the pain later, time with a woman like Bethany could never be a mistake. Even if it set a bar I wasn't sure any other human could meet, it didn't matter. Long-term relationships weren't a world I'd ever navigate, anyway. She could set whatever bar she set.

Her and her lipstick.

"So," she said, brow drawn high, "what's this elusive business you occasionally have phone calls about? I know there's something besides the business you're testing with the Frolicking Moose. You're always mentioning Mallory."

I leaned back, laughing. A nugget of something glittering had come into her eyes. Was it jealousy? I hoped so.

"I worked for my sister-in-law, Mallory, who is the CEO of a tech company out of California. They just turned the corner into a billion-dollar business right before I came out here to Grandpa's cabin, thanks to a new sales force initiative I put into place."

Her eyes widened. "Geez."

"She's done well. And she's only thirty-six. She married my brother a while ago. They started the company together."

"You went from military to sales?"

He nodded. "A lot of headhunters pull military leadership into business jobs once we get out, particularly if you've lost a limb. It wasn't a hard process to work my way to where I ended up. I introduced Mallory to my brother Baxter when I met her on my first job after the amputation."

"Your personality certainly helps."

I quirked a brow with a sly smile. "Is that a compliment or tongue-in-cheek humor?"

She grinned. "Figure it out yourself. Do you like working with Mallory?"

"It was a job."

"So . . . no?"

Carefully, I leaned forward again. My job was complicated. There was a lot I loved about it. The security. The money in my account. Time with my sister-in-law and brother. The sense of supporting someone else as they achieved their dreams. But the daily grind, the office space, the sheer number of people always moving around me. I hated that. Measuring success was hard when a company was always scaling bigger.

Big numbers became just that—numbers. Success needed different indicators that were lost in a corporate climate. Life satisfaction. The number of employees assisted through marital issues. Other things.

But I didn't know if I hated it enough to leave it yet. Enter Pineville and the Frolicking Moose.

"A corporate world doesn't fill my happiness bucket, let's just say."

She tapped her crust on the box. "Why not?"

"It's a difficult funnel that forces your life to revolve around other people and their schedules. That's fine. I love to see other people succeed because of what I put into place, but there's no . . . open space."

"To move." Something flickered in her eyes, but quickly disappeared.

"Yes," I said quietly. "No freedom. Before I left, Mallory extended an offer to me. She wants to promote me to the Chief Revenue Officer over the company."

"Wow. Congratulations."

"Thanks."

"Are you . . . are you going to take it?"

"That depends very much on how things pan out with the Frolicking Moose."

Her jaw dropped. "You're kidding."

"Not kidding."

"That's not fair! There's enough pressure as it is," she said, half-laughing. "You can't put that on me."

"Has nothing to do with you." I shrugged. "And everything to do with my setup. The Frolicking Moose will prove whether I can take my skills in the sales force and my knowledge of business and apply it to a brick-and-mortar Mom-and-Pop kind of shop. It's not always the same thing."

Her gaze tapered to slits. "You really are testing this with me."

"As previously discussed."

"Very diplomatic," she replied wryly, a laugh hidden in her voice. "I think I understand."

"Do you?"

"Maybe. Working for Mallory may be good for you on several levels, but it's not great. You don't want to give up something that promises stability and some level of passion, but not much else."

Startled, I nodded. "Yes. That's how it feels."

"It's how I feel about the coffee shop."

"Really?"

Her brow furrowed. "I love it because Dad loved it, but I don't want to be strapped to a shop my whole life."

"Then what do you want?"

She looked at me. "That's a great question."

"Do you have the answer?"

"Real estate."

"Really?"

She nodded. When she drifted into deeper thought, her lips twitched to the side of her mouth, and one side of her face wrinkled. I reached for my beer to keep myself from staring a little *too* intently.

"I want to sell homes, and I want to eventually carve out a niche in the high-end market. I love luxury houses. The feel. The theme. Merging functionality with beauty and art. It's a cool thing. Plus, I love the sales process for houses. It's a big part of someone's life. Whether it's a first-time home or the result of a lifetime of work. It's cool to be part of that. Plus . . . I never knew where my home was. Of course, it was with Dad. But he was military for a while. Pappa would come over while he was gone. Or I'd go to Mama's. It's just . . . I want to give people that security."

"I know the feeling," I murmured, unable to tear my eyes away from the dark lashes that contrasted with her freckled skin.

"With renovations?"

"Yes. I love it. I love taking raw material, infusing new life, and making something else out of it. Particularly when I can reuse what already exists. It's efficient and less wasteful and impacts everyone more positively."

"Sounds like your new business idea."

Startled, I blinked. Though I hadn't seen the parallel before, there definitely was one, and I made a mental note to follow up on that later. I didn't like the idea of such a big facet of me remaining undiscovered to me but apparent to everyone else.

"Yes," I said.

She smiled, as if she knew she'd caught me by surprise, and grabbed a second slice of pizza.

"Well," she continued, "your high-level position is certainly a far cry from renovating a cabin and selling it or trying to help small business owners save themselves. So, what's the big motivation behind the helping-small-businesses idea?"

"A high-level position is lucrative," I admitted. "There's something amazing about being able to scale that high, impact an entire culture or way of life within a business—which is really like a little city itself—and know that you're helping people be their best selves. Success is literally everywhere. But it's also isolating. It forces me inside all the time. Even though I work, I never feel like I'm changing *me*."

She seemed to mull that over. "Interesting. But working with smaller businesses can't come with much money."

"It won't."

"And?"

"And?" I repeated, laughing. "Money isn't the only measure of a good life."

"No, but it sure helps."

Debating over whether I should be totally honest or not, I let out a long breath. "Yes, I make a lot of money and I have sound financial investments right now. But I've never dreaded going to work more. Wished the next day wouldn't just be a repeat of the previous one. The *Groundhog Day* effect of working in corporate is killing my brain cells."

I forced a smile for some levity, but her expression remained as serious as I'd ever seen it.

"And moving around, saving people? That will help you feel better?"

"Freer, I think."

"But what if it doesn't?"

"Then I have new information, and I make a new plan."

She nodded once and smiled, but there was a distance to it. I quelled a rush of uncertainty. Something I'd said didn't sit well with her yet again, that much was clear. But I had no way of knowing what it was without asking. And that would obliterate this beautiful back-and-forth.

And imply that I cared enough to fix it, or stay.

Enough of that deep dive. Time to turn this back around to her.

"The big question here," I said as I shoved away the almost-empty pizza box. "Is what kind of movie you want to watch."

I tilted my head toward the couch. She slid her hand in mine without hesitation. My palm engulfed hers as I tugged her into the other room. Grandpa's old couch didn't look like much, but it was still the most comfortable couch I'd ever sat on. Plus, the cushions were weak in the middle, guaranteeing she'd sink closer to me.

"I rented four movies." I sat on the couch and pulled her next to me. "On the off chance you liked zombies, romance, football, or thrillers."

"All in the same movie?"

"No! Different ones. But that would be an awesome movie."

She grinned ruefully, but I could see the fatigue in her eyes. Just in case, I reached behind us, grabbing a blanket from a basket by the couch.

"And if I tell you I prefer romance?" she asked.

"We're all over it. I can deal with romance. Mallory used to have them playing in the background when she was stressed at work. Something about them calmed her down."

Bethany paused and pulled her knees to her chest. "What if I fall asleep ten minutes in?"

*That is my ultimate plan.*

"I fully anticipate you will," I said, laughing.

She smiled back wearily. "You choose, because I'll probably conk out."

"Zombies it is."

"Great," she muttered, "now I'm going to have nightmares."

*Also in my plans.*

"Nah." I grabbed the remote. "I'll keep you safe."

A wrinkle appeared in her forehead, then smoothed out. Without another word, she snuggled closer into my side. I draped the heavy quilt over both of us, and a little sigh escaped her as she burrowed in. My arm dropped naturally around her shoulders, pulling her close.

A cool mountain breeze whispered into the room as the movie began. Her warmth and the sweet scent of lavender melted me. I played with a lock of hair that spilled across her back, fascinated by the silky texture.

Bethany murmured something after the initial credits flickered away to reveal a dark mountain scene. But her body relaxed before I could decipher it, and when I glanced down, she was fast asleep in my arms.

I held her more tightly and wondered if maybe freedom was overrated.

# Chapter Twenty-Five

BETHANY

My eyes flew open.

Breath held, I stared at a dark, unfamiliar ceiling with shadows moving across it. Outside, flashes of lightning streaked across the sky, illuminating the room. A roll of thunder reminded me of Maverick's deep voice. Rain pattered gently against the windows, the drops tumbling over each other to slide down the glass.

A warm body stirred behind me. Maverick held me close to his chest, a protective arm around me so I wouldn't fall off the couch. I closed my eyes, dimly remembering our conversation over pizza.

Recalling Maverick at dinner, at ease but still somehow on guard, sent flurries through me. He spoke with such certainty. Here was a man who knew exactly who he was and what he wanted. Unfortunately, he didn't want a girlfriend with two kids and a shop.

Still, there was his arm around me. The warm caress of his breath on the back of my neck.

It impressed me—how he could figure out what he wanted and make a plan, and then let the plan unfold. Like success *sought* him out.

There was more at play here than just our simmering romantic tension or my desire to run my hands through his beard. The only thing I knew for certain was that Maverick would do what he wanted. He wasn't the type to be swayed. In the end, he'd stay or he'd go.

With the undeniable warmth of him wrapped almost entirely around me, I snuggled deeper into his chest. While I had it, I would soak it up. His arms felt deeply personal, although nothing but uncertainty loomed ahead. My place in his world was about as stable as a fault line.

In that moment, I didn't care.

I felt warm, safe, and comfortable. With my next breath, I slipped back into sleep, his name on my lips and a promise to remember the power of his touch forever.

* * *

"Are you and Mav dating?"

Lizbeth and I sat in the canoe on a calm lake, a hundred yards away from the shore where Ellie, Devin, and Maverick fished from a long dock. Every now and then, Maverick's baritone laugh rolled over the water. Lizbeth slathered more sunscreen on her freckled shoulders and stared at Maverick from behind the aviator sunglasses I'd loaned her.

"Uh . . ."

"I have romance-dar. Whenever something romantic happens around me, I pick up on it like a satellite. I saw the way he was ogling you in the shop on Friday. Plus, you were wearing that really red lipstick, and you only do that when you're *really* happy. And while I can't confirm it, I have my suspicions that you didn't sleep at home on Friday night, because the bed was still made when we got back. You never make the bed."

"Whoa. No snap judgments."

She held up two hands. "No one said the word *sex*, Bethany. Just sayin'."

"Because there was none."

She stared.

My response stalled in my throat, suspended like a rock. Maverick and I had made it abundantly clear that we weren't dating, but that hadn't stopped his hot look at me when he'd arrived. Or his intense study of my swimming suit.

How to explain that to Lizbeth when I wasn't even sure I understood it? *I'm crazy about him and want to date him with no hope of a future,* didn't sound great.

When Maverick showed up today, he'd laid a big, fat kiss on me while the girls were up in the car. I nearly lost all muscle control, which would have forced him to pick me up. Which, in hindsight, would have been great.

Missed opportunity.

"I know you have this whole back-and-forth thing going on," she continued, "but I'm telling you, it's getting old. Would you just admit it, already?"

"Not happening," I muttered.

She flashed me an amused look.

I dipped my canoe paddle farther into the water, casting a dancing ripple on the surface. "I don't know for sure what Maverick is thinking, but I know it's not a relationship."

"A flirt fest?"

"Ah . . ."

"Are you his friend?"

"Yes."

"Client, for sure."

My nose wrinkled. That didn't throw us in an ideal light, and friend was a little too *blah* for me. *Love interest* sounded as exciting as *middle-school crush*.

"Do we have to label it?" I asked.

"Yes."

I rolled my eyes.

"I can tell you what he's thinking," she said, leaning back and setting a floppy straw hat on top of her head. Lizbeth was all easy grace, like a young Audrey Hepburn. "This is a classic romance, Bethie. He's a troubled soldier returning from war with PTSD and a closed-off heart. Only the perfect, feisty woman who stands up to him when all the others won't will steal his heart. Just be sure to refuse his kiss and not be impressed with the glorious state of his body."

She clutched dramatically at her chest while I tilted my head back and laughed. Maverick had PTSD about something, all right, but I had my doubts it had anything to do with the war.

Her smug grin faded.

"Seriously, Bethie. Is he messing around, or what? Not that I'm complaining. I could listen to his voice all day, and Ellie isn't as tense when he's around. But he's got to pee or get off the pot, you know?"

While I didn't love the metaphor as it pertained to me, I could see where she was coming from. A thousand responses flooded my mouth, but I couldn't say any of them. They all revolved around two unexpected attachments that had fallen into my lap weeks ago. I didn't want Lizbeth to think they were a hardship in my life.

Besides, Maverick would roll through here once he finished his grandpa's cabin, girls or no girls.

"He's not the committing type," I said. "He mentioned not even having a place to live while he travels around fixing businesses. I hardly think he'd want to be calling home to a girlfriend while he gets his company off the ground. What we have is just . . . for fun."

Lizbeth lifted a hand as if I'd proven a point. "He's the stereotype! I told you."

"He is not," I muttered, splashing her with my oar. "He isn't troubled."

"But his heart is closed."

"His heart is . . . fine."

She smirked when the answer stuttered out of me, then her expression became serious again. "Maybe he's never felt love."

I groaned. "Those romances are filling your brain with utter mush. They're going to take you away from me if I don't start giving you something of substance to read."

A flash of fear appeared on her face but vanished just as quickly.

I let out a long, regretful breath. *That* had been really stupid. "I'm sorry," I said, shoulders slumping. "I shouldn't have said it like that."

Lizbeth gave a half-smile and a shrug. "It's okay. I know what you meant." But her voice sounded strained. Any hint of trouble and she panicked, though she tended to hide it well. "And you're wrong. I'm too brilliant for them to touch me intellectually."

She said it without malice or arrogance, and she was right. Lizbeth was borderline genius. She'd skipped two full grades in elementary school. If Mama hadn't died, this next year would have been her senior year in high school. Her quick mind computed at twice the speed of mine, which made her fairy-like creativity even more interesting.

"When are you going to college?" I asked, eager to change the subject.

"Dunno. Thought about testing out in a year or two, then applying around. I need to ace the SAT first."

"You could probably go anywhere."

"Probably."

*But I can't pay to send you.* The realization stuck in my throat. With a mind like hers, she might not need college money. She could get scholarships easily.

"What do you want to do?"

"Tech," she said. "Something with computers, most likely. I

have a lot of ideas, and I want to see more women leading in that world."

"Not writing?" I asked with a wry jab of the oar at her foot. She snorted.

"I want to *read* all the books, not write them. Besides, there isn't as much stability in a creative endeavor like that. I want to put the work in and know I'll get the result I expect. I want the comfort of the scientific process or the ritualism of code."

"I think that sounds awesome."

She grinned again, but her expression was far more subdued.

"But I still think Mav is holding a torch for you." She flicked at something under one of her nails. She never did let a topic go easily. "You need to pay attention to it because an opportunity to act may present itself, and I hope you do. I could watch those broad shoulders all day, baby."

"Holding a torch?" I snorted, dipping the oar back in the water. "Are you eighty-two?"

"It's what all the books say!"

I laughed again. "Okay, Grandma Myrtle. Thank you for that. Listen, Maverick is *holding a torch* for his business, not me. Maybe he feels a mild attraction to me because we're stuck in the same working space all the time. And maybe he kisses like fireworks and gangbusters, but that means nothing about longevity. We're having fun. Bottom line."

"Or," she cried, lifting a finger, "he's secretly pining for your love and doesn't know it."

I pretended to vomit off the side. She leaned forward, arms wrapped around her knees.

"You kissed. I saw it."

My gaze locked with hers. "What?"

She grinned, white teeth sparkling in the sun. "Friday morning."

"Geez, Lizbeth! You do have romance-dar. You were there?"

"I saw the light on downstairs, and you hadn't come to bed,

so I was going to offer to help with whatever you were doing. When I peeked in, you two were hot into it." She shrugged. "Who am I to interrupt a kiss like *that*?"

I struggled to remember everything we had spoken about that day, but I only remembered talking about Mama. My jealousy of Lizbeth and Ellie.

She frowned slightly, and my heart sank. She'd heard.

"We were always jealous of you, you know," she said quietly.

"Me?"

"We physically had Mama, but you had the rest of her. She was happy when you were there. Present. She spoke to us a lot, and we all played games and did things. But it wasn't like that when you were gone. After you left, there were a lot of sullen silences. Canned dinners. We rarely played games unless you were there."

My hands relaxed, and the canoe slowed. Ellie, Devin, and Maverick were specks in the distance now. We were the only people here, in a world surrounded by water.

"Really?"

Lizbeth swallowed hard. "It's like there were two of her. Mama when Bethany was around, and Mama without Bethany. She loved us, and she never neglected us, but she was never really *there* when you weren't. I think that's why Ellie loved her so desperately. We got so little of her. Ellie scrambled for any sign of affection from Mama since Dad is so . . ." She trailed off with a sigh. "Mama gave me books and gave Ellie the woods."

Stunned, I simply stared at her. What a tapestry this whole mess had become. All of it pointed back to Mama and whatever demons had pushed her to the horrible decisions that had harmed the rest of us. The flares of anger I felt toward her, however, always faded into resignation. This was Mama's legacy.

But it didn't have to be ours.

"Lizbeth, I had no idea. I'm sorry. I wasn't the best big sister in the world."

"What was . . . what was she like before we came along?"

My forehead scrunched, trying to remember. "She was shadow and light. Maybe that sounds dumb. I just remember moments of deep joy and moments of total despair. There was either goodness or terror. I was only with her until I was six or seven. That's when Dad took me back, and she let me go."

"She told me about that time. That you lived out of the car. She burned through your Dad's money at first, then worked as a prostitute to get gas money for the next place. On good nights, she said, she'd be able to get dinner and a motel room."

My back stiffened. I'd always suspected, but Mama had never betrayed herself. I couldn't help but wonder why she'd told Lizbeth, of all people.

Hopefully to keep her out of that life.

"Yes," I whispered. "I remember sitting in the car, waiting for her to come back. Being confused as to why she had to go at all, and why Dad wasn't good enough. Then he showed up, and everything changed."

"He did you a favor," Lizbeth muttered darkly.

The truth swept through me in a long, cold rush.

"I know."

* * *

"Things are progressing nicely." Maverick tutted under his breath as he studied one of his favorite spreadsheets. "We're already seeing signs of progress, even with the minor improvements to your ordering process. You had a $23 profit yesterday."

His jaw flexed as he thought, a funny little tic I liked to watch for. I straightened from where I stood behind the counter, the greatest vantage point from which to see him. Lizbeth watched me with a smug expression every time she caught me staring his direction.

Which was a lot.

"My bank account will hopefully notice."

Maverick stood from the table and stretched with a smile. His torso and shoulders elongated, and it took all my considerable mental energy not to stare at the gap between his belt and shirt that revealed his abs. I tossed a rag toward the sink to distract myself, and it landed on the spigot.

"Did you already fill out your spreadsheet today?"

"Yes, Mom," I drawled.

In truth, the spreadsheet he'd made me was kind of nice. I liked a centralized place to look at my business numbers. Something similar might come in handy with real estate. I'd been pondering ways to adapt the system. In truth, however, I had no idea what would translate to real estate. All those dreams were just that . . . dreams. Until I could get my license, it was just a hope.

Although his organization of ideas had been imperfect, Maverick had proven correct so far. Things at the shop didn't seem quite so bleak. The operations manual had exposed a lot of issues and forced me to find solutions. A lot of those solutions meant losing less money. While things were more organized and I had *some* semblance of cash flow, there was a lot of room for improvement.

Relentless as usual, and far too handsome in a pair of glasses he only occasionally wore, Maverick folded his arms. Despite our snuggle session Friday night and lake day on Saturday, he was all business now that it was Monday again. He stood in the middle of the coffee shop, legs braced slightly apart. The power pose did funny things to my stomach.

Why did Lizbeth have to be reading in the corner?

I couldn't help but wonder if *she* was why he was acting so professional. So far today, he'd given no indication that we had any nonwork connection. I'd noticed that about him. Work time was focus time.

An array of marketing ideas lay sprawled in front of me on

the counter. Each idea was written on an index card, and I kept moving the cards around to re-prioritize them. Lizbeth and I had been debating back and forth about how to get more people into the shop.

*Book club* said one card near the top. *Birthday parties. Better pastries. BOGO sales. Wedding catering*, which didn't make any sense, but she'd insisted I keep it. "Don't dismiss ideas, Bethie," she'd muttered. "There's brilliance on each card."

"Think deeper," Maverick said now as he watched me regard each one for the fifteenth time. "What do people want when they come in, Bethany?"

The sound of my name on his voice purled like hot tea inside me. I blinked in a poor attempt to focus.

"And what do they need?" He tapped a finger on the counter. "This is Sales 101."

I frowned. "They want *coffee*."

Pretty simple.

Or was it? It must not be, or he wouldn't challenge me this way.

Credit card day loomed, and even though I spent time in my numbers every day at his insistence, I still felt sick to my stomach. My body had learned to be stressed the moment I thought about money.

"It certainly isn't fish," he said.

"Hey!"

Maverick held up two hands. "Listen, there comes a point where you have to look at your current assets and optimize those. That's the next stage in my process, and that's where we're at now. All the markers are present to indicate you're here."

He scribbled something on a notepad next to his laptop. He kept more notes than me.

"English, please?" I asked.

A hint of a smile ghosted his lip. "We're going to make your shop . . . better."

"And how will we do that?"

"Your decorations and . . . ambiance. I think we can improve the way things look around here and get more customers. More *loyal* customers, anyway. This ties into your marketing efforts and asks the same question: what do people *want*?"

Yikes. He'd gone right to my weak spot.

My few half-hearted attempts to move around what Dad had originally created in his manly, fishing-themed coffee shop had been minimal. Most of my time went into trying to keep this place floating. I literally hadn't once thought of revamping the inside.

"How do you *optimize* decorations?" I asked. Already, I felt my hackles rise.

"Improve them. But first, we need to step back. I'm getting ahead of myself again." Scribble, scribble on his little pad. "Let's figure out who your ideal client is, and what kind of ambiance they want. That's the goal today. Figuring out the answer to the question *who do you serve?*"

"That's easy! Everyone."

"Wrong."

I blinked. "What?"

He motioned to me with a wave. "If you didn't own this place, would you ever come here? You don't like sweet flavors, and you hate the smell of coffee."

"No," I said slowly.

"See? You don't serve everyone. In fact, your business doesn't even serve *you*. Which, let's not get into that right now."

"Okay," I drawled. "So, we don't serve everyone. What does that mean?"

Lizbeth peered out over the top of her book. "Please," she said to Maverick, "tell me you're going to encourage her to get rid of the fish." Her eyes darted to two plastic fish above the door. "I beg of you."

He winked at her.

My mouth dropped open. "The fish?" I cried. "Those are Dad's favorite!"

"They're hideous," Lizbeth said.

"They're . . ."

While I searched for adequate words to encompass the plastic replicas of leaping rainbow trout, Maverick nudged a nearby coat rack that Dad had bought at a secondhand antiques shop.

"This, for example?" he said. "Terrifying. Gaping fish mouths are holding the coats. They all need to go."

"No, please," I said, folding my arms. "Soften it for me, why don't you?"

"They're hideous."

"I was being sarcastic," I snapped.

Lizbeth tilted her head to the left. "Can that go too? All of them are ancient."

Dad had always loved board games, so a haphazard offering of them sat tucked under one of the tables. Every now and then, kids would stop in after school to caffeinate up for the rest of the day, playing Monopoly with ruthless vigor. Then they'd disappear to their gaming consoles at home.

By every once in a while, I meant once a year.

"Those are games!"

"They're for grandpas." She grimaced, then mouthed, *Sorry.*

"The rest of it isn't bad. Luckily, this isn't a structural problem. It's not like you need to re-carpet, or anything," Maverick said with a wary gaze. He didn't sound so convinced.

The wooden floor was scuffed but in decent shape. I moved to clean up two abandoned coffee cups off a cracked table.

Dad had always brought home coffee mugs as souvenirs from his deployments. When he opened the Frolicking Moose, he had over a hundred mugs that he put onto a cupboard in the corner. Time had whittled them down to about seventy-five.

*I take the world with me whenever I drink coffee,* he always said. It was definitely fun to pick your own mug. Those weren't going anywhere.

"Yeah," Lizbeth drawled, "it's all pretty gauche here, although I could live with the coffee mugs. You could potentially pass off all the decor and theme as a joke, but you'd need a few other things that are equally ridiculous—like a stuffed Sasquatch, or something."

My brain couldn't even process that.

"And that?" Mav pointed to a bulletin board covered with pictures of different types of fish, along with some lures. "What is that, anyway?"

"A lure exchange." I regarded it with a tilted head, my nose wrinkled. "The idea was fish and coffee."

"Fish and coffee?" Lizbeth whispered, horrified.

"It's not so bad! If fishermen wanted to try out different lures, they could come in and swap . . . and hopefully buy coffee. With the lake right there, he was convinced it'd work."

"Did it?"

"Ah . . . no."

I had completely forgotten it was there. Dad had been so excited when he called me with the idea. Taking it in from an outsider's perspective, however, I could see why it seemed . . . odd.

"Who is a customer that comes in here all the time?" Maverick asked.

"All the time?"

"Someone who genuinely loves coffee, pastries, and being with other people, even if they don't interact."

Well, no one who didn't feel some obligation to help me, like Jada and Millie. They were regulars, but I suspected more for my sake than their own.

Except . . .

"Someone who loves to read, perhaps?"

He shrugged. "Sure. Maybe they need the internet, like to be out of their house, want to be around other people. Who would use this coffee shop as a place to be social? A place to be seen, known, and heard. Somewhere to be safe. To belong. Somewhere to *go*."

With a quick twist of my lips, my gaze settled on Lizbeth.

Her eyes widened dramatically. "Uh, yeah!" she cried. "Finally, someone sees me as I really am! I freaking love coffee, and I'd never leave my armchair if you didn't force me. Millie gave me all the dish on the latest gossip this morning." She pointed saucily at us. "Give me a year, and I will run this town."

The expression on Maverick's face suggested he didn't doubt it for a second.

I spread my hands. "So, what do you want in a coffee shop? How would you decorate this place? What would you change? Feel free to take your ti—"

"Cozy. You need to cozy the *crap* out of this place."

The words flew out of her in a second, as if she'd already been thinking about this. Knowing how much time she spent in Dad's mustard-colored recliner in the corner nook, I wouldn't have been surprised. Lizbeth rose from the chair like a wood nymph.

She warmed to this at an alarming rate.

I unsuccessfully strove to quell a rush of panic as everything in the coffee shop met her scrutiny. Maverick watched with unbridled amusement.

"Cozy?" I repeated.

"Needs to be cozy. This is too . . ."

"Fishy?" Maverick offered. I glared at him. His lips twitched, but he offered no apology.

"Masculine," Lizbeth countered. "But yes, all the fish have to go. I have a Pinterest board on this already. Do you want to see it?"

"What?"

Maverick tilted his head back and laughed. Lizbeth sent him

a coquettish smile as she passed me her phone. She *did* have a Pinterest board, filled with images of arguably cozy shops. This was spiraling from bad to worse.

"I'm a dreamer," she said easily. "I like books, and I like pretty places. Since this is all I have to work with"—she waved a hand around—"I imagine myself in one of these other places. Anyway, more warm tones. The floor is beautiful, but needs a polish. I'd paint the walls, probably change from white to plum. Bookshelves on that wall, for starters. Keep the moose head, I actually think it works. We'll go with *rustic cozy*, and it's going to change this mountain forever."

She pointed to the fishy wall while I scrolled through the pins on her board.

Indeed, she'd thought this out.

The pictures showed warm lamps that cast buttery light. People milling around high and low tables. Chalkboards with fun writing and colors, instead of hastily scratched options. High class. In comparison, this place seemed . . . desperate.

"Wow," I murmured.

Lizbeth slipped over to one corner. "A lamp here. Maybe one with a silhouetted moose. You need to play more on your theme. And I think we amp up the mountain feel more. It's a bit lacking right now, but gives people the outdoor theme they come here for. That antiques store in Jackson City? We could refurbish from that with less than two hundred dollars. I'd bet my position as romance queen on it."

Maverick pointed at her as if to say, *Check her out?*

"She'll be unbearable after this," I muttered as Lizbeth studied the glass windows peering out on a hideous parking lot.

"We can do all that," Maverick said.

"With what money?" I cried.

He ignored me.

"Will you help, Lizbeth?" he asked.

She tossed a lock of hair over her shoulder. "You can't afford me, Mav."

Maverick laughed again.

Lizbeth rolled her eyes. "Um, yes, I will help you! This could be my big break into the interior-design space. Plus, then I can show all my Pinterest followers. They have ads there, you know. I could haul in some cash." She gazed at me from under thick, pale eyelashes. "Besides, we owe you, don't we?"

Before I could counter, she started prattling again, bouncing around the room. I let her live in it while I staved off the utter panic scalding my throat. It wasn't just the money—although that was part of it. It was the change. The shift. The loss of control as this all moved forward.

The total erasure of Dad.

We were getting rid of everything that made this place Dad's. The fish. The colors. The not-so-organized feel of clutter and coffee. It certainly wasn't impressive, but it wasn't a hole, either. Besides, I made great coffee, and that's all anyone cared about.

Right?

Maverick watched me carefully. I forced the thoughts back. I'd sort through them later, on the motorcycle.

No, I wouldn't do that, either, would I?

Panic squeezed my chest like a vise. I fumbled for my purse. Was it time to touch up my lipstick? Take a break?

Run away?

"Well," I said, my voice a little *too* bright, "let me think about this for a day or forty."

"You okay?" Lizbeth asked, studying me.

"Fine. I'm fine."

"That means—"

"I'm fine!" I snapped.

"Ookaaay," Lizbeth said, "while you have a mild panic attack, I'll get to work. But we're going to do two lists." She reached for my laptop. "One of things we can do right now, and one that will take some time and money to build out. I might be able to draw up a budget for draperies and—"

"Are you all right with this?" Maverick asked, moving to stand next to me. He propped his hands on the counter behind him, though he didn't take his eyes off Lizbeth as she honed in on the computer. Clearly, she didn't expect a response.

Lizbeth was a verbal processor. Instead of the quiet, she needed the chaos. Right then, I could have made do with a long stretch of highway and the rumble of the bike beneath me.

"Fine," I said.

"You're pale."

"I'm fine."

"And your knuckles are white."

A glance downward confirmed I was clutching the counter with a white-knuckled grip. Every muscle in my body felt like it was ready to spring. "It's . . . a lot."

"A lot of what?"

"Of . . . unexpectedness."

That wasn't a word. Or maybe it was. I didn't care, but I did try again.

"It's a lot of letting go."

He nodded slowly, seeming to roll that idea around his mind. "Or a lot of embracing the future. However you want to look at it."

My brow furrowed. I hated it when he acted like my mentor or pulled out some nugget of wisdom I didn't really want. I didn't want to be functional. I wanted to *feel*. Especially when I just wanted to rip the glasses off him and throw myself back into his chest. The temptation to send Lizbeth skittering upstairs with her ideas was nearly overwhelming. I held back because I didn't quite know where I stood with Maverick.

Strictly speaking, we were friends who would part as soon as he felt the need. We just happened to share a strong sense of attraction and kisses that would melt the panties off any woman.

"It's okay to *feel,* you know," I muttered a bit too sharply. *Defensiveness,* Dad always said, *means something is very wrong, Bee.*

Maverick grunted.

"I just . . . I feel sad. And not ready. To let go of all of this is to . . . kind of . . . you know . . . erase my dad from the coffee shop. And if he's not here, then he's nowhere, because this was literally all he had left."

"Not all." He kicked the side of my foot gently.

I frowned up at him. "You mean me?"

He nodded.

To that, I had no reply. Maybe he was right, but I wasn't ready to see that yet. A small part of Dad would always live on in me, but I couldn't *feel* that. I couldn't embrace it. That wasn't the tangible proof that he was still with me. Letting go of the only physical assurance I had of my father was too much. I'd already sacrificed his bike to a stranger.

Now I had to let the fish go.

"That feels hard," I said, swallowing my emotion. "Sad. It's too much. Besides, it's almost credit card day. How will I pay for all this?"

He paused. "You're right. It is sad, and it is hard."

"I'm not ready."

"Then don't do it."

"But the girls?"

He shrugged. "You don't have to do anything you aren't ready for."

Annoyance rolled off of me. "That's the thing, Mav. I don't get the luxury of freedom or walking away or minimalism. Not anymore."

My heels tapped on the ground as I did, indeed, walk away. A fire sparked under my skin, and I knew I'd regret throwing that back in his face.

Clearly, he didn't get it.

Maybe he never would. And he didn't have to get it, because that's the life he chose. No attachments. No expectations, no disappointment.

But it wasn't mine. Not anymore.

# Chapter Twenty-Six

MAVERICK

My exchange with Bethany kept me up until past midnight.

I'd totally messed up—I could own that. Sometimes I crossed the line between business and friendship when I was a bit too honest, or maybe just too blunt. Bethany had an emotional response to a situation that I hadn't pegged as difficult.

Most people loved redecorating. Fresh start, and all that. Didn't realize I'd pushed too hard, too fast until I saw the terror on her face. But I wasn't sure how to fix it, and I didn't like that. Somehow, I felt like I'd disappointed her. Which totally sucked. And it all came back to her proposal that we let our attraction show with no expectation of a future.

Because she was already forming expectations.

My phone beeped. I almost ignored it, but decided to make sure it wasn't my mother. Instead, Bethany's name showed on the screen.

I couldn't open the text fast enough.

*I'm sorry I was angry at you and stomped off like a toddler.*

Letting out a long exhale, I lay back. That wasn't what I'd expected. I started typing.

*Fault is mine. Should have been a little more compassionate. You're giving up a lot for these girls.*

Two full minutes passed before her reply came. I didn't notice how hard I was holding on to the phone until I forced my fingers to relax a little.

*You weren't entirely wrong in what you said. I get really annoyed with how right you are ALL THE TIME.*

Chuckling, I said, *I know. My family hates that about me too. Except Mallory. She loves it because I made her company grow faster.*

*I think . . . maybe I'm holding on to my dad too hard.*

My brow furrowed. What on earth to say to that? Of course she was holding on to him. He hadn't even been gone a year. But too hard?

Maybe.

Or maybe this was all a part of the process. I had no idea because I just avoided thinking about my father. She might have a leg up on me there. At least she let herself feel. I ran from it like a plague.

She'd lost so many people that I couldn't even relate. My palms started to sweat a little. She clearly needed something right now, and I had no idea what. Falling short here would only disappoint her.

No one had made me swim in deeper waters than this girl.

*I think you're surviving and doing a damn good job of it,* I finally said.

*Thanks. :)*

I could picture her lying back. I wanted to brush hair away from her face and cup her chin. The memory of falling asleep with her on the couch haunted me. My arms felt oddly cold and empty. Not wanting to let her go just yet, I said, *See you in the morning, Bethany.*

*Sweet dreams, Mav.*

Sleep finally slipped over me. My dreams were restless, filled with the expression on my father's face when he lay in his casket, and the coldness I'd felt radiate through me.

# Chapter Twenty-Seven

BETHANY

The rest of the week passed in a blur of stolen moments with Maverick as we made changes to the coffee shop. Maverick stole a kiss every time Lizbeth left to go to the bathroom or grab a new book. He took me to lunch one day and tried to figure out my favorite dessert, even though I didn't have one.

For a blessed week, I felt like I was floating. Life seemed suspended for a brief summer lull. I poked my head out of the haze of grief and soaked up all the love, attention, and touch a girl could ask for.

But Credit Card Day loomed large.

I tried not to think about it while preparing the store, while running through my numbers, or while Lizbeth and I hung flyers for a new book club at the coffee shop next month. Even though I checked twice a day to reassure myself that I had enough money, I still felt terrified.

Maybe the money would just . . . disappear.

Lizbeth, Ellie, Devin, and I bounced around antiques stores for several days, trying to find *funky-cabin-cozy*, as Lizbeth called it.

"It's your new vibe," she informed me. She set aside a

shrunken moose head that looked like a cross between a swamp souvenir and a voodoo doll. "Trust me, Bethany. I was made for this kind of work."

Although my heart prickled while it happened, I allowed Lizbeth to pull the ugly fish down off the wall. We had a solemn burial in the backyard that, oddly enough, made me feel a little better. Lizbeth brightened like a star, falling easily into her creative element. Piece by piece, the shop slowly pulled together.

My heart beat a sad, hollow staccato as everything changed.

Later that week, I stared at the calendar while the stench of paint fumes filled the air. We'd closed the store early so Lizbeth could start painting. She looked adorable in a pair of Dad's old overalls and a too-big shirt, her hair pulled into a high bun. Blue tape lined the floor and ceiling as she prepared to paint the walls a warm plum, accented by taupe.

Thanks to some donations from the local hardware store, whom my father had frequented, I'd only had to pay for paint— which left us with a hundred dollars. In Lizbeth's words, we were *investing in aesthetically pleasing decorations*. So far, that meant a silhouetted moose shade and an antique oil lamp.

The silence, punctuated only by the sound of Lizbeth laughing at her audiobook and Maverick speaking to his assistant on the East Coast, fell like a weight around me.

Time to do it.

No avoiding the credit card now.

The statement waited in my inbox, unopened because I'd been leaving it there for the absolute last moment. It would be due tomorrow. I'd have to pay online today to be safe, because I'd skipped last month.

Despite Maverick's attention to the finances, I still didn't want to see it. Didn't want to comprehend the enormity of the task that lay in front of me. It was so much more than just *this* credit card. There was still the mortgage. The line of credit at the bank. Saying goodbye to Dad.

This credit card just represented it all.

"This is irrational," I muttered.

But it felt as if my fate were somehow listed in the numbers.

I wiped my hands on my apron and drew in a deep breath. Sounds of summer rang from outside. Tourists gathering paddleboards from the rental shop next door. Trucks hauling boats to the lake.

A lovely soundtrack for such a horrible task.

With a deep inhale, I grabbed my computer, opened my email, and stared at the message on top.

*Credit Card Statement Available.*

I opened the statement and skimmed to the bottom of the page. Total due: $39,987.

Monthly charge: $3,700.

My breath stalled in my chest. Maverick made me go through my numbers every day. But transfers and credit card processing fees and months of drowning made it hard to trust anything. I opened another tab, navigated to Dad's business bank, and logged in. A spinning wheel filled the screen before the accounts revealed themselves.

My breath caught.

In the account that I would pay the credit card from was $3,725.

Not only was there enough to cover the credit card payment for the month, but twenty-five dollars left over. That meant I'd made twenty-five dollars in profit.

This stupid coffee shop had actually made money. This crazy business actually *worked.*

Tears thickened my throat, making it difficult to breathe. My vision swam. This worked. I looked up to tell Lizbeth, but the words didn't come out.

We'd not only pulled a small profit, we'd covered expenses *and* charges. That meant Maverick's plan had already started to turn us around. The proof lay in front of me. If we continued on this path, I would have the evidence I needed to keep the girls. Eventually.

"It's working," I whispered.

Lizbeth glanced up, one eyebrow raised. She pulled an earbud out. "What?"

Clapping, I twirled in a circle. Ellie peered at me from the pantry, where she tied lures with Devin. They'd rigged a little office out of a lamp and a bag of coffee beans.

Whooping, I typed in the numbers, hit send, and made the credit card payment. Then I slammed the laptop shut and started to dance.

"We made twenty-five dollars!" I cried. "We made *money!*"

Lizbeth's eyes widened. Even at sixteen, she got it. She knew that this meant we had a fighting chance against Jim. With a cry, she turned on the old radio and cranked the music. A fast-paced song filled the room, and we started to dance. Ellie and Devin joined in, whirling and bumping around the chairs, bright with laughter.

A lightness filled my chest as I grabbed Lizbeth and Ellie in my arms and spun. Maverick stepped outside the office with a questioning expression. I grabbed his hand and pulled him into the dance.

"We made a profit!" I cried over the music. "I made the minimum payment *and twenty-five dollars!*"

His expression brightened. "Yeah?"

"We're doing it! We're turning this business around!"

He twirled me with the music. Our dance party blared out the windows as we celebrated our massive success in the summer sunshine.

* * *

A week later, I bit my bottom lip. A half-grin lived on my face as I stared at my text message exchange with Mav.

. . .

*Hey Mav. You're taking tonight off from renovations, right?*

*Yep. Waiting for some stain to dry. Appliances are being delivered tomorrow.*

*Want some company? I'll bring dinner.*

*Bring yourself first.*

My thoughts spiraled like birds when I arrived at his place. The expiration date was coming up on our whirlwind . . . romance? Adventure? On the drive over, I'd promised myself to enjoy every minute. Because, eventually, this would end.

Eventually.

In the future.

At some possibly soon point that I didn't want to acknowledge. Because putting in new appliances wasn't the first step of a house refurb, that was for sure.

With a sigh, I stepped out of the car and grabbed a to-go box of pasta in one hand and a breadstick bag in the other. Maverick opened the door before I could knock. Dust coated his features, highlighting a knee-weakening smile.

"Welcome."

I held up my offerings. "I bring sustenance. In the form of Italian food."

He tossed the food on the counter and grabbed my wrist. "Bring me this first," he murmured, then spun me around, caught me against his chest, and captured my lips in a hungry kiss.

Heat pooled in my belly as his hands brushed my face, cupping them with gritty warmth. He backed me into the wall. All the air rushed out of my lungs. I grabbed his shoulders, heady with the scent of him. Maybe *goodbye* wasn't coming too soon. No one kissed like that who didn't mean it.

Who was about to say *goodbye*.

No one kissed like that *ever*.

Like a fool, I entertained the thought that he might stay. Flip houses with me. Like Chip and Joanna Gaines, only in the mountains. When he deepened the kiss, I wrapped my arms around him. My thoughts dissolved. The rough feel of his hair on my palms sent fire through my fingers.

He pulled away with a self-satisfied grin. I stood there a second, heart racing.

"Whoa," I whispered.

"Maybe you need to have Lizbeth go to Jada's more often." He laughed but didn't let go. The deep roll of his voice made me shudder. I would never get enough.

"If this is what I get from it, we'll just have her move in."

He tightened an arm around me and pulled me in for a second searing kiss, setting fire to my skin. He set me free and held me back all at the same time. The odd distance between us during the day melted away.

Several breathless minutes later, the kiss slowed. I blinked, staring into his eyes in something like shock. But I didn't have any words. His expression softened as he rubbed a thumb over my bottom lip.

"Why do you look so serious all of a sudden?" he whispered.

"Because you make me feel serious things."

"Same." With a lopsided smile, he threaded his fingers through mine, then tugged me away from the wall. "C'mere. I have something to show you."

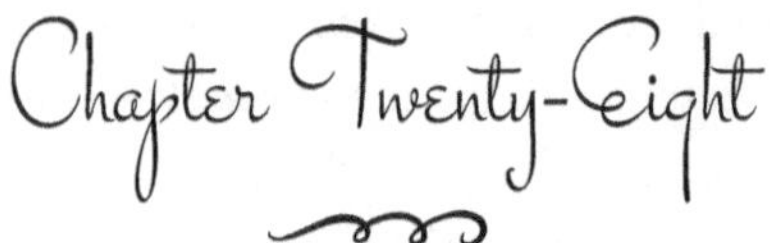

# Chapter Twenty-Eight

MAVERICK

I'd longed for Bethany's hand in mine. The oddly grounding effect of her smell. Just knowing she was there, even if we didn't say a word. I'd never just wanted to be around a woman before. Not like this.

Her kiss-stung lips looked almost too tempting to ignore as I led her through the house, toward the back rooms that faced the forest. Had she worn yoga pants on purpose? I wouldn't put it past her. She drove me crazy.

The house had been a vanity project. A delay. Something to do while I ensured the coffee shop could stand on its own two feet. Something to keep me here until I figured all of this out. But now? Now we knew the plan worked.

This was where I started to wrap things up, I imagined.

She'd made a full credit card payment. The leniency from the bank for the next six months would buy her time to get debts paid down. She would earn enough to support the girls if they lived at the coffee shop. Their new marketing efforts, aided by some discreet consulting help from one of my friends at corporate, would bring more people in. Her shiny new systems guaranteed a greater return on investment.

It wasn't perfect, but it was just enough.

Right now, Bethany needed it.

Shoving thoughts of the future aside, I slowed. She stood so close to me I could feel her heat. Wanted to run my hands through her hair again. I kept them locked at my side, her fingers tangled in mine.

"Here." I pulled her into the doorway of a room on the left. "Let me know what you think."

She stepped inside, then gasped. My anticipation smoothed into relief when she gaped at me, wide-eyed.

"What's this?"

"A bookshelf."

"Well, obviously it's a bookshelf. Did you make it? It's . . . gorgeous."

She slipped inside, walking around the five-shelf stand that I'd put together. If she wanted rustic, this was certainly it. Knotted wood stained dark in a charming style. I leaned against the doorframe, content to watch her.

"Lizbeth would die," she murmured.

Her fingertips trailed the wood as she walked in a circle around it. I almost felt those same fingers in my hair again. I shoved my hands in my pockets to keep myself from slamming her against this wall too.

"Good, because it's for her."

Bethany paused, head tilted. "For Lizbeth?"

"Well, for your shop, but I figured Lizbeth would need somewhere to put all her books when they officially moved here." I shrugged, completely unable to read the expression on her face. She drew in a deep breath, regarding the bookshelf as if she'd never seen one before.

"Moves here," she murmured. "Yes."

There definitely wasn't room in that tiny attic. The coffee shop had space. I'd purposefully made it the exact right size to put against the far wall, near Lizbeth's chair. But she might not have noticed that yet.

She began to say something, then stopped. *We can't take it,* I imagined her thinking. *We have nowhere to put it.*

The fact that she hadn't said it yet meant she wasn't ready to hear my other offer.

"It's not finished." I let out a breath. "It still needs some more love on the scrollwork and a couple good coats of stain. But it will be soon."

Her shoulders relaxed slightly. "How long will that take?"

"A week."

She didn't look at me. "And the house?"

"It's mostly done. The appliances are coming in tomorrow. A few cleanup things that I've paid some contractors to come do. It's more management for me at this point. I've taken a back seat on the work so I could be at the Frolicking Moose and prove this other business idea out. It's moved . . . quickly here."

"Lizbeth will love it," she said softly.

My contract with Bethany had moved faster than I'd expected. We'd shifted the Frolicking Moose into a better position quickly. Establishing the timeline had helped, and it was great to know it could be done in less than a month. But it meant my departure was lingering in the near future.

And I was a coward because I couldn't say it to her. *I'm leaving soon.* With a welcoming kiss like that, I'd thrown down mixed signals all over the place. *I'm leaving* on one side and *kiss me breathless* on the other.

But she'd agreed to this.

Something seemed to shift in her in that moment, as if she'd made a decision. No sign of trouble loomed in her bright face. She smiled, meeting my gaze without a qualm.

"It was very kind of you, Mav. Thank you. Seriously."

"It was my pleasure."

"Ready to eat?"

"That entire box of spaghetti, yes."

With a soft laugh, she followed me out, winding back through the house to the kitchen, which smelled like marinara now. She paused, staring curiously across the room, and pointed.

"That's an internet modem."

"Yes. Right next to it is a window, and it sits on a table, and—"

"No, that's a *working* modem."

I whistled. "Nothing escapes you, does it, sharpshooter?" I said, reaching for a plate in the kitchen.

Her gaze tapered, nonplussed by my poor attempts to turn this into something humorous, when, in fact, it might be creepy.

"*Does* it work?" she asked, hands on her hips.

I tossed a cheap plastic plate onto the counter next to her. "You can thank it for the late-night text marathons."

"How long have you had it?" she cried.

"Almost two weeks."

"But you've been coming to the shop for all that time."

"I still wanted my Pineville office." I pretended to take offense. "Where else could I possibly find such spacious accommodations?"

"Your closet is more like it," she said with wry humor. The glint in her eye told me she wasn't angry. "You've been paying me to use my tiny little office that even a mouse would feel claustrophobic in when you could have more conveniently worked from this gorgeous house?"

"That isn't what I was paying for," I said quietly.

She looked away, gaze distant. My stomach knotted. I had to force down hot acid in the back of my throat. *She's in a good place,* I reminded myself, *and I'm no hero. I'm here to help her find success, and then I'm out. No expectations. She's known that.*

Her parents had left her with a real mess, and I couldn't save her from it. But I could help her see what real success looked like, and she was well on her way now. Best to bow out before expectations bred deeper disappointments.

Because in my world, they always did. And those disappointments led to much scarier things than a broken heart. Bethany deserved better.

Desperate to head back to the safety of our banter, I gave her a quick wink.

"C'mon. I'm starving, and I have a chocolate pie that needs to get in my belly once we're done with this. Let's take this onto the porch."

# Chapter Twenty-Nine

BETHANY

I wanted to kill him.

He kisses me like that, then shows me that bookshelf? The house? Tells me that he's going to leave in a week?

Total. Jerk.

My rage was short lived, and futile. I'd brought this on myself, and blaming him wouldn't do any good. I'd willingly checked into Heartbreak Hotel, and now I had to live with it. Sooner than I'd expected, unfortunately. My heart felt like he'd taken a cheese grater to it.

*This is the beginning of the end.*

All I really wanted was more of Maverick. All of Maverick. My wasted expectations were futile. Maverick would give whatever he would give, then run.

The cycle was established. Running away to the Army. Running from Mallory. Now, he would run from me. Or was it even fair to say that? We had . . . what? Not a relationship. Shared affection, perhaps, but no commitment.

"So," I said through the uncomfortable, vise-like feeling around my neck. Based on his wary expression, my forced casualness didn't fool him, either. "What's next for you?"

He nodded and sipped at a beer he'd grabbed from the fridge. Sunlight filtered through the trees near the back porch, overlooking the mountain ridge that fell into more mountains. This house had to be worth at least half a million dollars.

"I'm looking at some places in South Dakota," he said slowly, hedging. "I think just another week will do it."

"And you have internet. The operations manual is done, and I've organized my books so the girls and I can eat every day. Even if I haven't figured out the whole health insurance issue. But I have that insurance broker's number, so . . ."

He met my gaze, nodding. For a long moment I held it, arrested by the uncertainty I saw there. Everything felt too big all of a sudden. *Goodbye* lingered like a hummingbird.

"Bethany—"

"Don't." I held up a hand, panic in my voice. "Please, don't. This is . . . I agreed to this. I just have to accept it now. I get that. Just . . . give me some time to wrap my head around it." My voice softened. "This is harder than I thought it would be, and I knew it would suck."

He paused, studying me. "All right. Well, I wanted to show you one more thing tonight." He grabbed an envelope on the table and slid it to me. I withdrew a folded sheath of papers and opened them. It took me two full scans to understand the paperwork.

"A rental agreement?"

He sucked in a slow breath. "I've decided to keep the property a little bit longer. Rent it out instead of sell it. I think, given the market, I could make more money off my investment in five years. It's a buyer's market now."

The market wasn't great for sellers, but it wasn't bad. I doubted five years would gain him much, but one never knew. My eyes skimmed the paperwork until they tangled on some numbers at the bottom.

Rental agreement: $125 a month.

But that was ridiculously low. In fact, that was—

Oh.

The implication hit me all at once. He was keeping the house so *I* could rent it.

For $125 a month.

Something hot ballooned in my chest. I slid the papers back to him, my lips pressed together.

Mixed signals alert. What was I supposed to do with this?

"I don't know anyone who's looking," I said stiffly.

"Bethany, I . . ." His nostrils flared. "I'm not great at these conversations."

"I know. It's why we never had any."

His shoulders lifted as he took a deep breath. "I thought it might help until you get back on your feet. You can rent this place for a low cost and—"

"I'm not *off* my feet," I snapped.

He lifted an eyebrow.

"I'm not! The store had a twenty-five dollar profit last month. That's twenty-five dollars that has never happened before. We bought a beautiful rug with it, if you're asking. If your numbers don't lie, I'm on track for a hundred-dollar profit next month. That will help pay for new clothes for school next year. It will only keep growing. That's after I get paid, which means we're fine."

"For now. But raising kids means a lot of unexpected things pop up. You're living in a single room with two teenage girls."

"Oh? Is that right? Thank you for mansplaining that to me."

His gaze tapered to dangerous slits.

"Why do you care?" I asked, voice shaky. "You're leaving. And soon. Much . . . much sooner than I thought."

His voice deepened to a roll of thunder. "That doesn't mean I'm heartless."

I turned, unable to face him.

"We both agreed this thing between us would be just what it

is. I've accepted that you feel like you have to move on. That there's nothing to keep you here. This? This rental agreement just . . . muddies the waters."

"Bethany, I want you to be safe."

"Then stay." I whipped around. "Stay. Live in this house and travel to your next job, but come back to me. Let's make this real. You and me. Committed. Dating. Figuring out if our lives can merge in a way that makes both of us better people. Long distance sucks, but it couldn't be worse than this. We can make it happen. Success seems to just . . . *flow* to you."

The air crackled with tension. Troubled ridges formed on his forehead. This wasn't fair of me to ask. I knew that, deep down. He had never indicated he wanted a relationship, and it was dirty of me to try.

Still, the power between us couldn't be denied.

If I didn't try, I'd never forgive my cowardice. And at least, this way, I could live with myself.

"It's not that simple," he said.

"Why?"

"Because . . ."

A cold feeling washed over me. "You're going to accept the position and work for Mallory?"

"No." He ran a hand through his tousled hair. "I mean . . . maybe. I haven't decided officially."

My heart felt swollen. Heavy. This was all my fault. I should never have let it happen. Let my aching heart fall hard again. It was like I wanted to remain broken.

"Bethany, if I stay, then you and I are going to fall deeper into . . . whatever this is."

I paused, expecting him to finish, but he'd stopped.

"Wouldn't that be the point?"

"That comes with expectations."

"Like?"

He stood. "Like commitment and affection and time and . . . expectations."

"You didn't mind that affection twenty minutes ago when you slammed me against the wall."

"Not just that kind of affection. But intimacy. Depth. I can't control those variables. With successful ventures come expectations. The more successful you are, the more people want out of you. Eventually, you can't live up to what they want, and everything suffers. Marriages fall apart. Love burns out. I've seen it time and time again with business, with Mallory, with Baxter. With my parents. I don't want that for you."

"This isn't a business, Maverick!" I cried. "This is your life. It's my heart."

He faltered. "See? Expectations."

The pain in his gaze stopped me flat. I had no idea what to say next. Maybe he was right. Maybe he wasn't. But the only thing I knew was that he was leaving. Just like Mama. Just like Pappa. Just like Dad. In a strange, backward way, I understood it. I had created this situation, not him.

Stupidly, I realized that I'd been hoping I would be enough for him. That he'd change his mind because our great match was enough to make him stay. But that wasn't how this worked. People brought their own issues into relationships. I'd been idealizing him out of desperation.

Out of loneliness, I had created this monster.

Maverick was afraid of failure, bottom line. That fear was bigger than me. I swallowed hard, barely keeping my composure. Perhaps he was right. This wouldn't be a good thing. Me, so desperate for love. Him, so desperate for success and freedom. We were oil and water.

Fire and ice.

That ancient bad mixture that felt so good.

"I understand," I whispered.

The anguish in his eyes tripled. He reached for me but stopped halfway. "Bethany, I . . ."

I stepped back.

"Good luck, Mav. I think it's best if we part here. It's only going to be worse for me, so I'll ask for your compassion in this. But . . . I just . . . I want you to know that you never disappointed me. The only thing I wanted from you was for you to show up, and you did that. So . . . thank you."

His face fell, and his coiled body didn't move.

I stepped back, my legs colliding with the chair. Hot tears welled up in my eyes. I blinked them away, my emotions wildly unbound. "I need to go."

When I moved to leave, his hand on my wrist stopped me. I looked back in wordless question.

"I wanted you to have the first pass at the rental agreement," he continued, as if everything that lay between us suddenly wasn't there. But his eyes didn't quite meet mine, and the knot in my chest tightened. "I wanted to . . . I wanted to help."

Hanging on to the last vestige of my pride, I said, "The offer is kind. I appreciate the place of care that it originated from, but I'm able to take care of myself and the girls without you. Just like you wanted."

His expression clouded. I felt the crack all the way down the center of my heart. I slipped through the house, walking away as fast as I could. He followed, not saying a word until I reached the door.

"Wait."

My hand gripped the doorknob. I felt a traitorous fluttering in my chest at the sound of his voice. Maybe he'd say it. Stop me. Confess whatever fear paralyzed him.

"Can I say goodbye to the girls?"

Pain I hadn't felt since Dad died filled my chest again. I wanted to say *no*. I wanted to tell him to just go and stay away.

Seeing him again would be torture. It would be hard enough being in the coffee shop without him.

But Lizbeth and Ellie had experienced enough loss without closure.

"Tomorrow afternoon is fine."

The feeling of his eyes boring into my back followed me to the car. I shut the door, turned the key in the ignition, and pulled away with full composure. He hadn't budged. Always stagnant. Alone in his isolated bubble.

The bubble that outrated me.

All of us.

Everyone.

The tires skidded on the rocks as I peeled away with a sob.

# Chapter Thirty

MAVERICK

She drove away.

A cloud of dust whirled behind her car, which quickly disappeared among the trees. The whispered remnants of her words and the inescapable sense that I had just made a mistake haunted me.

She didn't get it yet.

She didn't understand that expectations led to disappointment and, ultimately, heartbreak. In the end, she'd be better off without me failing her. The way I had constantly failed Dad, which led to his ultimate demise.

The right thing had never felt so awful.

# Chapter Thirty-One

BETHANY

My head pounded the next morning.

Despite lying awake until 2:00 a.m., tears silently soaking my pillow, more grief lingered behind my eyes. My rage at our conversation had ebbed into a low, pulsing heartache. How had I fallen so hard? He'd invaded my life and painted himself all over it, and now he'd leave. Everything in Pineville had echoes of Maverick. The grocery store. The bar. The Italian restaurant.

Even the coffee shop still smelled like him.

By three, I gave in and headed downstairs to make the frappuccino bases for the day. The quiet repose was a welcome escape, so I flipped the sign on, tied my apron, and turned to my to-do list. If some random trucker wanted to stop by and get some caffeine, I'd take their money. While I worked through the daily preparations, my traitorous mind spun over his kiss. The heat in my belly.

To shove the thoughts away, I looked at my bank accounts.

The morning rush came and went. I moved through it like a machine. Ellie and Devin showed up at seven. They were playing out in the reeds five minutes later. Lizbeth popped awake around eleven, while I shoved caffeine into the hands of as many people as I could, silently tallying the dollars.

*Operating expenses covered for the day.*
*Sixty dollars in sales tax.*
*My broken heart will never heal.*
*Thirty to the credit card.*
*I'll sell this place to forget him.*
*Forty to the line of credit at the bank.*

I called a local bakery in Jackson City and discussed selling their goods. While we worked out a delivery schedule and a cost table, Maverick fluttered through my mind. Erasing Dad's favorite scone from the chalkboard sent physical pain shooting through my core. I bit my lip to keep from crying again. I thought I heard Maverick shuffle in the office, and turned that way. My heart plummeted to see it dark and empty.

When a clang sounded at the door, I jumped. Lizbeth glanced at me from the top of her book.

"Just the mail, Bethie," she said, turning another page. "You're twitchy today."

She'd been studying me all day. I'd felt her eyes on me. I hadn't mentioned Maverick yet. Couldn't bear to force the words out. But I felt a moment of panic when his truck pulled up in the parking lot. My cracked heart split down the middle. I ripped the apron off and threw it at Lizbeth.

"I'm sorry," I whispered. "I can't."

She looked up at me in surprise as I rushed into the hall, hurrying up the spiral stairs. The door below opened as I sat at the top of the steps, folding my knees into my chest. Maverick's low voice rumbled as he spoke with Lizbeth. I bit down on my jeans to muffle a short cry.

Tears trailed down my cheeks, soaking my knees. I tried not to hear his words.

Several minutes later, Lizbeth appeared at the bottom of the stairs. The door chime rang, indicating his final departure. She looked up, then climbed toward me. When she reached the top, she sat down and folded me into her arms.

I fell into her embrace with a muffled sob.

"There's always pain and struggle in the books I read," she whispered against my hair. "The heroine has to go through something dark before the light comes. Before she figures out what she needed to know all along. Maybe that's where Maverick is. Maybe that's where *you* are. Some writers call it the *dark night of the soul.*"

My throat choked as I spiraled back over the last year. Dad's heart attack. Dropping out of college. All the lonely nights in his coffee shop. The weight of crushing debt. The destructive emptiness of living alone, with no one to touch. No one to be part of my team. Then Lizbeth and Ellie's arrival.

And the final blow: Maverick leaving.

It was more than heartbreak over Maverick that poured out of me now. It was *everything.* Losing the motorcycle. Dad disappearing out of the coffee shop.

Maverick leaving meant that my team was really and truly gone. As if there was something broken inside of me that kept anyone from staying.

"I . . . I think my heart is going to break," I whispered. "And it's all my fault."

Lizbeth folded me against her, and I cried.

* * *

The next day, I clutched an official-looking letter from an attorney. The coffee shop purred quietly in the background, the air thick with the scent of a new brew Lizbeth had started advertising on our shiny new Facebook page.

My stomach churned as I stared at the return address through bloodshot eyes. *Riverdale.*

"Oh no," I muttered.

This could only be from Jim.

Lizbeth didn't look up from the laptop, where she was putting together a post about the Fourth of July sugar cookies we'd bought from the Jackson City bakery.

"What is it?"

"A letter. From your father's lawyer."

Her head snapped up. I stared at the words swimming on the page, my brain suddenly mush as I comprehended what they meant.

I tossed the letter at her. "He's threatening me through his attorney."

"To send us back?"

"No. Just you." I shoved away from the table and started to pace. Ellie was curled up on the bed upstairs, watching a movie with Devin while the hot, afternoon sunshine warmed everything with choking heat.

My brow furrowed. "It doesn't make sense. He's only claiming you, though. Why?"

"Because he isn't Ellie's dad."

Lizbeth said it with all the emotional inflection of a rock. Her expression didn't waver in the slightest as she stared at the letter, although my jaw almost dropped to the floor.

"What?" I screeched.

Lizbeth sighed, hugging her book to her chest. She looked at me uneasily, then pushed the letter my way again.

"Mama had a . . . thing . . . for the neighbor. He was a widow. They'd talk every now and then when he came to borrow a tool from Dad or something. She'd cook big dinners and take some over to him. That kind of stuff. She didn't act on it at first, but then . . ."

"She did."

Lizbeth nodded with a sigh. "Yeah. For a while. Dad didn't find out until right before Mama died. The night she died, in fact."

My already-aching heart sank a little deeper in my chest. "Is that why she was driving away?" I asked, puzzling out what I'd learned at the funeral. Mama had been in a terrible car crash, pulling out in front of a semi that her car couldn't outrace.

"Yes. From fighting with him," Lizbeth confirmed, a flash of something appearing in her eyes again. "She was angry; he was angry. They were both screaming for hours. When he found out the truth about Ellie, he went ballistic. Ellie and I hid in the forest for a while, until we heard the cops calling for us. That's when we found out that Mama had died."

I let out a long breath.

"Wow. Does Ellie know?"

Lizbeth shook her head, then shrugged. "At least, not that I can tell. I pulled her away before she could hear what they were arguing about that night. Mama never told her. Maybe Dad did. But I don't think so. He was never able to say the words, to admit it out loud. Even in his drunk rages, he never brought it up. Just blubbered and cried."

"Think he feels responsible for Mama dying?" I asked. "That's why he's drinking so much?"

Lizbeth shrugged.

"Wow."

Even though I tried to block it, Maverick's voice rose in my mind. *Expectations.* Mama had shattered her marriage vows for another man on her second marriage, defying expectations of fidelity. Maybe *she* was to blame for the situation we were in.

No, she didn't ask Jim to be drunk and abusive. If I knew anything, it was that.

But she sure hadn't helped anything, either. The memories flashed through me. The fear. Those long nights living in the car, waiting for Mama to come back.

No wonder Maverick ran from the depths of this crazy. From the carefully unraveling tapestry that Mama had built and left behind for us to bear the burden of. But that was Mama. In her mind, long-term consequences were for the birds. She had the here and the now, and that was it.

So many pieces clicked together. Jim's harsh treatment of Ellie. His sullen silences. His drunken rages. The way he took so much of his anger out on her.

"Mama was sick," Lizbeth whispered, terror in her voice, "and so is Dad. If I have to go back there, you'll never see me again, Bethie."

Gathering as much courage as I could, I pulled her to me, clutching her tight. "It will be over my dead body that he takes you, Lizbeth. I promise you."

"Maverick isn't here anymore. He was . . . he made me feel safer."

"I know." My heart cracked. "But we'll be fine. You'll never go back. This is just a formality, and it tells me that we need to get legal action going now. The business is profitable, even if by a small amount. Still, it's enough. I believe that."

She relaxed only slightly. Several moments later, she pulled back, tucking her hair behind her ear. "Can I go back upstairs and read for a little bit? The post is up."

"Of course."

Silently, she slipped up to the apartment. Seconds later, a pair of thudding feet appeared at the end of the hallway, and the back screen door slammed shut. Ellie and Devin must have escaped outside at some point. As if she could sense something bad had happened, Ellie stared at me in wordless question. New fly-fishing lures filled Devin's free hand, while a sleeping kitten was tucked firmly under Ellie's arm. She ran the tips of her fingers down its shaggy stomach, regarding me with wary suspicion.

Grief, when had she found a cat?

Devin stood next to her, one hand around her shoulders as if to protect her. They both had strangely somber expressions.

"Everything is fine," I said brightly, acting like I didn't see the new animal or the health code nightmare it would create. "You can keep playing."

Ellie wasn't fooled. I could see it in her eyes. She had a weird sixth sense about these kinds of things. But she said nothing else as she turned away and returned to the sunshine with Devin.

I stared at the letter with a churning feeling in my gut.

* * *

**Bethany:** Hey Kin. I want full custody of my sisters. Can we get the process started? I can promise to pay you $100 next month, and more after. But I'm otherwise strapped for cash right now.

**Kinoshi:** Of course. Don't worry about the money yet. Let's meet tomorrow. We'll discuss filing an application and start the process. Do you have proof of harm to them?

**Bethany:** From Jada, yes.

**Kinoshi:** I'll contact her to get the documentation. Any neighbors or other people who could also write statements or testify for you?

**Bethany:** Probably. I'll call.

**Kinoshi:** That would be helpful. Gather everything you can. I hate to ask, but can you prove that you'll be able to give them a better living situation?

. . .

**Bethany:** Yes. I can.

**Kinoshi:** Then we'll talk tomorrow.

**Bethany:** Thanks. Talk soon.

# Chapter Thirty-Two

MAVERICK

I left the day after my final confrontation with Bethany, but I only made it as far as Jackson City.

Grandpa's house would be finished soon enough. The staging team would move in furniture for the photos within the next forty-eight hours. I'd dropped the bookshelf off at Jada's and told Lizbeth about it when I stopped by the shop.

If I hadn't been so upset about Bethany, I would have felt proud of the house. Satisfied. But I couldn't feel much except agony.

If I stayed in Pineville, I'd see Bethany. If I saw her, I'd feel it all again. The pressure. The responsibility. The sense of impending doom that choked me. Her death would be on my hands if it ended the way others had . . . so, like a coward, I bailed.

Although I tried to push farther south, or west, or *anywhere* but here, dammit, I couldn't. When I steered toward South Dakota, my car wouldn't function. Or maybe my courage. Or maybe I just couldn't keep my foot on the gas long enough to make it onto the entrance ramp.

Bethany had given me the worst parting gift of all. Pain. The hurt in her eyes haunted me. Restless nights, fitful dreams, and a cumulative lack of sleep made me feel like a zombie. I shouldn't have cared this much. She knew this was part of the deal.

But I did care. A lot.

Work would save me. It always had. I forced myself to canvass Jackson City, studying shops from the outside, the way I had for Bethany's. Public records. Local gossip with other store owners.

Over two days at a nice hotel, I narrowed down three options that were clearly on their last legs, or would be soon. A touristy T-shirt shop that probably had seasonal issues. A restaurant with a limited menu and food that tasted like plastic. A knickknacks shop that appeared to be morphing into a glorified antiques store, but didn't really know what it wanted to be.

But the same thrill of an impending challenge didn't come the way it did with the Frolicking Moose. Because that challenge, I realized, had been more about Bethany.

Baxter called daily. Mom called hourly for a while.

Finally, Mallory called.

That one I picked up.

"Hey, Mal."

"What the hell is wrong with you?"

I winced. Despite the strength of her tone, I heard love in her words. All evidence to the contrary, I had deeply missed her and Baxter. Our board meetings. Late-night dinners of high-end sushi while we hashed out problems with the sales force.

I leaned back, resting my head against the seat, and watched a nightly parade that moved around the town square. Tourists clapped, enjoying the cheeky actors and cheap flares.

"Good to hear your voice too," I said dryly. "To what do I owe this pleasure?"

"Why are you ignoring the family?"

"I . . . needed some space."

"Bullcrap. You're running away again."

"I haven't decided on the promotion yet. I still have time left on my leave of absence. But I'm definitely leaning toward taking it."

She paused. "You did decide, Mav. When you took that leave of absence, you already knew. We all did. You're not coming back to work at Epsilon. Why do you think I was so pissed? My therapist said denial, but whatever. Go with that if it makes you happy."

"Maybe."

"Doesn't matter, anyway. The job is gone."

I sat up straighter. "What?"

"I gave it to José."

"José?" I cried.

"He'll kill it, and you know it. You bloody trained the man."

I closed my eyes. An unexpected rush of relief pulsed through me. José *would* kill it. He was made for the CRO position. He had a drive that I didn't. A love for corporate culture and all its weirdness at times. Despite my own ego, Mallory had made the right move. That meant I didn't have to go back. There was no proving myself there anymore.

With the elation came a heaping side of guilt.

"I'm sorry, Mal. I shouldn't have left you hanging."

"Mav, you needed an out. I get it, all right? This world isn't for everyone, and you've been looking strangled for a while, anyway. Ever since your dad's suicide, you've—"

"Stop. Stop saying it."

"No."

My hand gripped the steering wheel with white knuckles.

"He died, Maverick. He took his own life because he was in more pain than any of us could ever comprehend. Avoiding the issue is not going to change it."

I forced my jaw to relax before my teeth cracked. Trust Mallory to say it outright when the rest of us skirted the issue like old professionals.

Which, admittedly, could have been part of the problem.

"You know what else?" she said. "It had nothing to do with you, either."

"It did."

The words came out of me so fast they startled us both.

She let out a long breath. "Why do you think that?"

"Because I did everything he didn't want me to do." I pushed my palm into the steering wheel, grateful for some kind of hard feedback. "I focused on my grades instead of playing football. I didn't take Kelly Jones to the high school prom, even though Dad thought she was perfect. I joined the ROTC and became an officer instead of going to medical school. Then I blew up my leg in an IED and effectively crippled myself. Just like him. I was everything he never wanted me to be. The biggest disappointment."

My hands shook. I'd never said these things out loud. Bethany had pushed them to the forefront of my mind too much for me to hold them back now. Even though it sounded insane, I couldn't help the child-like fear that churned deep in my gut.

Dad's suicide was on my conscience.

"Dammit, Maverick. Is that what you've always thought? Is that why you're always running away when things get good or big? It's like you're afraid to be happy."

"No. It's what I've always *known*. Dad had expectations of me. I disappointed them at every turn."

Mallory hesitated, and in that long pause, I gripped the phone so hard my fingers ached. But I couldn't let it go, because it felt like *all* I had left.

"There was a letter," she finally said.

My brow furrowed. "What?"

"Your dad left a letter."

"No, he didn't."

"He did."

Stunned, I sat there for a full fifteen seconds. "Mom . . . Mom never told me that. She said . . ."

Well, she'd never really said anything about it.

"She never told any of you boys. I only found out by accident. She was signing something for me, and I saw it and—that doesn't matter. You know how she is. Regardless, she didn't want you to know because of what it said. So, I'm going to risk my own life and potentially make her angry with me and tell you that the note said he thought he had failed *you*. He felt like a failure as a parent, unable to run with you. To tackle you while you practiced football in the backyard. To . . . help you learn to walk again when you lost your leg. The very same thing you're feeling now is what your dad felt when he took his own life."

A long silence passed. It felt as if all the blood had drained from my head. I couldn't speak. Didn't know what to say.

"Mav, is it true? Did he fail you just because he didn't have use of his legs?"

Dizzy, I closed my eyes. "No," I whispered. "Not at all."

"The note said that he was so proud of you, his five sons. That you'd kept him going. He lived as long as he did because of how much he loved you. But he was in physical and emotional pain, and he said he couldn't fight it anymore. To him, it was the most compassionate route for everyone. Even though it wasn't. Mourning him opened up new wounds. Not sure if you've noticed this, but your family isn't great about talking over the hard things."

Snatches of my childhood came back to me. The night I told him I didn't sign up for football my senior year, I found him in the garage, sitting in his wheelchair, nailing a punching bag over and over, grunting with every *thwack* until he tired himself out. He'd stared at it, panting, his face etched with pain. I'd thought it was because of what I'd told him. Thought I had failed him again. That I wasn't who he wanted me to be.

But now I saw it differently. Maybe his rage hadn't been about me.

Maybe he thought I'd said no to football because of *him*.

"I'd like to point out," she said, breaking into my thoughts, "that I've met Kelly Jones. She brought cookies over after your dad's funeral. She's the spitting image of your mother at a younger age. Ever thought of that?"

A cold feeling trickled through my blood. He'd wanted me to take Kelly to prom because he couldn't dance with Mom anymore. Some subconscious dream of his own had pushed him to it. He hadn't seen it. None of us had seen it.

His frustration had nothing to do with me.

"You are no failure, Maverick. You are the greatest success of his life."

I clenched my teeth, feeling a wave of emotion I'd never given into before. Not since his funeral. It crashed through me. For a second, I couldn't breathe. Like a rip current, it threatened to whisk me away. I wanted to hit something. I wanted to fall in Dad's arms and let it all out. Tell him that I'm pissed, I'm sad, and I miss him like the hounds of hell.

I wanted to hold Bethany.

Finally, I managed to swallow and say, "I see."

"So, what does this mean?" she asked. "What's next for you if not working for us at Epsilon?"

The change of subject was a lifeline, and I grasped for it. "I'm starting my own company. Correction . . . have started."

"Competing?"

I snorted. "Of course not. I'll travel around, find failing brick-and-mortar stores, and resurrect them. Bring money back to the little people. Create success."

"Blah, blah, blah."

"Hey, don't be a hater."

"I'm not being hard on your idea. Sounds great, to be honest. But you sound as excited as a rock."

My mind flittered back to Bethany. If she wasn't part of my day, if I didn't have her to look forward to, then that adequately described my excitement about the job.

"Yeah. That pretty much covers it."

"You're playing small, Mav."

"I'm trying to figure it out."

"You're running. You and your proud minimalism and phobia of commitment. You're running like a scared toddler, that's what. And I know what that looks like, because Jameson has been crashing at our place with sweet little Sarah, and that thing is full of fire."

A sudden grin found its way onto my face. My spitfire niece, Sarah, had just earned her spot of honor on my left arm right before I came. She was fourteen months old, and *full of fire* was a perfect description. My brother Jameson had earned every second of it after his wild teenage years.

"I'm not running," I mumbled.

"That alone means you are, and that also means it's probably a woman. And one who actually stands a chance at meaning something to you. Are you already in love with her?"

I rolled my eyes. How was she always right? No wonder Bethany was annoyed with me so much. It *was* annoying.

"That's . . . oddly correct," I muttered.

"Don't act like this is my first rodeo. I can hear it in your voice. That bad, huh?"

"I messed it up pretty good this time."

"Get her back. Then bring her home so I can meet her already. Your mom will be . . . so happy. She worries about you."

"You'd tolerate her."

"Sure. Let her prove herself to me first, all right? In the meantime, get it together. Figure out what you *really* want. And remember, you're no failure, Mav. I would never have tolerated you otherwise."

"Thanks," I said wryly.

"Talk soon."

She clicked off without another word. I sat in my car until full darkness descended, stewing over a lifetime of incorrect thinking.

Somehow, this had gone oddly off course. For the first time, I realized that leaving Bethany had been the right thing to do. I hadn't been ready for her.

I had some demons of my own to chase. And they started back in California.

Time to confront my mom and see that letter.

# Chapter Thirty-Three

BETHANY

The cemetery lay in a patch of sunshine.

I crouched next to Dad's headstone, only a few paces away from Pappa's. Mama had been cremated, her ashes scattered to the river, the way she'd always wanted. A small stone tribute to her sat on Jim's property. Their neighbor had made it, his face tear-streaked when he brought it to her viewing.

Ironically enough, likely that was the neighbor who was Ellie's biological father.

For Dad, I'd chosen a massive headstone with a river carved into it, hints of fish in the peaked waves. The edges pressed into my fingertip as I traced each letter.

A dry, hot breeze brushed over my neck. I situated myself next to him, staring at the curves of his name. *Daniel David Beecham.* Talking to his headstone had never been a problem for me. I often came, spinning out yarns, laughing over memories, letting my cracked heart loose. Sometimes, on the slow days, it was the only real conversation I had.

Today, the words nearly stuck in my throat.

"I think I made a huge mistake, Dad. Huge. Boomer mistake, as you'd put it."

My jaw tightened as I thought about Maverick. Dad would have loved him. If Dad had ever met Maverick, he would have taken him from me. Between them, I never would have gotten a word in edgewise. The thought made me smile, but it quickly faded.

"I willingly fell for a guy who couldn't stay. I knew that. I knew he couldn't stay, but I let myself fall for him anyway. Maybe I was just that lonely. I rarely get hugs anymore, which is kind of my fault. I could find them. Millie would. Jada would. Stephanie would give me a hug, if I let her know I needed one. Kin would, even if that would get weird. But maybe it was desperation."

I gazed out over the low, aging gravestones to the forest beyond. A wrought iron fence circled this quiet place, just outside Pineville limits, inside the fold of the mountains. No one else was here but me. In the weeks since Maverick left, I'd questioned myself relentlessly.

Why?

Why had I let myself fall into him?

Why did I keep asking for heartbreak?

Had I been fair to Maverick?

There had definitely been some desperation. *Touch has always been your love language,* Lizbeth had said when she'd stayed up late to hash this out with me. The way a sister would. *I'll give you more hugs from now on. You need them.*

In the end, I could see that Maverick had done me a favor. I hadn't been ready for him. I'd been desperate for him. Eventually, it would have broken us up.

"I've asked myself if it was just desperation that led me so quickly into Maverick's arms. If it had been any other man, would I have done the same thing? But . . . I don't think so. I think I know why I did it." A tear trickled down my face. "Because he reminded me of you. He was on my team. He sparked life back into me when I'd felt dead for so many months.

He made me feel safe, and seen, and alive. I haven't had any of those things since you died."

I sniffled, turning to rest my head on my bent knees. "And now he's gone, and I'm sad. I only knew him for a few weeks but . . . it was still so real, Dad. So real for me. How many times can a heart break?"

The breeze rustled overhead again. I stopped breathing to listen. No words came. No representation of Dad appeared. Half of me had hoped for it. The other half thought I'd finally lost my sanity. The mounting pressure had broken my brain.

I blinked, then touched his name again.

"I'll be fine," I whispered. "Eventually. I always am. But that's not the only reason I came here today. I, uh . . . have a confession. No, I'm not pregnant." My lips twitched. "So, don't ask. I . . . changed the Frolicking Moose. It's been changing a lot, in fact. The fish are gone. Like, we buried them." The admission came out like a gasp. "Please don't haunt me."

Another stir of wind, gentle on my cheek. I laughed and wiped two tears away.

"The scones are gone, too, and Lizbeth painted the walls. I was fine with that. The place really did smell like fish, you know. I gave all your lures to Ellie. Because, honestly, Dad. Fish and coffee? That just *sounds* disgusting. She'll live up to your lures. She'll keep you going that way, won't she?

"Oh, and I maybe—but definitely did—sell the motorcycle. I'm also going to rent the attic of the Frolicking Moose out. Not sure if anyone will take it . . . but I'll try. Jada is letting us live in her basement until I can save up to get my real estate license. I've decided to push all our profits toward that once I get new school wardrobes for the girls. Kinoshi and I have filed for custody of the girls. He's taken us on as a pro bono case, if you can believe that."

A fluttering feeling moved through me. Quick. Light. How had I been so blind all this time? I thought I had been alone after

Dad died, but my team had always been around me. Millie. Jada. Kinoshi. Even Stephanie, at the restaurant. Hadn't she constantly brought me free meals? Jada gave me twenty bucks for a single coffee all the time. Millie brightened my day, sometimes stopping in to talk for an hour. Now Lizbeth and Ellie. I wasn't alone then . . . neither would I be now.

I had a team. And they had me.

"So . . . just waiting on word after the filing," I whispered, my throat thick with emotion. "Not sure what Jim will say, if anything. No sign of him yet, which is encouraging. I think we have a chance. I know it's what you would have done, too."

The usual stir of pain didn't pierce my chest. Just a hollow emptiness lived there now. Maybe that was better than the pain. Maybe it was nothing. But I had a feeling it was progress.

"By doing all of this, though, I feel like I've disappointed you. Like I've failed you by letting you go. By changing your dream into my own thing. By erasing you from my life by selling or removing all your things."

Another deranged giggle burst out of me. *This is the horrible feeling that Maverick must be avoiding. Disappointing someone you love so deeply.*

The emotion released something inside me. A dam broke in my chest. From it, a mixture of wrenching sobs and giddy laughter flowed out. I wasn't sure if I was terrified, or relieved, or finally totally crazy with grief.

But I sank into it.

"Please," I begged Dad when I calmed down. Tears flowed down my face unimpeded now. "Please just . . . don't be really gone if the coffee shop is different, okay? I know it doesn't make sense. It sounds insane. You're probably thinking, *You've lost your mind, Bee. Of course I'll still be around even if the shop doesn't smell like dead fish and old man.* But I just . . . I want to know that you're not really gone. There's still you somewhere, even if it's not the Frolicking Moose. Then I can move on. Then I can be the sister that Ellie and Lizbeth need me to be."

Another shift of wind ruffled my hair. I closed my eyes, letting it cool the tearstains on my cheek. The silence that followed sank all the way into my bones. I absorbed it, grateful for the peace. The quiet. The sudden fatigue that accompanied a crazed but necessary outpouring of emotion. I welcomed it. I felt lighter than I had in the ten months since Dad's death. Lighter, and stronger.

My eyes fluttered open when I felt a soft caress on my arm.

A bee lay there, wings gently fluttering. My breath caught as it traveled slowly up my arm, half-flying to my shirt, where it landed right over my heart. A sob broke from my throat. The bee remained, perfectly still, as my heart beat beneath it.

"Got it, Dad," I whispered, laughing. "Message received. I love you, too."

# Chapter Thirty-Four

## BETHANY

Early August sunshine cut through the windows, leaving the shop sticky with heat. My air conditioning struggled to keep up, which meant last month's two-hundred-dollar profit might end up going to AC repairs.

No, I'd figure something out. Swap coffee for their work, or something.

"What do you think, Lizbeth?" I asked, my head tilted to the side. "Should we do the Cut and Coffee event from six to seven or seven to eight on Thursday nights? Or six to eight? No, Thursdays won't work. That's bingo night at the community center. I think we'll have to do Wednesdays."

An almost-finished advertisement filled my computer screen. Millie and I had decided to host a cut-a-thon where people could buy coffee, get a discount on their haircut, and donate half the proceeds to the local food bank. Getting foot traffic into the coffee shop to show everyone the new baked goods was my idea. Buying mini cupcakes and giving out free samples was Lizbeth's. It was the perfect opportunity to show off the Frolicking Moose's new look.

Lizbeth lazily turned a page in her book, curled up like a cat on Dad's recliner. One leg bopped up and down. The plum-colored walls lent a newfound coziness to the shop. With one set of lights turned off, replaced by the warm glow of the lamp, the entire place felt calm.

She had weeded down the mugs to the best ones from Dad's collection—I willingly gave the rest to Goodwill—and used the rest of the space for donated books.

New games populated the coffee table, which Lizbeth had distressed. *Because, come on, Bethany. Crappy-looking furniture is the new thing.*

The sprawling, braided rug we'd found at a thrift store lay in a circle beneath her chair, which she'd scrubbed to a fresh shine with upholstery cleaner. It was shaggy in a totally chic way. Only the new designs on the chalkboard equaled it in terms of color, which Lizbeth had happily taken charge of. Her chalkboard palette grew in color every day.

The Frolicking Moose was officially rustic-mountain cozy. Dad would have loved it. I knew I did.

Main Street lay quiet. No customers had been in the store for an hour, which was a new record. Our marketing efforts had doubled revenue over the last four weeks since Maverick left. The new decor certainly had something to do with that.

The temptation to send Maverick pictures of the changes had been almost overwhelming, but I had refrained. He hadn't reached out to me, nor I to him. We'd both chosen our paths.

While I still ached for him, even after such a whirlwind affair, I couldn't be the one who went back. Honoring his need for space required nearly all my strength. The pine-scented candle that Ellie had chosen felt like a knife in my chest, even now. But I let it burn, because there was comfort in the loneliness for him.

He'd done his best in difficult circumstances, and I could see that now. These days, I tried to satisfy my need for touch through hugs with every willing customer or friend. A substantial number of people were willing to donate their hugs.

It helped, but it wasn't the same.

In the end, Maverick might have done the right thing. We hardly knew each other. He was used to a city life and a corporate world. For the next eight years, I was tied to this town, this shop, this path. Braiding our worlds would have been difficult, at best. He'd always live in my memory as a bright spot. An illumination. Downright magic.

Like lipstick that never faded.

Still, that didn't stop me from thinking about him. Where was he now? Some random town in South Dakota? Minnesota? I scoffed. No. Probably something less remote this time. He'd probably had his fill of small-town life for now. He was probably back in California with his family.

Did he want to go back to the city?

Any new tattoos? He'd have to have a new niece or nephew for that, which only highlighted how little we knew each other at all.

This had been for the best.

My attempts to make myself believe that only drove me deeper into a hole. Resignation didn't feel much better. No matter what I told myself, I *missed* him. The way he smiled. The look in his eyes when I chewed on my bottom lip—like he wanted to bite it too. I knew what my yoga pants did to him. It's why I wore them so often. He'd been more than my latest flame; he'd been my friend. I missed discussing the state of the store every morning. Asking questions about cash flow.

Knowing he'd have my back at the next bank meeting.

He'd been part of my team, and I missed that.

"Six to eight," I declared, forcing my mind back to work. "We'll do the Cut and Coffee from six to eight. We'll test it out and reevaluate later."

"Uh . . . Bethany?"

A tremor in Lizbeth's voice caught my attention. I glanced up. She backed away from the windows, her face as white as a sheet. Beyond her was a familiar, beat-up truck. My heart dropped into my stomach. The driver's door swung open with a groan, and a red-haired man staggered out.

"Jim," I whispered.

He wasn't sober, and he wasn't looking kind. I darted around the counter and bolted for the door, sliding the lock home. Seconds later, Jim slammed into the door with his shoulder. A low-throated bellow issued from him. His face pressed against the glass like a horror movie. Bloodshot eyes peered at me, gone with drink. A scruffy beard made his face look like orange sandpaper.

"Go upstairs," I said to Lizbeth, taking a few steps back. "Take my phone with you, and call 911. Tell them we need Sheriff Bailey here right now. Where's Ellie?"

Lizbeth stood frozen, her gaze locked on Jim. His vague shouts had ceased as they stared at each other. Sorrow appeared on his heavy brow. His breath fogged up the glass window.

She whimpered.

"Lizbeth!"

Startled, she came back to herself, looked at me, and whispered, "What?"

"My phone." I grabbed her arm. "Take it upstairs, and call 911. Tell them to send Sheriff Bailey right now. Where's Ellie?"

"I-I-I don't know. I think she's with Devin."

"Lizbeth!" Jim yelled. He slammed a palm against the door. "Let me in. Lizbeth is *my* daughter. You can't have her."

"Don't listen to him." I shoved her toward the hallway. "Go upstairs. Call 911."

"Maybe I can talk him out of it."

"No. You will *not* speak with him."

Lizbeth looked at me, then at Jim, and quietly disappeared,

eyes sparkling. When I turned back to the door, his nostrils flared.

"Give her back!"

"Get out of here, Jim. We're calling the sheriff, and he'll be here any minute now. Don't do anything you'll regret."

Jim stumbled back, screaming Lizbeth's name before he nearly fell off the porch. My heart hammered when Lizbeth appeared at the end of the hallway. Tears tracked down her face. "The sheriff is on his way, but he's up a canyon. It'll be a few minutes."

Great.

I licked my lips. "Thanks, Lizbeth. Go back upstairs. See if you can find Ellie."

"But—"

"I'll be fine. He's not going to come in here unless he breaks the glass down, and that would probably kill him. Go to the back door and see if Ellie is out there."

She stopped, torn.

"Do you trust me?" I asked.

Her lips parted. "Yes."

"Then go."

I turned to face Jim again, my knees shaking. No one walked by outside, which was good. This would be between me and him. All I had to do was buy time until the sheriff arrived. This would all be fodder against Jim in our custody case, which was already going better than expected, thanks to Jada's reports and a few neighbors contributing their testimonies. But this would seal it.

"Let's talk this out, Jim," I said through the window, but remained back. "I'm willing to listen to what you have to say, but you have to promise to stay calm."

He blinked rapidly, as if he couldn't focus. He leaned his forehead on the glass door to stare straight into my eyes. Darkness clouded his features. It was like staring into the soul of the devil.

"She's mine," he said. "Your whore of a mother cheated on me! Ellie can burn in hell, just like your mama will, but I get Lizbeth."

His gravelly tone set my teeth on edge. I pulled in a breath. "Mama was wrong. About a lot of things. Including cheating on you."

"Damn right!"

"I'm sorry that happened, Jim."

His eyebrows knitted together. "I loved her. I loved Kat." Like granite, his features hardened again. He slammed his hand into the door with a *crack* of his palm on glass. "Then she went and cheated on me for years! Right under my own nose. Right . . . right there."

"Fine, Jim. I'll keep Ellie. Will you give her to me?"

"Damn right you will."

"If I have Ellie, and you hate our mama, then why do you want Lizbeth?"

"Because she's mine! Mine. Mine. Mine."

"Lizbeth is going to graduate high school soon. You know she could have graduated next year if Mama hadn't died. She won't be around for long."

He paused, for a second appearing entirely sober. He tapped a yellowed fingernail on the door near my face, studying me closely. I almost thought I'd gotten through to him. That I saw a facet of something real in his dark, troubled gaze.

"Because I don't want to be alone, Bethie baby. And if your mama ain't here, then Lizbeth will have to do."

Revulsion crawled through me like a nest of spiders. I stepped back, ready to vomit.

"No!"

The shout came from just behind me. Ellie and Devin skidded into the shop from the hallway. Ellie growled, wide eyes tapering the moment she saw him. Jim's expression darkened immediately, clearing any flash of lucidity.

"The whore-child!" he screamed. His fist banged the door again. "There she is for everyone to see! Your mama was a cheater, and you won't be any better than her."

Ellie's hands tightened into fists at her side.

"Ellie," Devin said, putting a hand on her shoulder. "Let's get out of here."

"You hated me!" she cried. "I didn't do anything wrong, but you hated me."

"Paying for the sins of your mama." Jim stumbled to the side, leaning against the door to regain his balance. "You always will."

Ellie's nostrils flared. "I know you're not my father."

"Damn right I'm not!"

"You tried to kill me. To hurt me. To blame me for Mama's death, but it was your fault. You killed her! You chased her from the house. You told her you'd make sure she paid for her mistake. I heard you. Then she died, and it's your fault."

Jim paled. "I didn't kill her."

Ellie hissed through her teeth. "Murderer."

He slammed a fist into the glass, nearly cracking it. "Bastard child!"

"Hit me again," she called, "and I'll kill you. You'll never walk free again."

Jim reached into his baggy pants and yanked something out with a bellow. A gun appeared in his trembling right hand, pointed straight at Ellie's heart. "Not if you're dead."

"Jim," I cried. "No!"

Devin yanked Ellie back, throwing her behind him. I shoved them both into the hallway just as the percussive sound of a gunshot at close range blasted through my ears. An explosion of shattering glass accompanied it. I looked up to find Ellie and Devin on the ground in the hallway, eyes wide.

"Run!" I yelled.

Ellie and Devin tripped over each other until Devin shoved off the ground, grabbed Ellie's shirt, and hauled her to her feet. They disappeared out the back door and slammed it shut. I scrambled up as Jim advanced into the shop through the broken glass, gun trained on me.

"Don't move!" he screamed.

I froze. My heart pounded in my throat. Slowly, I held up both hands.

"All right," I whispered. "I won't move."

At my acquiescence, he stopped. He stood there, panting. His thin chest heaved up and down. A strangled sound escaped the back of his throat. A cry. Like a little sob. The gun wove back and forth in an erratic dance as he struggled to stay upright.

Finally, he leaned against a table.

"All right," I said soothingly. My voice and hands shook, but everything else seemed oddly clear. My thoughts were calm. My mind focused. My vision crisp and bright. "Calm down. We'll work this out, Jim."

"She lied," he whispered. Anguish filled his voice. "Kat lied to me. She used me. She gave me a daughter, and then someone else a daughter. Then she left. I loved her. I really loved her. She was the . . . only thing I ever cared about."

I stared at him, disarmed. A sniveling sound came from his throat as he lowered the gun.

His head bowed. "She's right. I'm the reason Kat is dead. She left . . . because of me. I . . . my fault."

"Jim . . . Mama wasn't perfect. You didn't deserve what she did to you."

"No."

"She got in that car. She chose to drive away."

A low, keening sound filled the air. A flash of black appeared just behind him, followed by a war cry. A thin cord wrapped around his neck, yanking him to the ground. The gun went off again. The floor splintered. Chunks of wood flew into the air.

Jim screamed, and blood sprayed from the top of his right shoe.

Ellie shouted as Jim fell back on her, struggling to pull her arm away from his neck. A string she'd kept in her emergency weapons stash tightened around his throat. Devin appeared through the front door, a thicker rope in his hands. I shot to my feet, kicking the gun away from Jim as Ellie pulled harder on his throat, feral determination in her gaze. He clawed at her hands with his freakish nails, drawing blood. But his alcohol-laced attempts were too weak to dislodge her.

Seconds later, Devin tried to hog-tie Jim's hands. Police sirens sounded outside as Jim's eyes rolled back in his head. His body slackened. Devin stared at him, hands shaking. Blood still poured out of Jim's right shoe, pooling on the floor.

I crouched next to Ellie. She held on to him still. Her entire body was rigid, as if she couldn't release him. Her teeth dug so far into her bottom lip that I could see her bleeding.

I put a hand on her shoulder. "Let him go, Ellie."

Her frightened eyes, filled with grief and terror, found mine. "I can't," she whispered. "I'm too scared."

"You can. It's going to be okay now. He's going to be in prison for a long time. He'll never see you again."

"Am I going to prison?"

"No."

"Have I killed him?"

"Not yet."

"Will Devin be in trouble?"

"No."

I squeezed her shoulder. She panted, looking to me for consolation.

"It's okay. I'm Team Ellie. I've got you. I'll take responsibility if I have too, but it won't come to that. All right?"

Chest heaving, she let out a long, shaky breath, then released him all at once. She slid away with a cry, as far away as she could scramble. Shards of glass lay beneath her, but she didn't notice them. When her back collided with the wall, she looked at Devin. He crossed the room, crouched next to her, and put his arms around her shoulders. Then he sank to the floor at her side, both of them trembling.

Sheriff Bailey appeared in the doorway, gun drawn. "Bethany?"

A lightheaded feeling rushed over me. Everything seemed to move slowly now, every sound amplified. The smell of gunpowder sharp in the air. Lizbeth shuffled up behind me with a low, muted sob.

"Bethie?"

"I'm fine," I managed to say to Sheriff Bailey. "He . . . he shot himself in the foot the second time. None of us are hurt."

Sheriff Bailey surveyed the scene, then strode over, glass crunching beneath his boots. After picking the gun up off the floor, he placed a hand on my shoulder. Like a shock wave, my stunned paralysis faded. I sucked in a sharp breath.

The girls. I had to get it together

"You're going to be okay," he said, voice low and firm. "We have an ambulance and help on the way. You're safe now."

His words echoed in my mind.

*You're safe now.*

I whispered, "Thank you," then reached back and grabbed Lizbeth by the arm. I pulled her into me, and then I held out a hand for Ellie. With a cry, she jumped to her feet and buried herself in my arms with her sister.

The two of them clung to me and cried while I held them close.

* * *

The next hour and a half passed in an odd blur.

Sheriff Bailey spoke on the radio. Ellie trembled against me, her teeth rattling like old bones. Lizbeth gazed on as they carried a half-conscious Jim to the ambulance. The sound of crunching glass rang in my ears. Deputies swarmed the shop. Flashing lights. The quiet chatter of people in a subdued environment. It moved around me like a storm. I stood at the center, something inside me ready to break.

*My team is coming,* I thought. *My team is coming.*

They came.

I don't know how much time passed, but Millie appeared first. Devin ran to her, his face ashen. Ellie followed him with a sob, throwing herself into Millie's arms. Millie spoke quietly with me as I explained, clinging to her son and Ellie. She admonished them both, hugged them, and then cried.

After they both gave their explanation to the deputies, Millie took them home.

Jada showed up next, eyes wide. While Lizbeth spoke with Sheriff Bailey, Jada hugged me so tight it hurt. When Lizbeth finished, Jada retreated to take her home with the promise to take good care of her and stuff her full of comfort food.

"Got plenty for you, Beth-baby," Jada murmured quietly into my hair. "Come home when you can."

That left me in the middle of the coffee shop with Sheriff Bailey.

Once the girls left, my composure faded. A low tremor started in my legs. With every passing moment, it crept higher. My knees knocked as Sheriff Bailey asked, "Do you have somewhere you can go?"

Tears clouded my eyes. No Dad. No Pappa. No comfort on this horrifying day. Where would I go now? I didn't want to be around the girls. Didn't want them to see me totally shatter and collapse like a dying star. They needed to recover without guilt.

I needed space to think. To breathe. To not think about

them, and focus only on me. They were safe. A hotel. I could find a hotel room. Or just drive somewhere. No. I couldn't drive. Not like this.

Maybe I could go upstairs and lock the door.

I opened my mouth to respond, but a voice from outside stopped me.

"Bethany?"

Maverick slipped past the deputies sweeping up the scattered glass and paused in the doorway. His fear-filled gaze slammed into mine. The burning terror in my chest broke. I reached for him.

He grabbed me a second before I collapsed.

"Lizbeth called me." His arms tightened, and his broad shoulders swallowed me. He alone held me up. "I hauled down the canyon from Jackson City, but there was a slow car and . . . she said Jim was drunk and had a gun. She . . ."

He surveyed the coffee shop over the top of my head.

I molded into him. My body shook until my teeth chattered. I felt cold all over, strangely distant, able to think only one thought.

*He came back.*

Vaguely, I heard the deep rumble of Maverick speaking to Sheriff Bailey. Felt him pick me up and take me to his truck. He set me on the seat next to him and drove with his arm around me. Trees flashed by. I kept my eyes closed and held on to him.

# Chapter Thirty-Five

## MAVERICK

Bethany's teeth clattered as I carried her up the stairs and onto the deck. Her hands felt like ice through my shirt. I lowered us onto a deck chair in the sun. A tear slipped down her cheek as she looked at me with soulful, terrified eyes.

"Jim," she whispered. "H-he—"

"I know."

"I thought we would die. I thought . . ."

A lock of hair fell into her eyes. I tucked it away. "You saved them, Bethany. You did so good."

"B-but I could have. He could have. It . . ."

I trapped her hands in mine, pressing a kiss to them. "It didn't. Everyone is safe. He won't ever hurt you again."

Tears filled her eyes. She reached out, brushing my cheek with a feather-light touch. "You came back."

"Nothing could have stopped me. I'm Team Bethany all the way."

With a cry, she closed the distance between us. Her lips claimed mine. She kissed me with all the frantic passion of someone who'd faced death and come out the victor. I wrapped my arms around her and pulled her close, not satisfied until every part of her pressed against me.

"I'm sorry, Bethany," I whispered. She pulled away, hazy with fear and passion. "I was such a fool."

"No." She trailed a hand down my face. "You were right. I still had things to work out. Things to . . . face."

Overwhelmed, I grabbed her chin, pressed a kiss to her forehead, and tucked her into my arms. With a sigh, she rested her head against my neck. Her trembling slowed.

"My dad committed suicide four years ago," I said.

She paused but didn't look at me. Grateful, because that made it easier, I pressed on. The words tumbled out. I couldn't have stopped them if I wanted to, and I didn't.

"It was just after Mallory and Baxter announced a devastating loss their company, Epsilon, suffered as a result of a failing sales force. They weren't sure the company would recover. I'd been working as a sales manager with another company, so they recruited me. I took over their sales team. Within a year, they'd grossed their first million."

Her shoulders relaxed. She laid a hand on my chest. Her eyelashes fluttered as I explained what I was doing in Jackson City. The call with Mallory. Sensing that my voice calmed her, I kept going. Told her about my family. My four brothers. How much I'd adored my father. How I'd gone home to hear it all out—all the gory details—with my mom. We'd called a family council and hashed it out. Finally, my family had spoken about the everything.

Ugly, healing tears were shed.

"My dad always talked about me going to medical school. Working with people like him who'd lost movement in their legs. Doing research with stem cells to figure out a cure. But I didn't. He had a lot of ideas for me that I didn't pursue, and I thought I'd disappointed him. My dad was my hero, working legs or not. I assumed I'd failed him. But I was wrong."

I blew out a long breath. She reached around me, tightening her hold.

"I wasn't a failure to my father, and I'm not responsible for his death. As crazy as it sounds, I thought his suicide was about me. But it wasn't. It had nothing to do with me at all. I thought his disappointment in my choices was what pushed him over the edge."

Bethany tensed for a moment, then turned. Her bright, aquamarine eyes blinked at me, and she rested her chin on my chest.

"You were afraid something terrible would happen to me, just like your father."

"As insane as it sounds, yes."

"It doesn't sound insane. Grief makes you think crazy things, Mav."

"I'm sorry, Bethany."

She leaned forward, pressing a gentle kiss to my lips. "There's nothing to apologize for. We both had things to sort out."

I held on to the small of her back. Afraid I'd lose her. Afraid this would just disappear. "And what did you sort out?"

Her expression eased into a half-smile. "The Frolicking Moose is rustic cozy, I sell the best-rated pastries in Jackson City, and I learned that my dad isn't in a coffee shop." She touched her heart. "He's in here. In me. Always."

How could any work have been more important than this woman?

"Above all that," she murmured, her gaze on my lips, "I realized you're the member of my team I want the most. I don't need you, Mav. I want you. That's infinitely more powerful, I think."

I smiled, brushing a lock of hair out of her eyes with my fingertips. "I want to be on your team."

"Even if there are two other people on it?"

"Even if."

"You are my team," she whispered. Sparkling tears filled her eyes. "Because you came back."

I pressed my forehead to hers. "Do you know that I love you? That it terrifies me in the most frightening, wonderful way possible? That I love you more than anything I've ever loved in my life?" A wry expression crossed my face. "Full right leg included."

Her lips pressed together as if suppressing a smile. "Not as much as I love you, Mav."

The pad of my thumb rubbed her bottom lip.

A tear spilled down her cheek. "Hold me?" she whispered.

I tightened my grip until there was no space.

"Forever."

She fell into hot, cleansing sobs on my chest until long after the sun faded. When she fell asleep, curled on top of me like a kitten, I carried her into the bedroom. I set her gently down, grabbed a blanket, and lay next to her. She burrowed into my neck with a sigh.

Finally relaxed, I fell asleep with her tucked safely in my arms. The way I planned to do for the rest of our lives, in this very house.

That was an expectation I'd never let go of.

# Chapter Thirty-Six

BETHANY

**Four months later.
Christmas Eve.**

The *pop* of a cork exploded in the coffee shop.

Lizbeth held out a cup, hopeful eyebrows raised. "Is that champagne?" she asked. "Does Bethany officially adopting us mean you'll finally let me try it?"

Maverick laughed but showed her the label on the bottle of sparkling cider.

"Nice try, Liz."

He poured the cider into five flute glasses, then passed them out. I winked at him, grateful to have him back. He'd just returned from buying a house in Jackson City that we'd start flipping in early January, after our first holiday together. Lizbeth already had Pinterest boards for the interior. Ellie couldn't wait to build a chicken coop in the back before it sold.

He'd consulted with two other companies in Jackson City over the past four months. Their business revenue was on track to double within the next five months. He liked it well enough to continue, but his real heart-and-soul was in home restoration.

Ellie sniffed the cider, then recoiled and shoved it back. I chuckled as I accepted mine. My aversion to sweet food must be somewhat genetic. For this kind of celebration, I'd make a happy exception.

"To new beginnings," I said, lifting my glass. Hung on the wall in a position of honor was the official declaration Kinoshi had brought over this afternoon.

I was a mama-sister.

Lizbeth grinned. "To new parents. May you pay me more in allowance than the former ones did."

Ellie just lifted her eyebrows, as if she merely tolerated our celebration. Devin leaned over to whisper something in her ear. She grinned a megawatt smile, giggling under her breath. Maverick put his hand on the small of my back, pulling me against him.

I silently toasted Jim's sentencing, which we celebrated in addition to the finalization of the girls becoming my legal dependents. *May he rot in prison for decades,* I thought to myself. Maverick and I would toast to that later, when the girls weren't around.

"To—"

A motorcycle revved its engine in the parking lot. I rolled my eyes. What idiot drove a motorcycle in the middle of winter, anyway?

"Do they not see the *closed* sign?" I muttered, glancing out the new windows.

Then my blood turned cold.

A twentysomething guy with dark hair pulled to a stop just outside. Maverick's younger brother, Benjamin. I'd met him twice now. He threw his legs off a very familiar motorcycle. I straightened.

"Is he . . ."

Maverick grinned as he took a sip of sparkling cider. "Yep."

My feet propelled me forward several steps. "That's a . . ."

"Yep."

Lizbeth, Ellie, and Devin flanked me at the window as Benjamin pulled his helmet off and set it on the bike. His shoulder-length hair shifted in the wind as he strode toward us. Benjamin had never been charming like Maverick. He was more intense. Brooding. His budding career as a jiu-jitsu fighter meant he stalked instead of walked. Still, he'd been the warmest person in Maverick's family so far.

Meeting Mallory loomed on the horizon, but I felt no fear.

All words fled my mouth when Benjamin peered into the coffee shop. A half-smile tugged at his face when he saw me pressed against the glass like a two-year-old.

"Maverick," I whispered.

"Yes?" he drawled from right behind me.

"That's not just any Indian Boulevard motorcycle."

"Nope."

I turned around to ask how he'd found *my* bike. Dad's bike. The exact bike I had sold to a total stranger months ago. And Maverick was kneeling on his left leg, a familiar blue box in hand. A squeak peeped out of me when I recognized the unique color.

*That* was a Tiffany's box.

Lizbeth, Ellie, and Devin stood behind him now, grinning from ear to ear. Maverick smiled. The certainty and depth in his eyes made my heart hum.

"Mav?" I whispered.

"Bethany, will you be part of my team? Forever?"

The box opened onto a glittering collection of gems that trapped a gasp in my throat. Tears filled my eyes as I brushed past the box and put my hands on his face.

"You found my dad's bike."

His grin widened. "Yes. I hired someone to track down the

owner, and I made an exorbitant offer. He sold pretty quick. Did you see this box?"

"Yes. But the bike—"

He tilted his head back and laughed. Then he leaned closer, gaze narrowed. "Are you going to say yes or no?"

"Yes!"

"To be clear, is that a yes to the bike or a yes to the ring?"

"To both," I cried, laughing. "Yes, Maverick! I want to be a part of your team forever."

He stood, scooping me up in his arms, and laid a kiss on me that sent tingles all the way through my toes. I laughed against his lips, deliriously happy as Benjamin opened the door, admitting a cool brush of wind across the back of my neck.

"She say 'yes'?" Benjamin asked.

"You bet she did," said Lizbeth.

Maverick ended our kiss an hour too early when Devin and Ellie made fake gagging sounds. I smiled, enjoying the warm flow of his breath on my cheeks.

"I love you, Mav."

"Not half as much as I love you."

"Sure you want to commit to this?" I asked, glancing around the shop.

"I've never wanted anything more."

"Great!" Shoving away from Maverick, I whirled around and skipped outside, snatching the keys from Benjamin. "Now get me on that bike already!"

# About the Author

Katie Cross grew up in the mountains of Idaho, where she still loves to play when she gets the chance.

If she's not finding the nearest taco, she's probably hiking in the Colorado mountains with her three vizslas (you read that right), two dogs, and hottie husband.

Her favorite food is everything. She's a sucker for romance, though she seems like a toughie. And when it comes down to it, being present in the moment is her favorite thing to do.

To learn more about Katie, visit her website, katiecross-books.com.